THE WITCH OF BRUGES

OLIVIER VAN GIERDEGHOM

Title: The Witch of Bruges.
Original title: De heks van Brugge.
Author: Olivier R. F. Van Gierdeghom.
Design & Cover: Olivier R. F. Van Gierdeghom.
Editor: Morgane Leblon.
Keywords: detective, witches, Bruges, LGBTQ+.

ISBN 9789493427099
Depot D/2025/15500/08
FF - Crime & mystery fiction
FIC022020 - Fiction / Mystery & Detective / Cozy
FIC011000 - Fiction / LGBTQ+ / General

Printed in the EU on 100% recycled mixed paper stock.

www.kabouterpers.be | www.witchofbruges.be

OLIVIER VAN GIERDEGHOM

THE WITCH OF BRUGES

kabouterpers®

JADE

In a crystalline prison breathed a forgotten key trapped in jade, its ancient form a beating heart of ghostly green light that only began to unravel for the few eyes that could see what others chose to ignore.

Elisabeth Vantomme, museum curator of the Bruges Museum of Ethnic Culture, nervously tucked a strand of grey hair behind her ear. Something about the artefact made her deeply uncomfortable. If the scholarly catalogues were correct, this was merely a rare ceremonial object from the classical Maya period.

"Everything sorted with the insurance?" she asked the woman beside her, whose navy-blue suit and sleek hairstyle radiated an aura of cold efficiency.

"All documentation is entirely in order, including the special clauses for objects of historical value," replied Arianne Vermeer, the prominent insurance broker who had insured the exhibition. Her voice was emotionless, clinical. "The mayor arrives in twelve minutes and seventeen seconds. The fireworks are scheduled for immediately after his speech."

Elisabeth nodded in agreement, but the oppressive sensation in her chest remained. She gently stroked her forearm, where a series of small, perfect circular burns were visible—each surrounded by a strange, green rim.

"It's not just an art object, you know," she whispered, almost to herself. "I only touched it once, with gloves, and that night...

That night, I dreamt things I cannot describe without losing my sanity."

Arianne's eyes narrowed, her posture subtly shifting. "Have you communicated these... observations to third parties?"

"Only to you. You insured the transport. I thought you ought to know."

Something flashed in Arianne's eyes—not concern, but calculation.

"The object is entirely safe," she declared, her voice even colder than before. "Let us focus our attention on the official opening."

At the main entrance, a black cat slipped unnoticed between the guests' legs. Strangely enough, the animal seemed to move purposefully, its amber eyes fixed on the central display case where the jade artefact gleamed. The cat settled on the first-floor balustrade, from where it had a perfect view of the coming events.

"Ladies and gentlemen, it is my great honour to officially open this extraordinary exhibition, 'Mayas in Bruges'."

Mayor Robert Maillard beamed in the spotlight, his voluminous figure wrapped in a drab suit, his hand gestures clumsy as he delivered his speech. The elite of Bruges—politicians, entrepreneurs, artists—sipped champagne and applauded politely.

In the central exhibition room, Kaylee Mendoza gestured wildly in front of her iPhone. Her bright pink winter coat with leopard-print trim contrasted dramatically with the subdued outfits of the older guests. Her face, perfectly contoured for the camera, glittered with strategically applied highlighter.

"OMG, this is literally the thing, you guys!" she said into the microphone, her voice cracking with excitement. "The legendary Maya jade cocoa bean that allegedly has low-key magical powers. I am shook!" She zoomed in on a small jade sculpture in a central display case, shaped like a cocoa bean and covered with intricate inscriptions that seemed to glow even under the party lighting.

Simon Laurent stood alone by the window, watching the party guests. His perfectly cut cashmere jumper emphasized his

athletic build and his handsome face bore an expression of refined boredom, but his grey-green eyes missed nothing—including the movements of the black cat that no one else seemed to notice.
The phone buzzed. A message from a number simply saved as "Contact":

"Is it authentic?"

Simon's lips curled in a subtle smile. He typed:

"Confirmed. The object is genuine. The resonance is unmistakable. Execute plan during fireworks."

Mayor Maillard concluded his speech with a joke that elicited polite laughter. "And now, ladies and gentlemen, whilst we look forward to the spectacular fireworks display above our historic city, I invite you to examine this fascinating exhibition more closely. The Mayas believed that this cocoa bean was not merely a religious artefact, but a literal key to another world."
Elisabeth Vantomme stiffened. She had not informed the mayor about this specific Maya legend. Her gaze met that of Arianne Vermeer, whose face remained a mask of calm, but whose eyes now alertly scanned the room.
The crackling of the first firework made the windows tremble. The mayor smiled broadly.
"Ladies and gentlemen, I invite you to join me on the terrace for a toast whilst we enjoy this spectacular fireworks display, specially organized in honour of this remarkable exhibition."
The crowd flowed enthusiastically outside, champagne glasses in hand, faces lifted to the colourful explosions in the sky. The exhibition room quickly emptied, with only a few security guards remaining at the entrances.
Simon Laurent stayed inside, ostensibly absorbed in conversation with a younger local politician, but his eyes continuously scanned the room. The black cat now sat on a high ledge.
When the last group of guests reached the terrace, Simon pulled a small transmitter from his pocket and subtly pressed

a button. Almost immediately, the lighting in the exhibition hall flickered, as if there had been a sudden power failure. A man in a museum staff uniform—a disguise, perfectly executed—slipped into the room from a side door. With quick, practised movements, he deactivated the central display case's alarm system, opened the glass, and took the jade artefact with gloved hands. The entire process took no more than six seconds.

When the light stabilized again, the man slipped away with the artefact through a staff door, exactly as planned. Simon took a sip of his champagne, the perfect embodiment of ignorant nonchalance.

On the terrace, voices rang out with excitement and festive noise. Only an elderly woman with a wicker basket had not gone outside. She stood in a corner of the exhibition room, hidden behind a pillar, her sharp eyes witness to the entire operation. The Yorkshire terrier in her wicker basket made a soft, warning sound.

Outside, the fireworks reached a crescendo of explosions and colours. The guests applauded enthusiastically, completely unaware of the theft that had just taken place.

Somewhere in the city, a young sports athlete and pizza delivery driver named Finn De Wulf bolted upright in his bed, bathed in sweat, his eyes glowing, his lips murmuring in a language he had never learned.

#ARTTHEFT

In his luxurious flat on the Eiermarkt, overlooking the historic facades of the city centre, Simon Laurent stood at the window, his silhouette outlined against the rainy Bruges skyline. He wore a merino wool jumper that accentuated his athletic build, and his designer jeans cost more than the monthly salary of the average citizen.

His fingers caressed the small jade object resting on his palm, the cocoa bean that seemed to pulse gently in the subdued light of his stylishly furnished sitting room. The ancient Maya inscriptions on the surface glowed with a subtle, green energy that reflected in Simon's eyes, transforming from grey-green irises to something hungrier, more unnatural.

"Perfect," he whispered, satisfaction in his voice almost sensual.

He placed the artefact carefully back on the bookshelf, seemingly casually between his academic works and sports trophies, as if it were nothing more than an ordinary souvenir. The perfect spot—hidden in plain sight, something no ordinary person would look at twice among the prestigious books on international law and political theory.

Simon picked up his phone and opened the latest news report about the museum robbery. With an amused smile, he took a screenshot of the article and posted it on his Insta Stories, accompanied by a carefully composed message:

"😱😱Shocked by the theft at the Museum of Ethnic Culture. The Maya exhibition was one of my favourites. I hope the police catch the culprits soon? #art-theft #bruges #culturalheritage"

Almost immediately, the phone vibrated with a notification. A message from Kaylee Mendoza:

"OMG, so awful!! That's so sus!! 😱 I was there that evening for the fireworks. Want to grind together for those exams tonight? No cap would be absolutely fire! 👀"

Simon's lips curled in what resembled a smile, but was more an expression of predatory calculation. Kaylee—so predictable, so hungry for recognition and affection. Her constant social media presence and her talent for unintentionally gathering useful information made her a valuable tool in his arsenal. Kaylee was always online.

He typed a vague confirmation, vague enough to keep her hungry, but not so explicit that it constituted a promise. The message that Kaylee was on her way for their "study session" had put him in an excellent mood. She would be a perfect distraction.

LINA

One month later

The wind clawed at the centuries-old facade of Wijngaardstraat 12. The hand-painted signboard reads 'Dreams of Lina', purple letters that flapped gently in the February cold. Inside, in the warm cocoon of the chocolate shop, shadows danced over the wooden panelling when an occasional horse-drawn carriage passed by.

Lina Vandevelde breathed out slowly, her fingers drumming on the rowan wood counter. The rare wood, according to old legends, a protection against dark magic, was an heirloom that had circulated in her family for generations. Her blue eyes followed the rhythm of the rain striking the window. January was always difficult in Bruges, but this January—the first without her mother—felt like a pool of quicksand in which she was slowly sinking.

She brushed a loose strand of light-brown hair behind her ear and focused her attention back to the praline in front of her. With surgical precision, she applied a touch of edible gold with a fine brush to the surface, creating a pattern reminiscent of ancient Maya symbols.

Sophia would have done it more perfectly, she thought bitterly. Her mother had hands that never trembled, even in her final days.

The memory came unwanted, but inevitable: *"Mum, you must rest," Lina had urged, trying to take the copper mixing bowl from Sophia's trembling hands.*
"There's no time left for rest," her mother had replied, her voice weak but determined. "The dreams are growing darker, Lina. The Laurent boy is getting closer than his father ever did."
"That's the fever talking," Lina had said, though she knew it wasn't true.
"Listen to me," Sophia's hand had gripped Lina's wrist with surprising strength. "Ingrid knows where the golden key is."
"Ingrid? Ingrid Vermeulen? That eccentric old woman with her annoying little dog and her endless gossip?"
Sophia had smiled weakly. "She's more than she appears, as we all are." She pointed to the corner of the room, where there was nothing but shadows.
"The silver key... you must always wear it. Never take it off, not even for... oh!"
A sudden attack of pain had made her body convulse. Blood had appeared on her lips. She fell to the floor.
"Mum!" Lina had grabbed her phone, but Sophia had stopped her hand.
"Too late," she had whispered. "Listen... the mayor... don't trust him completely. And remember: if a werewolf comes, let him in. He is the key to..."
But what the werewolf had been, Lina had never known. Sophia's eyes had opened wide, staring at something Lina couldn't see. And then, with a final trembling sigh, she had departed.

"Still busy with mayoral veneration?" The voice that broke the silence was rich and nasal, dripping with sarcasm.
Lina looked up. On the counter lay a black cat stretched out, his tail swishing with the precision of a metronome. His amber eyes, too human for an ordinary animal, observed her with a mixture of affection and impatience.
"This order must be perfect, Morpheus," she replied, her voice soft but determined. "The mayor is an influential man in Bruges."

"And a man with the taste buds of a twelve-year-old after a bag of Haribo," mewed the cat, his tail now swishing faster. "Your 'pearls before swine' mentality is admirable, but useless. Your mother would have said—"

"Leave my mother out of this." Lina's fingers tightened around the brush, a drop of golden paint falling onto the marble like a precious tear.

The cat stilled, his ears flat against his head. Sophia Vandevelde's death was a boundary he wouldn't cross. Not when the pain was still so fresh.

"I was there, you know," he said eventually, his voice softer than usual. "In the corner of the room, when she... went. She saw me, even when you couldn't. She knew the truth of what's coming."

Lina raised her head. "You never told me you were there."

"There are many things I don't tell you," the cat replied enigmatically. "That's the nature of my service to your family. Half-truths, subtle hints, strategic revelations."

"And insufferable arrogance, please keep in mind that," Lina muttered, but there was affection in her voice.

She continued working in silence, her hands now steady again, as she placed the final praline in the golden box.

"You don't have to bear every burden alone," Morpheus said eventually, his tone softened to something almost kind. "You're the last of your line, but not alone."

"I know," she breathed. "But the dreams are growing darker, Morpheus. And since that theft at the museum..." Her voice trailed off.

The cat's eyes narrowed. The jade cocoa bean—stolen during the New Year's celebration, vanished without a trace.

"The Laurent boy grows stronger," said Morpheus. "His family has waited generations for this moment. They have resources, influence. And now they also have the jade key."

"Then we must protect the other two keys," Lina replied, her fingers automatically grasping the small silver cocoa bean hanging on a chain around her neck. "And we must find the golden one before they do." The bell above the door suddenly chimed. A gust of cold air made the candles flicker. An elderly woman stepped inside, wrapped in a raincoat so bright yellow it hurt the eyes. Her face, heavily made up despite her age, radiated an almost childlike excitement. In her arms, she carried a wicker basket, from which the nervous face of a small Yorkshire terrier peeped.

"Lina, love!" The woman's voice was loud enough to wake the dead, her Bruges accent thick as cream. "Have you heard yet?"

Morpheus had already vanished, a black flash that ducked under the counter, his tail the only indication of his presence.

"Good afternoon, Ingrid." Lina smiled politely, her professional mask seamlessly in place. "What news brings you today?"

Ingrid Vermeulen, Bruges' walking gossip sheet, leaned so far over the counter that her bosom came dangerously close to the pralines. She pressed a hand to her chest, a gesture Lina had seen many times before. Her perfume—an intoxicating floral scent—overwhelmed the subtle aromas of the chocolate shop.

"It's dreadful," she muttered, her voice dropping to a dramatic level. "The mayor's in the hospital. Poisoned!"

Lina's heart skipped a beat. "Poisoned?" she repeated, her fingers unconsciously grasping the silver cocoa bean. "That can't be. I've only just prepared a box of pralines for him."

"Yes!" Ingrid's eyes grew wide as saucers, gleaming with a perverse excitement. "That's just it! They say it was chocolate! From your shop!"

For a fraction of a second, Lina thought she saw something in the old woman's eyes—a spark of intelligence, of calculation, that didn't fit her facade of senile curiosity.

She's more than she appears, Sophia had said. But what did that mean?

The world slowed down, colours faded at the edges of Lina's vision. From under the counter came a soft, almost inaudible growl—Morpheus, his senses picking up what people couldn't see: the sudden shift of energy in the shop.

"That's impossible," said Lina, her voice calmer than she felt. "My chocolate brings dreams, not poisoning."

"Well," Ingrid leaned even closer, her voice now conspiratorial, "strange things are happening in Bruges these days. First that stolen Maya thingy from the museum, now this." She paused, for effect, whilst stroking her Yorkshire terrier lovingly over his shivering head. "When I was walking Pouffe by Our Lady's Church, I saw something. Something big and black, skulking along the walls. Too big for a house cat, too small for a dog."

The Yorkshire terrier in the wicker basket began to tremble violently, a low, soft sustained whine escaping from his small throat, his eyes rolling wildly.

"Your imagination's playing tricks on you, Ingrid,". Lina said automatically, but her gaze shot briefly to where Morpheus was hiding.

"Perhaps," Ingrid straightened her back, clearly offended. "But when the police come here soon, they won't be wondering what I'm imagining, but what you've put in that chocolate, young lady. Mark my words. I'm off."

With that parting shot, she turned and strode to the door, her high heels clicking on the wooden floor.

Morpheus leapt back onto the counter, his form fluidly changing to a shadowy, half-human shape with the same amber eyes now at eye level with Lina.

"She saw me," he hissed, his voice deeper in this form. "At the museum, that night of the theft."

"What were you doing there?" Lina's voice was sharp.

"I felt it, Lina." Morpheus moved like a whisper between crowded thoughts. "The artefact called to me. The jade cocoa bean, it's a key to the underworld, just like yours." He pointed to the silver pendant around her neck. "And now it's gone, and the mayor poisoned with chocolate supposedly from you."

"This is no coincidence," whispered Lina, her fingers drumming on the centuries-old counter in a nervous rhythm. "Someone's trying to get me out of the way. Someone who knows what I am, what we guard."

She stared at the box of pralines she had just finished, her thoughts racing. If someone had used her chocolate to poison the mayor, then this was more than an attack on her reputation. It was an attack on the source of all magic in Bruges, on the fragile connection between worlds that had been guarded by her and her ancestors for centuries.

"We must discover the truth," she decided, her voice hardened by determination. "And quickly."

NIGHT ROUND

It was past eleven when Finn De Wulf laboriously climbed the stairs to his attic room. His Club Brugge tracksuit was soaked from the pouring rain, his muscles screaming for rest. As a second-year sports science student, he was used to physical exertion, but the combination of morning lectures, afternoon training, and evening work as a delivery driver for Presto Pizza pushed even his athletic body to its limits. He'd popped home because his bike chain had finally snapped—he'd have to make the last delivery on foot.

He threw his wet jacket over a chair and examined the damage to his last delivery—a pizza that had shifted in the box, the cheese stuck to one side of the cardboard. Finn swore softly. His boss would deduct this from his tips.

He checked his phone again for the delivery address.

```
Eiermarkt 7, Flat 3B. Large pepper-
oni, extra cheese. URGENT. Customer:
Laurent, S.
```

The address was nearby, one of those luxury flats around the city square. Perhaps a good tip, if he was lucky.

Finn shut the door behind him and stepped into the rain, not knowing that this delivery would change his life forever.

BENEATH THE SKIN

It wasn't raining anymore—it was pouring. Water streamed down Finn's face as he ran through the glistening streets of Bruges, one hand protectively over the pizza box. The Eiermarkt was deserted, the terraces abandoned, only the golden lights behind windows indicating there was still life in the city. Flat 3B turned out to be on the top floor of a renovated medieval building with a marble entrance that belonged more in a museum than a residential block. Finn looked at his soaked tracksuit bottoms and worn trainers, the muddy prints he was leaving on the gleaming floor.

Brilliant. A posh complex.

He pressed the intercom beside a brass nameplate: 'S. Laurent, J.D.' It took a moment before there was a response.

"Yes?" The voice sounded refined, slightly irritated.

"Presto Pizza, for Mr Laurent?"

"I haven't ordered any pizza."

Finn frowned. "Eiermarkt 7, flat 3B? Simon Laurent?"

A brief silence. "Come up. Third floor."

The door buzzed open. In the lift, Finn checked the order on his phone. Eiermarkt 7-3B, customer Laurent, S., payment on delivery. He was at the right address. Perhaps someone had played a prank?

The lift doors opened onto a short corridor with only one door. Before he could knock, it swung open.

Simon Laurent wasn't what Finn had expected. Early twenties, about Finn's age, but that's where any similarity ended. He wore a fine woollen jumper that probably cost more than Finn's monthly student loan, his dark hair perfectly styled despite the late hour. But it was his eyes that made Finn stiffen—grey-green, intelligent eyes that evaluated him from top to bottom with an intensity that felt almost physical. *Simon caught Finn staring. God, he was gorgeous.*

"You're soaked," said Simon, his voice warm and hoarse.

Finn recovered himself. "Sorry about the confusion. There's a pizza ordered in your name, but if you say you didn't—"

"Come in," Simon interrupted. "It's clearly a mistake, but you can't go back out in this storm." He stepped aside with an inviting gesture.

Finn's suspicious nature warred with his practical side. The thought of a dry, warm place won over his wariness. He stepped into the flat.

The space was a study in elegant minimalism—high ceilings, designer furniture, books in languages Finn didn't even recognize. And there were many books—the entire back wall was a bookcase, filled with what looked like legal texts and philosophical works. One object caught his attention—a small jade sculpture on a prominent shelf. The thing seemed almost to pulse in the soft light.

"Put the pizza down. I'll pay for it, even though I didn't order it." Laurent went to a sleek open kitchen. "Coffee?"

"No, thanks. I should get back—"

"That storm's only getting worse. They've forecast wind gusts of seventy-five miles per hour. One cup?" He was already reaching for two designer mugs before getting an answer.

Finn looked at the window, where rain lashed against the panes. His phone pinged—a weather alert. *Severe storm warning. Stay indoors if possible.*

"Alright, one cup, then." Laurent beamed. His teeth were perfectly white. "Sports programme? Judging by your tracksuit."

"Sports science, second year." Finn suddenly felt conscious of his worn Club Brugge tracksuit. "Part-time. This pays the rent."
"Impressive. I know few students who combine full-time study with work." Laurent handed him a cup of fragrant espresso. "I'm reading international law. Final year."
Finn took a sip. The coffee was rich and complex, nothing like the watery stuff in the university canteen. "Can you explain the 'J.D.' on your nameplate?"
"Juris Doctor." Laurent sat in a leather armchair and gestured to the sofa opposite. "Take a seat. You can't drip all over a stranger's property."
"This probably wasn't what you expected for a Thursday evening," said Finn, carefully settling on what was likely a priceless designer sofa.
"On the contrary." Laurent's smile deepened. "I find unexpected encounters fascinating. Life's full of... interesting turns."
There was something in the way he spoke, an ambiguity that Finn couldn't place. He took another sip of coffee and felt a strange warmth spreading through his body—too intense for ordinary caffeine.
"What sort of sports science do you do exactly?" Laurent leaned forward, his eyes never leaving Finn's face.
"Biomechanics and sports psychology. How the body moves and responds to..." Finn paused. The room suddenly seemed to spin. "What's in this coffee?"
Laurent looked innocent. "Just a few special herbs. An old family recipe. It helps you relax after a long day."
Finn tried to stand, but his limbs felt heavy. "I... should go." His words sounded slurred, even to his ears.
"You're not going anywhere, Finn De Wulf."
Laurent's voice was different now. Softer. More controlled. "Not in this storm. And not in this condition."
"How do you know my name?" Finn had never given his name.
Laurent stood up and walked towards him, moving with the grace of a predator.
"I know many things about you. You live alone. Your father left when you were ten. Your mother died two years ago. And you

have a... fascinating medical condition that manifests with the lunar cycle."

Finn's heart began to race. No one knew about this. No one except his mother, and she'd taken it to her grave.

"I don't know what you're talking about," he protested.

"Of course you do." Laurent stood over him now, his fingers lightly stroking Finn's cheek. "You're a werewolf, Finn. A beautiful specimen, even in this human form."

Finn's vision began to blur. The room spun faster. The jade sculpture on the bookcase seemed to glow brighter, pulsing in the same rhythm as his heartbeat. He felt an unwelcome wave of heat course through his body, a tingling in his fingertips where his nails began to change.

"What have you done to me?" he hissed.

Laurent knelt before him, their faces now level. "I've only helped you show your true nature, Finn De Wulf. And you're even more beautiful than I'd dared hope."

The last thing Finn saw before darkness claimed him were those grey-green eyes, gleaming with a hungry intensity that had nothing human about it.

BITTER AFTERTASTE

Lina stood before a massive mirror in her private room behind the shop, her fingers tracing the edges of the silver cocoa bean resting against her throat. It was late, the sort of late that brought the city to slumber, where even the night animals held their breath. Rain came down in buckets.

"The toxicology results are in," said Morpheus, now in his human form seated on an antique chest. "You were right. It wasn't your chocolate that poisoned the mayor."

"Of course I was right," murmured Lina, "my chocolate isn't poisonous."

"Technically, he's not dead."

"Technically, I have no need for your semantic corrections." She turned to face him. "What was it then?"

"A synthetic belladonna variant, mixed with something old." Morpheus jumped up, his movements fluid as smoke. "Something I haven't smelled myself in centuries. Maya origin, presumably. But the strange thing is... it looked identical to your chocolate. Same shape, same packaging."

"Someone's counterfeited my packaging."

"Not just someone." Morpheus picked up an old book from a nearby shelf. "Only someone who knows the secrets of magical chocolate could make such an exact replica."

Lina walked to a large globe in the corner of the room and spun it. The globe opened like an egg, revealing a series of

vials and small tools. "The last time belladonna was used to poison chocolate was in 1982, when my mother was nearly murdered by Theodoor Laurent." She took out a small bottle with a dark liquid. "History repeats itself."
"You think the son is continuing his father's fight?"
"The Laurents have tried to wipe us out for generations, Morpheus. They believe that what we do—maintaining the connection to the dream world—is a form of parasitism. A contamination of human consciousness." She let a drop of the liquid fall onto her tongue and closed her eyes. "We must find Simon Laurent."
"And then?"
Lina's eyes opened again, now harder than before. "Then I determine whether he's behind the theft of the jade artefact. And whether he tried to murder the mayor and frame me."
"And if he is?"
"Then I do what my mother would have done." She clenched her fist and the vials in the globe trembled. "I protect the dream world, at any cost."
Morpheus grinned, his amber eyes glowing in the twilight. "You're becoming more like Sophia every day. She'd be proud."
"She'd tell me I'm reacting too emotionally and doing too little research," Lina corrected with a faint smile. "Come, we have work to do."
She walked to the antique bookcase against the back wall and pulled at a yellowed volume titled "Theobroma: Food of the Gods". With a soft click, the bookcase slid aside, revealing a narrow spiral staircase descending into darkness.
"Laurent first, or the mayor?" asked Morpheus as they descended the stairs.
"The mayor. If anyone knows who poisoned him, it's him."
"You don't trust him."
"My mother said I should be wary of him. That was her last warning." At the bottom of the stairs, a massive door opened onto a space that couldn't have existed according to the physical laws of urban planning. A round room, lit by candles that burned not downwards but upwards, surrounded by walls

covered with maps of a city that looked like Bruges but subtly different—streets that didn't exist, buildings in impossible places, and everywhere small points of light that pulsed like stars. In the centre stood a scale model of the city, so detailed that even the smallest roof tile was represented, so lifelike that the water in the canals actually seemed to flow.

Lina bent over the model and placed her silver cocoa bean on what represented the Lake of Love. A network of glowing lines spread from that point, like veins of light running beneath the miniature streets.

"Ley lines," she said barely audibly. "The magical currents beneath the city have been disrupted since the theft. Look." She pointed to a dark spot in the network, exactly where St John's Hospital stood. "The mayor is there, and there's a blockage in the flow."

"The poisoning was magical, not just physical," Morpheus concluded. "Someone tried to silence him."

"Or extract something from him," Lina nodded. "The question is: what does Robert Maillard know that's so dangerous to the thief?"

She closed her eyes and placed her palms on the model. "When my mother was dying, she warned me about something coming. Something dark. The dreams foretold it. Now the jade artefact is stolen, the mayor poisoned, and my reputation under fire." Her eyes opened, now intensely blue like a southern sea. "This is no coincidence. This is a pattern. And I'm going to discover who's behind it, before it's too late."

Morpheus watched as Lina navigated the complexity of magic that had been perfected by generations of chocolate makers. She was younger than her mother had been when she took over, yet already formidable. But even she didn't know everything.

He knew there were things he couldn't tell her yet. About the prophecy that spoke of three keys and a wolf. About her true role in what was to come. Concerning the blood that would be required to flow.

Some truths were still too heavy for her shoulders, some secrets darker than chocolate.

SURRENDER

Finn, against his better judgement, stopped fighting. The sensation coursing through him was different from his usual transformations—no pain, no struggle, but a kind of liberation, like a door finally opening to a room he'd always tried to ignore.

Simon's lips found his, and the kiss was electric, a shock straight to his core. It was nothing like Finn had experienced with previous partners—this was raw, intense, almost transcendent, as if they were sharing electricity instead of breath. Their bodies moved together as if performing an age-old ritual, a dance written into their DNA long before civilization imposed its restrictions.

Simon's hands glided over the contours of Finn's now half-transformed chest, his fingers tangling in the dark hair growing there. "So warm," he murmured against Finn's skin. "You smell of forest and earth and... wildness."

The words unleashed something in Finn, an animal intensity he'd always tried to suppress. With a half-smothered growl, he pushed Simon against the wall, their bodies entwined in an embrace that was both desire and struggle.

Simon's laugh was soft and dangerous. "There it is," he whispered. "The beast beneath the surface. You don't have to hide it, Finn. Not from me."

And at that moment, Finn believed him. He was so used to hiding his true nature, so used to fear and shame, that Simon's pure acceptance—no, his celebration—of Finn's wilder side felt like a revelation. Finn unconsciously pushed his hips forward, clenched his buttocks, and in no time his throbbing erection demanded to be freed. A wave of shame overcame him that his body had agreed to every new touch without asking his permission.

"You're perfect as you are," Simon whispered against his ear, between kisses and caresses. "Human and wolf, civilization and wildness. You don't have to choose, don't have to suppress one side. You can be whole, complete." Simon pulled his jumper over his head, and with his bare torso came an expensive cedar wood cologne. He rubbed rhythmically over his polyester tracksuit bottoms, glanced at Finn's eyes, and began sucking him like a pro.

And though part of Finn knew this was manipulation, that there was an agenda at play, he couldn't deny that Simon's words resonated with a truth he'd always longed to hear. For one night, in that luxurious room with its confusing mix of desire, drugs, and magic, Finn allowed himself to believe that there could exist a world where he didn't have to decide, didn't have to hide, didn't have to fear.

It was a lie, of course. But like all the best lies, it contained a core of truth he would never forget.

Finn's consciousness returned in fragments, like pieces of a burnt film. He woke up in a strange bed, Egyptian cotton sheets soft against his naked skin. Naked skin?

He shot upright, his heart pounding. He was naked. In a strange flat. And beside him lay Simon Laurent, also naked, his slender body half-covered by the sheet, sleeping like a contented predator.

What have I done?

Images flashed through his head. Simon giving him coffee. The conversation. Then... heat. Desire. Pain and pleasure mingled into something entangleable. Simon pressing him against the wall, whispering about his "fascinating nature", his fingers gliding over Finn's changing skin.

The drug in the coffee.

Finn closed his eyes, memories struggling to the surface. Laurent had done something. It seemed at first like a love bite, but there was a quick cut. A vial collecting blood. His blood.

Finn felt his shoulder and found a fresh wound, already healing thanks to his accelerated healing ability. Laurent had stolen his blood, and Finn knew instinctively that this was important. Dangerous.

He looked around the room, searching for his clothes. His gaze fell on the bookcase he'd noticed earlier. The green object drew his attention like a magnet.

As quietly as possible, he slipped out of bed and crept to the bookcase. The object was jade, shaped like a cocoa bean and covered with strange symbols that seemed to dance in his peripheral vision. It was exactly as that little influencer had described it in her livestream. The stolen museum piece.

An intense shiver ran through his body. This wasn't an ordinary art object. It *called* to him, in a way he couldn't explain. The same unnatural attraction he felt during the full moon—a primal call that awakened his deepest instincts.

Behind him, Laurent moved, mumbling in his sleep. Finn froze, but the man only turned over. This was his chance.

As quickly and quietly as possible, he gathered his scattered clothes and put them on. His phone and wallet were still in his trouser pocket. Looking at the door, he briefly considered taking the object with him, but something held him back. If Simon was the thief, and Finn stole it, he'd be the next suspect. No, he had to tell someone what he'd discovered. But who? The police? They'd never believe him.

At the door, he suddenly remembered Laurent's words: *"You're a werewolf, Finn."* How did he know that? No one knew that, except...

A strange feeling of deja vu washed over him. His mother on her deathbed, whispering about a woman in Bruges who would help him, a chocolate maker, someone who knew the truth about what he was.

"If you're ever in danger, find Lina Vandevelde."

The name flashed through his head like an electric shock. Lina

Vandevelde. The chocolate maker who was now being accused of poisoning the mayor.
With a last glance at the sleeping Simon, Finn slipped out of the flat. He had to find this Lina, before Simon discovered he was gone.
The storm outside had finally subsided, but a new storm was building in Finn's chest. For the first time in his life, he wouldn't run away from what he was, but towards it. Literally.
He began to walk through the empty streets of awakening Bruges, like a wolf on the prowl.

MR.PERFECT

Kaylee Mendoza lay on her bed in her small but trendily furnished student room. It had been raining all evening and staying in was the advice. Her walls were practically invisible behind the collage of posters, cuttings, and Polaroids of her friends. Her pink duvet was strewn with study books she'd been ignoring for hours, and the soft glow of LED lights shaped like pink cacti provided the perfect atmosphere for mindless social media scrolling.

With one hand, she held her iPhone aloft, whilst with the other, she mindlessly drank a sugar-free energy drink. It was nearly midnight, but sleep wasn't on her agenda. There were still too many profiles to check, too many messages about collabs and sponsors to send.

"Let's see what Mr Perfect's up to," she said childishly to herself, her painted nails tapping on the screen as she navigated to Simon Laurent's profile.

His feed was sparse but stylized—an aesthetic whole of architecture photos, legal books artistically arranged on antique tables, and occasional selfies that looked as if they'd been taken spontaneously but were clearly carefully composed. Just enough personality to be interesting, but mysterious enough to remain intriguing. His latest post was a photo of a rare legal book in leather binding, with a cryptic caption: "*Veritas in tenebris lucet*"—truth shines in darkness.

Kaylee rolled her eyes, but still pressed the heart. "Que isso, what pretentious BS.," she said aloud to her empty room. "But why are you such an unbelievable HOTTIE? Spill the tea, honey. Mama wants juice." She rubbed her thigh with one hand and let her hand rest between her legs as she fantasized further.

She typed a conspicuously innocent comment:

> "Living for this content! Absolutely bangin' 🖤✨"

Followed by a DM:

> "Have you checked out the new Coffee & Law spot on Katelijnestraat yet? Major study vibes, I'm always incredibly productive there.
> Maybe see you there sometime?
> No pressure tho! 😊"

It was her third message of the day. The first two were still unanswered. Today was proper desperate.

She scrolled further through his profile, stopping at what she now considered 'her crush'—a photo from two years ago during a swimming competition. Simon in tight swimming trunks, his body defined and glistening with water, his hair slicked back, a rare, genuine smile on his face. Next to him stood another young man, equally athletic, with an arm casually around Simon's shoulders. They'd won the relay together, according to the caption.

She'd tried to find the other boy on social media, but he seemed not to exist—no Instagram, no Facebook, no TikTok. It was as if he were a ghost, an anomaly in Simon's carefully curated online existence.

"Who are you?" she whispered, zooming in on the mysterious friend's face. The boy was handsome, with an openness in his smile that completely missed Simon's usual thoughtfulness. "And why are you the only one who can make him laugh like that?" She'd studied this image so often she could describe every pixel. It interested her not only because she was hopelessly in love with Simon—which she absolutely was—but because she smelled a mystery. And if there was one thing Kaylee loved, besides likes and followers, it was a good mystery. 'Mmm. Proper juicy,' she moaned.

With a sigh, she swiped away from Simon's profile and opened her feed. The statistics were impressive for an international student: 330,000 followers, an average of 4,500 likes per post, collaborations with four local boutique brands, and an ongoing contract with a Belgian chocolate brand.

"Girl power," she said to herself, a mantra she'd picked up from her favourite reality show and used liberally as personal encouragement. Her parents would have a heart attack if they knew how she talked when she was alone, but the ocean between them offered a freedom she cherished. She studied searching for new ideas and scrolled through reels of people popping pimples, dressing up their cat, diving into a vat of slime, half-naked boys making breakfast whilst staring at the camera, half-naked boys making breakfast with their dog...

Her finger paused on a photo posted twelve hours ago by her younger sister Gabriela. She stood on Copacabana Beach, sun in her hair, surrounded by laughing friends, with Rio's iconic skyline in the background.

A stab of homesickness and guilt pierced Kaylee's carefully constructed façade. Gabi was only seventeen, but her face already carried the adult determination that characterized their mother. She studied hard, helped in the family shop, and dreamed of the same opportunities Kaylee had received—a scholarship to a European university, a ticket away from the limitations of their middle-class existence in Rio's suburbs.

Kaylee's fingers hovered over the screen, hesitating. She should have video-called her family yesterday, but had cancelled for a beer brand launch party where influencers got free drinks. She'd told herself that networking was important, that she needed to make contacts for her future, but the truth was simpler: the party sounded more fun than an hour listening to her parents asking when she was finally going to get serious about her studies. Furthermore, she typed a message to her sister:

> "Miss you sm! You look absolutely fire! 🔥 FaceTime sesh soon? Drop me a time that works!"

Then she scrolled on, but the photo stuck in her mind. The contrast between her life here and what she'd left behind was sometimes overwhelming. In Bruges, she was Kaylee Mendoza, a rising influencer, the Brazilian girl with the perfect mix of exotic charm and European sophistication. In Rio, she was just Catarina, daughter of an office worker/surf coach/shop assistant and a nurse, a girl who'd been lucky with a scholarship and who must never forget how much her parents sacrificed so she could seize this opportunity. That's why Kaylee put so much effort into her social media because if that worked she might have a steady income so she wouldn't have to go back home.

Two worlds, two identities, neither entirely true nor fake. Sporadically, she wondered if anyone—Simon, her followers, even her flatmate—really knew who she was. Or if she'd become so used to creating content that she could no longer see the distinction herself.

Her phone vibrated with a notification: Antoine from Confiserie du Cygne 'The Swan' had responded to her DM.

> "Chère Kaylee! I have something special for your new video. Come by the day after tomorrow for an exclusive tasting. This will be your superior video yet!"

Excitement pushed aside her melancholy. Exclusive content! Antoine was a charmer and his chocolate was Instagrammable. This was accurately what she needed to reach 100K followers before her birthday next month.

She quickly tapped an enthusiastic confirmation, her thoughts already on the outfit she'd wear and the perfect angle to film the pralines. Her gaze slid once more to her sister's photo, a brief flash of the home she'd left behind for this new world of possibilities and complexities. “Slay all day,” she murmured, half to herself, half to the girl she’d once been. “But please remember why you’re here.”

She closed Instagram and opened TikTok. There were still at least a hundred videos to watch before she’d even consider going to sleep. And maybe, if she were lucky, Simon would finally reply to one of her messages.

A girl could always dream.

HAPPY PILL

The workshop behind 'Dreams of Lina' was filled in the morning with the soft sound of Lina's voice dancing through the warm air. She'd pushed aside the worries of the previous evening. She sang in a language no human had spoken for centuries—ancient Maya words mixed with melodies that sounded like flowing water and rustling tree leaves.

Her hands moved in perfect harmony with her voice, stirring in a large copper cauldron where a deep, almost purple chocolate mass slowly melted. Steam rose in spirals, responding to her song as if it were a living being, listening to her voice.

Morpheus, stretched out on a high shelf between pots of exotic herbs, observing her with half-closed eyes. His tail swayed slowly back and forth, the only indication that he wasn't sleeping.

"Ik-nal-le ku-kulel," sang Lina, her voice rising in a crescendo as she sprinkled a handful of dried flower petals into the mixture. "Tsa-lik beh u k'a-lik yaah."

Life returns again, clear the path of pain.

She added a pinch of cinnamon-like powder, then a drop of a shimmering liquid from a small bottle on the shelf. The chocolate pulsed once with a deep, amber light.

"If you're going to dance, you could at least sing something more exciting," Morpheus remarked dryly as Lina began to hop around the cauldron, her movements light and rhyth-

mic. "Something with a beat. Disco, perhaps. Or hip-hop."
Lina smiled without losing her rhythm. "I doubt 'Stayin' Alive' has the same healing properties as a thousand-year-old Maya blessing," she replied, now spinning with each step.

"Technically speaking," said Morpheus, slowly stretching in the way only cats can, "the song 'Stayin' Alive' is perfectly suited for people struggling with life-threatening illnesses. It's in the title."

Lina's smile widened as she added a pinch of crumbled lava blossom—a plant that only grew at the edges of volcanoes in the Underworld, its rare leaves a brilliant red reminiscent of the first morning light.

"This batch is for the children's ward at St John's Hospital," she explained whilst continuing her dancing movements around the cauldron. "Children who are losing the will to fight because the treatments are so harsh."

Morpheus rolled his eyes theatrically. "Ah, of course. And your magical chocolate will have them dancing through the corridors, abandoning beds, astonishing doctors."

"Not quite," Lina replied, amused by his cynicism. "It will simply return taste to their world. Literally—many of these children lose their sense of taste through treatments—but also figuratively. It will subtly shift the chemical balance in their brains, brighten their outlook, help them find pleasure in small things."

"Medicine in chocolate form," said Morpheus mockingly. "How... predictable."

"Effective," Lina corrected, now rhythmically tapping on the cauldron with a wooden spoon. "Ku-ku-lel, ku-ku-lel, ti'-ik ki yetel ki'imak olal." *Come back, come back, fill yourself with joy.*

She moved faster now, almost dancing on her toes around the cauldron, her purple velvet cloak swirling around her like an exotic flower opening in the first sunlight. It was a sight few were privileged to see—Lina in her element, unguarded, completely surrendered to the magic of her craft.

"You look like a demented ballerina enchanting a witch's cauldron," Morpheus observed. "Bit over the top, don't you think?"

Lina laughed aloud, the sound echoing through the workshop.

"Jealous because you can't dance with those four left paws of yours?"
"Cats are the most graceful creatures in the universe," Morpheus replied haughtily. "We simply don't dance for an audience. It's beneath our dignity."
"Says the cat I saw chasing a ball of tin foil yesterday."
"That was a tactical exercise. Entirely different."
The chanting reached a climax, and Lina's dance became faster, more intense. The chocolate in the cauldron now began to glow with a warm, golden light that made the entire room gleam. With a final high note, Lina stopped, her arms stretched above the cauldron, her eyes closed in deep concentration.
The glow retreated into the chocolate mass, absorbing into every molecule. It became dark again, but in a deeper, richer way—like the night sky full of stars instead of simple darkness.
"Finished," Lina sighed, opening her eyes. She picked up a set of metal moulds from a nearby shelf. Instead of the traditional hearts or curves one would expect from a chocolate maker, these moulds had the shape of large pills and capsules.
"The 'Happy Pill'," she announced as she poured the now perfectly tempered chocolate into the moulds. "Medicine without side effects, joy without crash, hope without illusion."
"Except a chocolate hangover after eating a dozen in one go," Morpheus noted, but his tone was softer now, almost respectful.
"That's why each patient only gets two," Lina smiled. "One for the body, one for the soul."
She carefully placed the filled moulds in the cooling chamber, her movements now precise and methodical, a contrast to her earlier dance. When she turned around, she saw that Morpheus had jumped down from his shelf and was inspecting the now empty cauldron.
"You have a talent for it," he said, and for once, there was no sarcasm in his voice. "Your mother would be proud."
Lina felt a stab of emotion at the rare sincerity. "Thank you," she said simply.
"Well," Morpheus continued, breaking the moment with his

usual sarcasm, "if this chocolate-medicine business doesn't work out, you could always start a career as a dancer. Though I'd recommend taking some lessons first."

Lina threw a tea towel at him, which he nimbly dodged with a fluid movement. But she was smiling, knowing that beneath his cynical façade, Morpheus knew as well as she did that what she'd just created was truly magical.

After cooling, she would pack the chocolate pills in small boxes, each decorated with hand-painted butterflies and stars, with a handwritten note: "Take twice daily, with a sip of wonder."

Next week, a nurse from the children's ward would tell her in confidence about a seven-year-old girl who had laughed for the first time in months, about a teenage boy who had started drawing again, about parents who had tears in their eyes seeing a spark of zest for life return to their children's eyes.

By then, Lina would already be working on the next batch, dancing around her cauldron, singing in a language as old as time itself, whilst Morpheus provided commentary from his shelf—a ritual as old as their friendship, a dance of creation and magic disguised as everyday life.

BITTERSWEET

After his nocturnal escape from Simon's flat, Finn wandered through the misty morning streets of Bruges, his thoughts' chaos of confusion and fear. The jade cocoa bean, the stolen museum piece, Simon's manipulation, the blood he'd taken... it was all too much to process.

He had to find that chocolate shop, had to discover who Lina Vandevelde was and why his mother had said he should seek her out if he was in danger.

A sudden downpour drove him under the awning of a small café on the corner of the Dijver. Whilst he stood there, trying to sort his thoughts, he heard a cheerful, loud voice from inside the café.

"...and then I told Marie that her husband wasn't just having 'late meetings', but that he sits with that new barista at 't Hoekje every Wednesday! And not for the coffee, if you catch my drift!" Finn checked his phone, his battery died.

Shrill, cackling laughter followed. Finn looked through the window and saw an elderly woman in a strikingly bright yellow coat seated at a table with what looked like a morning club of Bruges ladies of a certain age. A small wicker basket stood beside her chair, in which the nervous face of a small Yorkshire terrier peeped.

The woman leaned forward, her hand theatrically beside her mouth, as if she were about to share a great secret. "And did you know the mayor's been to that new chocolate shop twice this week already? Not for the history, if you ask me. That shop girl with her short skirts..."

The other women giggled like schoolgirls, completely taken with the storytelling performance of this cheerful gossip.

The rain lessened and Finn was about to leave when the café door swung open and the old woman stepped out, her wicker basket with the little dog on her arm.

"Ah, you must be Anna's boy!" she said without preamble, in a tone as if greeting an old friend.

Finn stiffened. "How did you know my mother?"

The woman laughed, a surprisingly youthful and hearty sound. "I know everyone, love. That's my speciality. Ingrid Vermeulen's the name, and this here is Pouffe." She held up the basket in which the little dog trembled and stared at Finn with heightened intensity.

Finn instinctively stepped back. Animals usually didn't like him, could smell his werewolf nature, but this dog seemed more... interested than afraid.

"No worries, he doesn't bite," Ingrid assured him. "Unless I tell him to, of course! Ha!" She laughed again at her joke. "So, you're looking for Lina Vandevelde, yes? The chocolate shop with the purple sign?"

"How do you know that I—"

"Wijngaardstraat 12, the side street that ends at the Lake of Love," Ingrid interrupted, a hot pink lacquered finger pointing upwards. "You can't miss it. And tell her Ingrid sent you, then she'll know you're to be trusted."

Finn blinked confused. "But I haven't even said that—"

"Things happen in Bruges," said Ingrid, her voice suddenly more serious, her eyes sharper and less vague than her theatrical behaviour suggested. "Things that most people don't see or don't want to see. Your mother knew that. I know that. Lina knows that." She patted his arm. "And deep under those cheap sports shirts you always wear, you know it, too."

Before Finn could respond, she turned and walked towards the Rozenhoedkaai, her bright yellow raincoat a beacon in the

grey morning, her voice already loud again as she answered her phone: "No, Marie! I'm telling you, it wasn't the baker's wife, it was his wife's niece! The one with the short haircut, you know!"
Finn stared after her, feeling as if he'd just met a small tornado. But despite her eccentric behaviour and apparent superficiality, she'd told him exactly where he needed to go.
Wijngaardstraat 12. Lina Vandevelde.
With a last glance at the glowing yellow spot that was Ingrid, he set course for the chocolate shop, his senses on high alert and his curiosity piqued by this strange, all-knowing old woman who knew exactly who he was and what he was looking for.

Whilst Finn walked through the misty streets of Bruges, heading for Lina, his thoughts drifted back to a moment, years ago, when the world still seemed simpler.
He was fifteen, maybe sixteen, and it was a rare day when his mother had time off from work. Anna De Wulf worked as a nurse in shifts, her life dictated by the unpredictable rhythms of the hospital. But that day was different. She'd taken him to the Sonian Forest, an ancient wood not far from Brussels, for what she called a "special walk".
"Come on, sleepyhead!" his mother had woken him that morning, her voice warm and energetic. "The day waits for no one, and we have much to discover!"
Finn had groaned, his teenage body protesting against the early hour. "It's the weekend, Mum," he'd moaned, burying his head under the pillow.
But Anna De Wulf wasn't the type of woman who gave up easily. She drew the curtains open, let the morning light stream into the room, and playfully tugged at his duvet. "The forests are waiting, Finn. There are things I need to teach you, now that it's almost time."
Those last words had made him look up, curious despite his sleepiness. "Time for what?"
She'd only smiled, a mysterious expression that in-

trigued him. "You'll see. Put your walking boots on." Finn had dressed while grumbling, but by the time they were in the car, his natural enthusiasm had won over his teenage rebellious attitude. His mother had that effect on people—her joy was infectious, her energy inexhaustible.

The drive to the Sonian Forest was filled with their usual conversations—school, his football team, her stories about the more humorous aspects of hospital life. But there was something different about her that day, an underlying intensity that Finn couldn't quite place.

They parked at a secluded entrance to the forest, far from the main paths where tourists and day-trippers gathered. Anna took an old rucksack from the boot, heavier than Finn had expected when she handed it to him.

"What's in here? Rocks?" he asked jokingly.

"Tools," she answered simply. "Things you need to learn to use."

The forest welcomed them with the mild temperature of early autumn, a carpet of fallen leaves rustling under their feet. Anna led him off the main paths, seemingly moving randomly between the old beeches and oaks, but Finn noticed she regularly looked up at the sun, using its position to keep course.

After about an hour's walk, they reached a small clearing where a crystal-clear stream meandered through the moss. Here, Anna stopped and sat on a fallen tree trunk.

"Come, sit," she invited, patting the spot beside her. "It's time we talked."

Finn, now genuinely curious, obeyed. "About what? You've been mysterious all day, Mum."

Anna smiled, but there was a seriousness in her eyes he rarely saw. "About your inheritance, Finn. About what it means to be a De Wulf."

"Our family history?" he asked, slightly disappointed. He'd expected something more exciting after all this mysterious business.

"Yes and no," she replied. "It's more than just history. It's... a condition we share. A gift, some would call it a curse, that flows in our blood."

Finn felt a strange tingling down his spine. "What do you mean?" Instead of answering directly, Anna took a small penknife from her pocket. With a fluid movement, she made a small cut in her palm. Finn startled, but before he could protest, she held up her hand so he could see it.

The cut, which had seemed fairly deep, was already closing. As he watched, the wound faded before his eyes, until there was nothing but a thin pink line, and even that faded quickly.

"How..." he began, but words failed him.

"De Wulf is not merely a name, Finn," his mother said softly. "It's what we are. Or partially, at least."

"I don't understand," he said, but part of him did, a deep, instinctive part that had long known there was something different about him, about his mother, about the way they experienced the world.

"You'll understand soon," said Anna. "You're standing on the edge of considerable changes. Your body will transform in ways you can't predict, more than with other boys your age."

Finn's cheeks coloured. "Mum, if this is a puberty talk, we already had that in year five, and I really don't want to—"

Anna laughed, the sound echoing between the trees. "No, Finn, not that sort of change. Although that's part of it too." She became serious again. "I'm talking about your first transformation. It usually happens around your seventeenth or eighteenth, often triggered by intense emotion or stress. For me, it was when I was eighteen, during my final exams. Perhaps for a girl... or a boy, or both."

"Transformation?" Finn repeated, his throat suddenly dry. "Like in..."

She nodded. "Like in werewolf, yes. Although that word carries a lot of baggage thanks to films and folklore. The reality is... more complex."

Finn didn't know whether to laugh or run away. This had to be a joke. His practical, sensible mother, a nurse no less, was telling him she was a werewolf? That he would become one?

"You don't believe me," she stated, reading his reaction. "That's all right. I didn't believe my mother either when she told me. But I wish

I had. It would have made that first night much less traumatic." It was the honesty in her voice, the absence of any humour or mockery, that made Finn hesitate. His mother was many things, but she wasn't a liar, and certainly not a cruel joker.

"Let's say I believe you," he said slowly. "What does that mean for me?"

Anna opened the rucksack and began taking out various items—a leather bracelet with strange symbols, a bottle with liquid, herbs bundled with string, a thick notebook with yellowed pages.

"It means you must learn how to live with it," she said. "How to control the changes instead of being controlled by them. How to use your sharpened senses, your accelerated healing, your increased strength—without being discovered, without becoming a danger to others."

"It sounds like you're telling me I'm a superhero," said Finn, half-joking to hide his nervousness.

She smiled warmly. "In some ways, perhaps. But with great power..."

"Comes great responsibility," he finished automatically, rolling his eyes, thinking of the Spider-Man films he'd devoured as a child.

"Exactly." She picked up the notebook and handed it to him. "This was your grandmother's, and her mother's before that. It contains everything they learned about our... condition. Techniques to control transformation, herbal mixtures that help with the pain, places where it's safe to transform."

Finn took the book, leafing through the densely written pages full of diagrams, notes, and what looked like recipes. "This is mad," he muttered, but without real conviction.

"I know," said Anna, taking his hand. "And I wouldn't be telling you this now if it weren't necessary. But I see the signs, Finn. Your hearing's getting sharper, isn't it? And your sense of smell. You have bursts of anger that seem to come from nowhere. Dreams about running on four legs through an endless forest."

Finn looked up, shocked. She was describing exactly what he'd experienced over the past months, chang-

es he'd written off as normal puberty things, or perhaps excessive energy drink consumption during exams. "How do you know that?" he whispered.

"Because I went through the same thing," she answered simply. "And my mother before me, and her mother before her. We're an old bloodline, Finn. Not cursed, not blessed, just... different." She stood and reached for his hand to pull him up. "Come. There's much I want to teach you today, practical things that will help you when the time comes."

The rest of the day was intensive training in survival and self-control. Anna taught him how to tell which plants were edible by smell and taste, a skill that, according to her, was essential for a werewolf who might find himself alone in the wilderness after an unexpected transformation. She taught him breathing techniques to calm rising anger, which according to her was the biggest trigger for unwanted transformations.

"I need time to myself once a month," she told him as they walked along the stream. "I always say I have night shifts, but actually, I go to a remote cabin in the Ardennes. It's safe there, far from people. A place where I can be free in my other form."

"So you really do change into a... into a wolf?" Finn asked, still struggling with the concept.

"Not quite a wolf, not quite human. Something in between. And yes, it hurts, especially in the beginning. But there's also freedom in it, a connection to something older and wilder than our modern world. It has its price, but also its gifts."

Finn tried to imagine his practical, caring mother as a mythical creature, and found it hard to reconcile the two images. Yet, there was a part of him that instinctively responded to what she was telling him, a part deep in his blood that resonated with her words like a tuning fork on exactly the right note.

As the afternoon passed into evening and the shadows in the forest grew longer, they sat by the stream's edge, eating the wild berries and mushrooms Anna had gathered. It felt primitive and strangely familiar at the same time. "There's something else you need to know," said Anna, her tone suddenly more serious. "There are others like us, but not everyone is friendly. Some see their nature as a curse and hate themselves for it. Others embrace it too fully and lose their humanity."

"Sounds like an X-Men film," Finn tried to smile, still taking refuge in humour.

"Life imitates art, or the other way around," she beamed. "The point is, you must be careful. Trust your instincts, but don't be naive."

She paused, as if weighing how much she should tell. "If you're ever in real trouble, if you feel unsafe or if there are... problems after your transformation, there's someone you can trust in Bruges."

"In Bruges?" Finn asked, surprised. "Who?"

"Her name is Lina Vandevelde. She runs a chocolate shop. She's... like us, but different. She understands things that even I don't fully understand. She can help you in ways I can't."

"A chocolate shop?" Finn couldn't keep the scepticism out of his voice. "What can a chocolate maker know about..." He gestured vaguely towards the moon, still not entirely comfortable with the W-word.

Anna smiled mysteriously. "Much more than you'd think. Sweet secrets often hide the deepest truths."

They walked back in comfortable silence, Finn's head spinning with all the new information. At the edge of the forest, just before they reached the car park, Anna stopped and placed a hand on his shoulder.

"I wish I could make this easier for you, Finn," she said, her eyes soft with love and concern. "But the only thing I can give you is knowledge and support. The journey itself is yours."

She took out a small leather bracelet, decorated with what looked like a small silver wolf's head. "This was your father's. He wore it until the day he decided he couldn't live with what he was. It helped him stay calm during the full moon. Perhaps it'll do the same for you."

Finn took the bracelet, surprised. His father had left them when he was ten, and his mother rarely spoke of him. "Was he... like us?"

Anna nodded. "Yes. But he fought against it, hated the part of himself he couldn't change. Eventually, that hatred destroyed him from within." There was deep sadness in her eyes. "Promise me you'll never try to be what you're not, Finn. Promise me you'll learn to accept both parts of yourself."

Finn closed his fingers around the bracelet, feeling a strange sense of connection with the father he'd barely known. "I promise," he said, and he meant it, despite all the doubts and questions still haunting his head.

On the way home, he fell asleep in the car, the notebook clutched tightly to his chest. He didn't dream of monsters or transformations, but of a peaceful forest where he ran on four legs, free and fearless, with his mother running beside him in a form that was both strange and familiar.

When he woke, they were home, and the world seemed both the same and completely changed.

Now, years later, walking through the misty streets of Bruges, Finn felt the silver wolf pendant he wore around his wrist—he'd eventually worn the bracelet together with various festival bands that somewhat hid the bracelet from the curious. His mother's words echoed through his mind: "If you're ever in real trouble... there's someone you can trust. Her name is Lina Vandevelde."

He'd forgotten that name in the trauma of his mother's death and the struggle with his first full transformations. Only when he'd heard it from that eccentric old woman in Bruges had the memory returned.

"You were right, Mum," he said barely audibly in the mist. "About everything."

The morning air in Bruges was ice-cold, crystal blue after the night's storm. Finn shivered as he stood before 'Dreams of Lina', the purple sign swaying gently in the winter wind. The shop was still closed, only a faint light visible behind the stained-glass windows.

The night full of strange dreams and more-intense-than-normal sensory perceptions had exhausted him. He was barely

rested after his escape from Simon's flat, too obsessed with what he'd seen and the urge to find this Lina Vandevelde. *Why had his mother mentioned her name on her deathbed?*
Finn breathed deeply. The air around the shop smelled different from the rest of Bruges – richer, sweeter, with undertones of spices he couldn't identify and something ancient, like parchment and charcoal. His heightened sense of smell, always stronger in the days around the full moon, picked up details that normal people missed.
He knocked three times on the door – harder than intended. A long silence followed. He was about to walk away when he heard footsteps approaching. The door opened a crack.
A pair of penetrating blue eyes studied him – alert, calculating. They belonged to a woman in her late twenties, with light-brown hair in a loose bun. She wore a purple velvet cloak that seemed made for another century.
"We don't open until eleven," she said, her voice soft but powerful.
"Are you Lina Vandevelde?" asked Finn, suddenly uncertain about his mission.
The woman opened the door slightly wider. "Who wants to know?"
"My name is Finn De Wulf. I... this sounds mad, but my mother mentioned your name before she died. She said I should find you if I was ever in danger."
Lina's posture changed subtly. "De Wulf?" She studied his face more carefully. "Who was your mother?"
"Anna. She died two years ago."
Something flashed in Lina's eyes – recognition? "Wait here." She closed the door.
Finn stood dejected on the doorstep. Had he made a mistake? But a moment later, the door swung fully open.
"Come in," said Lina. "The streets have ears in Bruges."
The inside of the chocolate shop was like a time capsule – antique counters of dark wood and glass, copper instruments that gleamed in the soft light, and the smell... the smell was intoxicating. Chocolate, but deeper, richer than anything Finn

had ever smelled. He felt light-headed from the intensity.
"You don't look your best," Lina observed as she led him to a small table at the back and indicated a chair. "When did you last sleep?"
"Last night. Or rather, I tried to." Finn pulled his jacket tighter around himself, suddenly shivering. "I was at Simon Laurent's. In his flat."
Lina stiffened. "Laurent?"
"He'd ordered a pizza. Or rather, someone had placed an order in his name. It was a trap." Finn felt his cheeks burn. "He... he drugged me. Knew things he couldn't know. About me, about what I am."
Lina suddenly seemed older, her face more severe. "And what exactly are you, Finn De Wulf?"
Finn hesitated. He'd kept this secret his entire life, but this strange woman with her intense eyes seemed to know exactly what he was struggling with. "I'm... I'm not entirely human. At the full moon, my body changes. Since puberty. My mother called it a family curse. She had it too, but could hide it better than I can."
"A werewolf," said Lina, not questioning but confirming. She crossed her arms. "What happened at Laurent?"
"He gave me coffee. It brought... the beast out, even without a full moon. And then..." Finn struggled with the words. "We had sex, I think. But during... he took blood from me. He filled a small vial. My memory's a bit fuzzy."
Something dark passed over Lina's face. "Forced blood extraction. Classic Laurent tactics." She turned and walked to a copper kettle sitting on an antique stove. "You were lucky you could escape. Most... guests of the Laurents don't wake up."
"There was something else," Finn added. "In his flat. There was a jade sculpture, shaped like some sort of bean. It attracted me in a way I can't explain."
Lina turned abruptly, her eyes wide. "You saw it? The stolen Maya artefact?"
"I think so. It seemed to glow in the dark."
"And it... called to you?" Lina's voice was soft, almost reverent.

"Yes. How did you know that?" Instead of answering, Lina pushed back the high collar of her cloak, revealing a silver chain with a small pendant. It was a silver replica of the jade object Finn had seen – the same cacao bean shape, the same strange inscriptions, only smaller. It glinted in the morning light with an unnatural brightness.
"Because you, Finn De Wulf, are more than just a werewolf. You're a Bearer."
A shadow moved at the edge of Finn's vision. He turned instinctively, his muscles tensing. From nowhere, a black cat materialized on the table, its amber eyes observing Finn with unnatural intelligence.
"He smells like Laurent," said the cat in a deep, sardonic voice. "And a hint of fear. Interesting combination."
Finn jumped up, his chair clattering on the wooden floor. "Your cat... talks."
"And you turn into a wolf at full moon," Lina shot back. "We all have our peculiarities." She placed a steaming mug in front of Finn. "Drink this. It'll neutralize the after-effects of what Laurent gave you."
"Shut your mouth, pizza boy, before you catch flies," Morpheus remarked, his feline eyes gleaming with amused disdain. "Never seen a talking cat that transforms into a shadow demon? Typical humans – always amazed by the most mundane things."
"Mundane?" stammered Finn, finally finding his voice. "I wouldn't classify 'a talking cat that transforms into... whatever you are' as particularly mundane."
"And I wouldn't consider a boy who turns into a furry biting machine every month as an authority on what's normal," Morpheus retorted, in the tone of someone explaining that water is wet.
"I'm not a 'furry biting machine'!" protested Finn, indignant.
"Of course not," Morpheus consoled, his voice dripping with sarcasm. "You're a majestic, elegant predator who happens to have an unfortunate allergy to full moons and silver cutlery. My apologies for the terminological inaccuracy."

Lina sighed deeply. "If you two are finished with this fascinating debate on taxonomy, perhaps we could return to the not unimportant fact that someone has tried to poison the mayor and blame me for it?"
"She started it," Finn grumbled, pointing at Morpheus.
"He," corrected the shadow cat with a raised eyebrow.
"Pardon?"
"He. I identify as male, thank you very much. Just as you identify as human 29 days per month and as 'I suddenly have lots of hair and an unreasonable need to howl at the moon' on day 30."
"I don't howl at the moon!"
"Of course not, you just serenade her. Thoroughly different."
Lina put her hand over her face, but not before Finn caught a glimpse of a suppressed smile.
The liquid in the mug was dark as coffee, but smelled of chocolate, herbs, and something earthy that Finn couldn't identify. He hesitated.
"It's not poison," Lina assured him. "If I'd wanted to harm you, I wouldn't have let you in."
Taking a deep breath, Finn took a cautious sip. The flavour exploded on his tongue – rich, bitter, complex, with a warmth that spread through his body. Immediately he felt the fog in his head clear, the trembling in his muscles diminish.
"What is this?" he asked, gripping the mug with both hands.
"Xocolatl," answered Lina. "The original drink formula of the Maya. Long before Europeans mixed cacao with sugar, it was drunk as a herbal brew with medicinal and... spiritual properties."
"Spiritual?"
The cat hissed.
"She means magical. Not that dancing new-age spirituality."
"Thank you, Morpheus. Always so helpful," Lina said.
Finn looked between them. "Right, so we have talking cats, werewolves, stolen Maya artefacts and magical chocolate. Is anyone willing to tell me what's going on?"
Lina sat opposite him, her hands flat on the ta-

ble. "What do you know about dreams, Finn?"
"Dreams? You mean, whilst sleeping?"
"Not ordinary dreams. The deep dreams. The dreams that make your spine tingle, that stay with you for hours afterwards. The dreams in which you fly, or discover underwater worlds, or... run as a wolf through endless forests." Her eyes bored into his. "Those dreams."
Finn felt a sudden heat in his chest. How did she know about his wolf dreams? Those dreams he'd had since childhood, long before his body began to change?
"What do dreams have to do with this?"
"Everything." Lina leaned forward. "Dreams aren't brain activity, Finn. Or, at least, not only that. They're literal connections to another reality – the Underworld, as the Maya called it. A parallel realm where everything that can be dreamed exists."
The cat – Morpheus – jumped onto Lina's shoulder, his tail swishing. "And the only reason you, with your limited human brain, have access to it is thanks to us."
"Us?"
"Chocolate makers," Lina clarified. "Or rather, Dream Weavers. My family learnt the art from Maya priests – chocolate that doesn't just taste, but opens doors to the Underworld. To dreams."
Finn stared at the nearly empty mug in his hand.
"This chocolate..."
"Is merely a weak echo. A medicinal mix. But yes, it contains the basis of what my family has been making for generations – chocolate that strengthens the connection between worlds." She pointed to the silver pendant at her neck. "This is one of the three Keys that the Maya made to regulate that connection. The silver cacao bean, in my family since it was made."
"And the jade version I saw at Laurent's..."
"The jade key, stolen from the museum just over a month ago." Lina's voice hardened. "The third, a golden bean, disappeared centuries ago. Together they can be used to permanently open the gate to the Underworld... or permanently close it."
Finn tried to process this. "And Simon Lau-

rent wants to close this... Underworld? Why?"
"Because the Laurents have always believed that dreams are a weakness," Morpheus growled. "An infection in human consciousness. They want a world without imagination, without magic, without possibilities. A world they can control."
"And what does this have to do with me? Why did Laurent take my blood?"
Lina and Morpheus exchanged a look. "Because you're a werewolf," Lina said finally. "A being that exists in two worlds. Your blood has... properties that can strengthen or weaken powerful magic."
Finn let this information sink in. It was mad, and yet... it fitted. The wolf dreams he'd always had, the strange attraction to the jade object, the knowledge Laurent had about him.
"Wait," he said suddenly. "You said Laurent poisoned the mayor? Not you?"
"Finally he's asking the right questions," Morpheus murmured.
"Yes," Lina confirmed. "Laurent – or someone working for him – counterfeited chocolate that looked like mine, and gave it to the mayor. A double strike – trying to eliminate an important person and blame me for it."
"But why the mayor?"
"Because Robert Maillard knows more than he should," said Lina. "He's one of the few people in Bruges with conscious access to the Underworld. I suspect he's seen something – something that threatens Simon Laurent."
Finn tried to process this bizarre information. He stared at the black cat studying him with those strange, intelligent eyes.
"And you?" he asked Morpheus. "What are you in all this?"
The cat grinned, revealing unnaturally sharp teeth. "I'm a servant of the Underworld. A... link, shall we say, between worlds. The Maya called my kind 'bixan' – shadow walkers. Your culture would call me a demon, or a deity, depending on how polite you want to be."
"Morpheus has been connected to my family for generations," Lina added. "He helps us maintain the balance between worlds."

"In exchange for cream and a warm spot by the fire," the cat added as a reminder of their arrangements.
"So, you're what... four hundred years old?" Finn asked the feline figure.
"Four hundred and eighty-three, to be precise," Morpheus responded dryly.
"Cool. So you lived through the plague. And Spanish flu. And—"
"And now TikTok dances. Truly, human civilisation reaches ever new depths."
"Says the cat who licks his own arse for a quarter of an hour each day."
"Twenty minutes, thank you. I'm thorough. And before you ask: no, I don't have Instagram for cats, no Insta-paws or whatever you lot have invented. The last time someone tried to photograph me for social media, I pissed in his expensive trainers."
"Back on topic. What do you want from me?" asked Finn De Wulf. "If all this is true, why would I get involved in your... magical war?"
"Because Simon Laurent took your blood without consent," Lina said seriously. "Werewolf blood, used in a ritual, can have catastrophic consequences. Not just for you, but for everyone in Bruges." She stood up. "And because your mother Anna wanted me to help you. She knew what was coming. Dream Weavers like her often have prophetic dreams."
Finn felt his heart skip. "My mother wasn't a chocolatier."
"No, but she was a natural Dream Weaver. Rare, but it does happen." Lina's eyes softened. "I met her several times, when you were still a child. She came to my mother for help understanding your... condition."
"You knew who I was when I came in."
"I had a suspicion. The De Wulf line is old, one of the few families with the true werewolf mutation rather than a curse or infection."
Finn tried to understand all this. "So what now? You expect me to... what? Help you stop Laurent? How?"
Lina smiled, and for the first time Finn saw genuine warmth in her expression.

Morpheus said: "You need to shower. You still smell of Eau Laurent, and that's really quite unpleasant for my sensitive nose."

Despite everything, Finn felt a smile tug at his lips and his stomach muscles contract. "Is he always like this?"

"No," answered Lina. "Usually he's much worse."

"Charming," Finn spoke indistinctly.

"After a shower and rest," Lina continued, "we're going to the hospital. If the mayor's awake, he's our best source of information about what Laurent's planning."

"And if he's not awake?"

"Then we'll have to find another way to reach his dreams." Lina's face hardened. "A dangerous way."

UNHAPPY GAY DAY

Three years ago

"Make a wish, Finnie-boy!"

Finn looked with mixed feelings at the eighteen cheap candles stuck into the supermarket chocolate cake – more than his mother could really afford this month. The small flat felt even smaller with the five lads from his football team standing awkwardly around the kitchen table. He'd deliberated for ages about whom to invite, or whether to invite anyone at all, but ultimately, he'd just bitten the bullet under social pressure.

He took a deep breath, his wish already prepared in his head. *That I can just be who I am. That it'll be chill someday.* He blew out all the candles in one go, which earned a sort of half-hearted round of applause.

"Here," said his mother, handing him a simple kitchen knife. "You get to cut the first pieces."

Anna De Wulf looked tired, but she curled the corners of her mouth – a smile that didn't quite reach her eyes. She'd been pulling double shifts at the hospital to pay the rent since Finn's father had buggered off. Finn knew she'd really tried to make this birthday a bit special, despite everything. He cut the cake into exactly equal pieces, counting carefully – one for each guest, one for his mother, one for himself. No leftovers, nothing wasted. That was something he'd had to learn young.

"So," began Marco, the team captain and by far the coolest lad in the group, as he took a bite of his cake. "Is that Isabelle coming tonight? Thought you'd invited her?"
Finn felt his cheeks warm, but he'd expected this question. Isabelle was the girl the whole school thought he fancied. He'd never denied that rumour – it was easier than dropping the truth.
"Nah, couldn't make it," he answered quickly, knowing he'd never invited her. His eyes shot involuntarily to Daan, the quiet lad from the neighbourhood who'd been at his school before Finn transferred to the sports programme. Daan was the only non-footballer in the group, and Finn's heart skipped a beat when their eyes met.
"Shame, mate," grinned Kevin, a defender with far too big a mouth. "Would've been a laugh having a bird here. Now it's all a bit..." He made a limp-wrist gesture that could only mean one thing.
"A bit what?" asked Finn, though he already knew the answer.
"You know," said Kevin, still grinning. "Gay shit."
The word hung in the air like a hand grenade with the pin just pulled. Finn's mother, who was fiddling around in the small kitchen, stiffened for a moment but said nothing. She knew, of course, but they'd never really talked about it.
"And what if it is?" The words tumbled out of Finn's mouth before he could stop them.
An awkward silence fell across the room. Marco's smile disappeared. "What d'you mean?"
Finn's heart was hammering like mad in his throat. This absolutely wasn't his plan. Not on his birthday, not in front of these lads. But he was so bloody tired of hiding, of pretending.
"I mean, what the fuck, what if it is gay? Or what if I am?" His voice cracked a bit, but he kept his eyes fixed on Kevin. The silence that followed was so thick you could cut it with a knife. Finn could hear his mother catching her breath.
"Wtf, are you taking the piss?" asked Jasper, the third lad from his team. "No," said Finn, his throat bone dry. "But I'm gay." Kevin's face twisted into a grimace. "Damn, bro, that's... Why

d'you invite us, then?" The question hit Finn like a punch to the gut. "Because you're my mates? I thought, anyway."
"Right, chill," said Marco quickly, always the peacemaker. "We're still your boys, yeah, Kev?"
Kevin didn't look convinced. "Course, whatever. But that doesn't mean I don't find it weird. Have you... have you been perving on us in the changing room ?"
"Oh my God, seriously?" Finn jumped up, his cake completely forgotten. "Is that really what you think? That I'm checking you out? Newsflash, Kevin, you're absolutely not my type."
"Easy, everyone," came Anna's voice from the kitchen. She came into the room, her face pale but determined. "This is still a birthday party."
But the damage was already done. An uncomfortable tension hung in the room, getting worse with every second.
Thomas, the fourth teammate who'd kept his mouth shut until now, suddenly stood up. "Cheers, this was brilliant. Think I'll bounce," he said, leaving his cake half-eaten. "Um, happy birthday and all that, Finn."
Kevin and Jasper quickly followed, muttering similar bullshit excuses. Only Marco remained sitting, clearly torn between loyalty to his friend and pressure to go with the other lads.
"You don't have to stay," said Finn, his voice now hard with the emotion he was trying to push away. "Go on with your homophobic mates."
"They're not... it's just a shock, yeah?" Marco stood up too. "Allow them some time to process it."
The door slammed shut behind the four footballers, and the silence in the flat was suffocating. Anna came and sat next to Finn, put a hand on his shoulder.
"Sorry, love," she said softly.
"It's alright," Finn replied automatically, though they both knew it was bollocks. He looked up and saw that Daan was still sitting at the table, his cake untouched, his eyes wide with... not disgust, Finn realized, but understanding.
"You already knew," said Finn, not a question but a statement.
Daan nodded slowly. "Had a feeling. Doesn't bother me, for

what it's worth." Finn was overwhelmed by gratitude, followed by a strange sort of relief. If this was the end of his friendships, sod it. At least one person had stayed.
Later that evening, after Daan had left with a sort of awkward bro-hug and a promise to text later, Finn sat alone on his bed. His phone lit up with a message from Marco:

> "Sorry about today. I still think you're chill. The rest just need time."

It was more than he'd expected, but less than he'd hoped for. Tomorrow at school the whispers would start, the looks. The rumour would spread like a virus – Finn The Gay – and everything would be different. The football team would be awkward, the changing room a no-go zone. His phone pinged again. This time it was Daan.

> "Wanted to say this earlier but didn't dare. I'm gay too. Thx for your courage today."

Finn stared at the message, a mix of emotions racing through him. Pride, fear, hope, regret. But also something else – a realization that he no longer had to fake it, at least not with Daan. He typed back:

> "Thx for stayin'. Means a lot."

What Finn didn't know then was that within a month the rumours would become so toxic that he'd quit football, that he'd lose Daan because he was too scared to be associated with "that gay bloke," that he'd flee into individual sports – fitness and running – and that he'd learn to hide his true self behind a wall of normal friendliness.
His eighteenth birthday – the day he'd finally dared to be himself – ironically became the start of a new period of hiding.

DANCE

The doorbell of 'Dreams of Lina' chimed cheerfully as a customer entered, a slender person in their early twenties with short, asymmetrical hair in a soft lavender shade – a colour dear to Lina's heart. They wore an oversized grey jumper over tight black leggings, with ankle boots that made them just a bit taller than they already were. Their movements had a natural grace that immediately reminded Lina of a dancer.

"Welcome," Lina greeted them with a smile, whilst placing a final praline in the display case. "May I help you with anything?"

The customer moved through the space with a suppleness that Lina had only seen in professional dancers, almost as if gravity had slightly less hold on them. She smiled as they approached the counter.

"I'm looking for something special," they said with a melodious voice. "Something that helps with..." they made a vague gesture with their hand, "dreams, I think? Someone at the dance academy said your chocolate can help."

Lina nodded understandingly. "Dreams are my speciality. Do you have a specific sort of dream in mind?"

As she spoke, Lina moved her head slightly, causing her hair clip – a small, finely crafted silver object in the shape of a miniature broomstick – to catch the light.

"Wow," the customer leaned slightly closer, eyes wide with admiration. "That hair clip is gorgeous!" They

smiled more broadly. "You've got excellent taste." Lina's hand automatically went to the clip – a magical object that could actually transform into a real flying broomstick when needed, but that wasn't something she usually shared with customers.
"Thank you," she said, genuinely pleased with the compliment. "I wear it almost daily. I got it from my mother." The customer nodded approvingly and then let their gaze drift over the pralines in the display case.
"So, tell me," said Lina, returning to the original conversation, "what is your dream? What do you hope to find in your sleep that might help you in your waking life?"
The customer hesitated. "I'm a jazz dancer," they began. "Or I'm trying to be one, anyway. I'd like to dream about... acceptance, I think? Confidence in who I am." Lina nodded encouragingly. "Those are powerful dreams. Acceptance is a gift we must give ourselves before others can do so."
"Exactly," the customer leaned slightly closer, as if sharing a secret. "My coach keeps insisting I should be more 'masculine' in my physical presentation and movements. Especially to be able to lift female dancers. He says the audience doesn't want to see someone with my..." they gestured towards their slim, androgynous body, "...appearance lifting those traditionally seen as 'more graceful.'"
"That sounds frustrating," said Lina with genuine sympathy. "He's trying to squeeze you into a corset that doesn't fit who you are."
"Exactly! I want him to accept that I can lift and support brilliantly without changing my physical appearance. I dream of dancing as myself." They straightened their shoulders slightly. "Oh, and I use they/them pronouns, by the way. Plenty of people make assumptions based on how I look."
"My apologies," Lina responded immediately, without a trace of discomfort.
They smiled, clearly at ease with her reaction. "No worries. It's refreshing when people just accept it without making a big deal of it." Lina let her gaze drift over the pralines, thoughtfully.

"I think I know exactly what you need." She picked up a small box and began carefully selecting specific pralines. "This one here," she pointed to a delicate praline with a spiral pattern, "helps strengthen your natural balance – literally and figuratively. And this one," she added a dark, almost black bonbon with a subtle golden shimmer, "opens dreams of self-acceptance, where you can explore your true self without others' expectations."

The dancer watched fascinated as she filled the box. "How do you know all this? Is it just marketing, or...?"

Lina grinned mysteriously. "Let's say, my family has understood for generations that chocolate can be more than just a treat. There's magic in connecting the senses with emotions, and in dreams we often find the answers we can't see in the waking world."

"That sounds almost too good to be true," they said, but there was a hopeful tone in their voice.

"Magic is just a word for things we don't fully understand yet," Lina replied, closing the box with an elegant purple ribbon. "And dreams are the bridge between what is and what could be."

The dancer nodded, as if this made perfect sense. "I hadn't actually expected you to be so... understanding. Not everyone in Bruges is so open-minded." "In my work," said Lina, handing over the box, "you quickly learn that people are as varied as the flavours they prefer."

"That's undoubtedly the sort of acceptance I'm looking for," they said, taking the box and pointing towards the till. "How much do I owe you?"

Lina named a price that was surprisingly reasonable for handmade chocolate, and the dancer paid with a smile. "Eat one just before bedtime," Lina instructed. "Let it melt slowly on your tongue, and think about what you want to dream about. The rest will come naturally."

"Thank you," they said sincerely. "Not just for the chocolate, but for listening. That's sometimes just as valuable." As they turned to leave, Lina added: "If your coach can't see that strength can take many forms, that's his loss. True strength doesn't come from how you look, but from who you are."

They paused at the door, a genuine smile on their face. "I think I need to write that on my mirror. See you next time. Are you still looking for help?"

"Yes, just for weekends and Wednesdays." They nodded. The bell chimed again as the door closed, and Lina was left with a warm feeling. It was customers like them who reminded her why she did this work – not just making chocolate, but helping people find their dreams, in whatever form they took.

Morpheus, who had observed the entire conversation from a sunny windowsill, opened one eye. "That was almost touching," he noted dryly.

"Even you have a heart, Morpheus," Lina replied, lightly extending her hand to scratch his head.

"Barely," he said, but leaned subtly into her touch. "Though I must admit there's something fascinating about how humans struggle with identity. Beings like me don't have that problem – we are what we are."

"And yet, you choose to spend most of your time as a sarcastic black cat," Lina observed with a smile.

"Style isn't a matter of identity, but of aesthetics," Morpheus replied haughtily, before closing his eyes again and pretending to sleep.

Lina's thoughts returned to the dancer as she continued with her work. In a world where the barrier between dreams and reality was growing ever thinner, it was encouraging to meet people who were already busy redefining their boundaries. Perhaps, she thought, that's where real magic began – not with spells or artefacts, but with the courage to be yourself, regardless of what forms others tried to impose on you.

STEAM AND SILENCE

The water from the shower in the sports facility streamed over Finn's tired muscles, washing away the sweat and exertion from the intensive training session. As a second-year sports science student, he'd learnt that pushing his body's limits was the only way to get stronger, but every so often he wondered if his lecturers took his... unique physiology into account.

Since his first full transformation five years ago, Finn had noticed that his body reacted differently to training. Muscles recovered faster, endurance was superhuman, but the tension between his human and wolf nature made him more susceptible to injuries if he wasn't careful. It was a delicate balance that his mother had tried to teach him, but which he was still refining.

He closed his eyes, let the water stream over his face when suddenly the memory returned unexpectedly.

A memory from last year, in this same shower room, but under very different circumstances.

He'd been alone, or so he thought, the last one remaining after an evening session. Most of the lights were already dimmed, the facility nearly closed. Finn had taken extra time, working on his fitness, trying to exhaust his body in hopes of sleeping better that night. The full moon was still three days away, but he could feel her influence already – a restlessness in his blood, a tingling under his skin.

The shower had helped, the water almost hot enough to burn, washing away the instability that bubbled in his muscles. He'd just closed his eyes when he heard a sound – a locker slamming shut, footsteps on the tiled floor.
"Thought I was the last one," came a voice, deep and with a slight Antwerp accent.
Finn turned around, surprised. He vaguely recognised the other student – Mathias? Matthieu? One of the third-year physiotherapy students. They'd spoken a few times in the sports café, superficial conversations about football matches and shared professors.
"I'm nearly done," Finn replied, suddenly self-conscious about his nakedness, though that was rarely a problem in changing rooms.
"No rush," the other grinned, beginning to strip off his training clothes. "Haven't even started yet. Coach wanted to go through some specific exercises for my knee rehab."
Finn nodded, not sure what the appropriate response was, and turned back under the stream. He wanted to reach for his shampoo when he noticed that the other student had chosen the shower next to his, despite twelve others being unused.
"Sánchez scored a cracking goal today, did you see it?" asked the student – Finn decided to call him Matthieu from now on, with his characteristic tattooed bicep of a Chinese dragon with some decorative Kanji characters.
"No, missed it," Finn replied. "Had lectures until six."
"Mental. I've got the clip on my phone if you want to see."
Finn turned slightly, frowning. Though male camaraderie in changing rooms was normal, this conversation had a strange energy. Or maybe it was his heightened senses, already more sensitive due to the approaching full moon, making him hyperaware of the subtle signals in Matthieu's posture, scent, heartbeat. There was desire there. Interest. And not just friendly.
"Maybe later," Finn replied evasively, moving faster to finish his shower ritual. He wasn't unfamiliar with male attention – his athletic build and sharp features attracted both women and men – but he was usually careful with intimacy.

His "condition" made complex emotional situations... risky. "You know," said Matthieu, his voice now lower, more intimate, "I've often noticed you during training. You're... intense. Focused. I appreciate that in a training partner."
The double meaning was now clear, an invitation hanging in the steam-filled space between them. Finn considered various responses, but before he could decide, Matthieu spoke again.
"Sorry if I'm reading you wrong. No problem if you're not interested." Finn laughed again, it was so clumsy.
There was honesty in his tone, a vulnerability that Finn found unexpectedly charming. And maybe it was the tingling of the approaching moon, or just the simple human need for contact, but Finn found himself responding in a way he hadn't expected.
"You're not reading me wrong," he heard himself say, his voice rougher than normal.
Matthieu's smile widened, surprised but clearly pleased. He stepped closer, water still streaming over both their bodies, steam rising around them. "Nice."
What followed was a dance of exploration – first cautious, then more desperate. Hands gliding over wet skin, lips meeting and withdrawing and meeting again. Finn was surprised by how natural it felt, how his body responded with a hunger he hadn't fully acknowledged.
Matthieu was experienced, confident without being pushy. When he went to his knees, looking up at Finn with a questioning look, Finn could only nod, his voice lost in the sensation.
"Better than fags after sport," Matthieu grinned, before taking Finn's cock into his mouth with a skill that suggested this wasn't his first such encounter.
The experience was intense, almost overwhelming for Finn's heightened senses. Every touch seemed amplified, every sensation multiplied. He had to fight to maintain control, to keep the wolf that always waited beneath the surface in check. His claws, which tended to extend in moments of intense emotion, pressed into his palms as he struggled to remain human. It was over quickly – too fast perhaps, a combination of Finn's lack of experience and the intensity of the moment.

Matthieu didn't seem disappointed, rising again with a satisfied smile, his arousal still clearly visible.

"My turn?" Finn offered, uncertain but willing. Matthieu shook his head.

"Cheers, but next time. We haven't got much time before someone comes to lock up." He leaned forward, pressed a surprisingly gentle kiss to Finn's lips.

"No stress. This was... nice." They dried off and got dressed as the caretaker came in to turn off the lights. The moment had a dreamlike quality, like something that happened in a parallel reality. When they reached the exit, Matthieu glanced around and handed Finn his phone.

"Feel free to put your number in," he said casually. "Or not. No pressure, but..." he laughed, "I wouldn't mind a training partner."

Finn hesitated only briefly before entering his number. He wasn't sure if it was wise, but there was a part of him that wanted more – not just the physical release, but the simple human contact, the connection he so often missed since his mother had died.

They went their separate ways, a simple "later" as the only goodbye.

Finn walked out into the cool evening air, his body relaxed, but his mind full of thoughts.

In the days that followed, Matthieu had texted him, and they'd met twice more for similar, quick encounters – once in a remote corner of the university library, and once in Matthieu's student room. It wasn't romantic, barely emotional, but it was human contact that helped Finn temporarily forget the loneliness of his existence.

Yet, each encounter left him with a strange emptiness, a feeling that something fundamental was missing. It was purely physical, without the emotional connection he craved in his deepest being. After their fourth meeting, Finn had decided not to respond to Matthieu's next messages. It wasn't fair to Matthieu, who was clearly satisfied with their arrangement, to project his complex emotional needs onto him. Besides, the tension of hiding his werewolf nature during intimate moments made it too stressful, too risky. Matthieu had understood, or at least accepted, with a simple message:

`"No worries. If you ever want to train again, you know where to find me. ;)"`

The shower water, now colder, brought Finn back to the present. He shook his head, amazed at how far away those memories felt, though they were barely a year old. Since his arrival in Bruges, since meeting Lina, and yes, even his complicated interaction with Simon Laurent, his old life seemed like a dream from another time.

He turned off the shower and began to dry himself, his thoughts still with the memory. It hadn't bothered him that Matthieu was a man – Finn had long ago accepted that men attracted him most. What had bothered him was the superficiality, the absence of real connection?

Now, standing in front of his locker, he wondered if he'd ever be able to have a completely honest relationship, where he could share both his human and wolf nature. Simon's betrayal – using desire as manipulation – had only strengthened those doubts. "De Wulf, are you coming, or are you going to stare at your locker all day?" His classmate's voice broke through his contemplations.

"Yeah, coming," Finn replied, running his fingers through his wet hair one last time. He closed his locker and grabbed his bag. As he left the sports hall, he didn't notice the dark sedan parked across the street, or the man inside taking photos of everyone entering and leaving the building, his camera specifically focused on Finn. Finn's phone pinged.

`"Hey. Simon, here. Everything alright? Let's meet. I'll treat you to an ice cream tomorrow at Maria's."`

Finn wondered how he'd got his number and eventually sent back a confirmation. Some connections were more complicated than they seemed at first glance, and some hunters had selected their targets long ago.

XOCOLATL LESSON

"So... I saw you were looking for someone for weekends and Wednesdays?"

Finn stood awkwardly in the doorway of the workshop behind the shop, his hands in his pockets, showered and dressed in clean clothes, his eyes curiously darting over the strange collection of apparatus, pots, and instruments that filled the space.

Lina looked up from the small tablet on which she was checking orders. "Yes, indeed," she said, evaluating him with a look that seemed to see more than just his appearance. "Are you interested?"

"Maybe." Finn De Wulf stepped further into the workshop. "I'm looking for something alongside my studies, and this sounds more interesting than delivering pizzas."

Lina nodded, put down the tablet. "It's not just selling," she warned. "You'd also need to learn about chocolate. The history, the techniques, the... unique properties."

"That sounds good," said Finn. "I'm a quick learner."

A small smile appeared on Lina's face. "Let's test that, then." She gestured towards a stool next to a large marble worktable. "Sit down. Your first lesson starts now, if you've got time."

Finn hesitated for a moment, surprised by her directness, but took the offered seat. "That's fine."

Lina nodded, satisfied, and moved to a copper kettle standing on an old-fashioned stove. She lit the flame underneath with a smooth movement and turned to a cupboard full of small glass jars.

"Did you know," she began, whilst picking up various jars and placing them on the worktable, "that what most people know as 'chocolate' barely resembles the original drink consumed by the Maya?"

"I know it was originally bitter," Finn replied. "And that they added spices and that."

"Spices, yes," Lina nodded, now opening a bag containing what looked like raw, dark beans.

"But it was much more than that. It was a sacred drink, a connection between the human world and what they called Xibalba – the Underworld." She smiled at his surprised expression. "They probably don't teach you that in history class."

She poured water into the kettle and added some raw cacao beans, along with various powders from the glass jars. The scent that emerged was rich and complex, but not like the sweet chocolate smell that Finn associated with chocolate shops.

"This," said Lina, pointing to the kettle, "is xocolatl. The original chocolate drink of the Maya and later the Aztecs. The name means 'bitter water' and that's accurately what it is." As she spoke, something strange began to happen with the vapour rising from the kettle. Instead of simply dissipating into the air, it seemed to take shape, thickening into what looked like small, moving images in the mist.

"The journey of chocolate," Lina continued, her hands moving through the steam as if she were conducting the images, "begins here."

In the steam appeared the image of a tropical forest, where cacao trees bore their strange fruits directly on their trunks. Finn watched fascinated as the scene unfolded in the vapour – hands harvesting the fruits, cutting them open to reveal the beans.

"The beans are fermented under banana leaves," Lina explained, her voice rhythmic and hypnotic. In the steam appeared beans covered with large leaves, time-lapse shown in seconds. "This is when the magic begins – the chemical transformation that changes ordinary seeds in their whitish flesh into something extraordinary." The images in the steam changed, showing how the fermented beans were dried in the sun, sorted, roasted.

"Each region, each climate produces a different flavour," Lina continued, her fingers now swirling through the steam, the image changing to different landscapes – rainforests, mountain slopes, coastal areas. "Cacao from Venezuela is different from cacao from Ghana, different from cacao from Ecuador. Like wine, chocolate is influenced by terroir – the soil, the climate, the environment."

Finn couldn't take his eyes off the vivid images dancing before him. "How do you do this?" he murmured.

Lina looked mysterious. "Chocolate has a memory," she said simply. "It remembers its journey. I just help it share that memory." The steam images changed again, now showing how the roasted beans were ground, first in large mills, later in finer machines.

"In Europe, chocolate was transformed," said Lina. "Sweetened, mixed with milk, formed into bars and bonbons. Swiss chocolate is known for its creaminess and vanilla additions. Belgian chocolate for its perfect balance and quality of contrasting ingredients. But originally..."

The images returned to an ancient Maya temple, where priests poured a dark liquid from a height, creating a foaming drink they served in simple earthenware cups.

"Originally, it was a sacred drink of the gods," Lina continued. "Bitter, spiced with chilli peppers and other spices, drunk during rituals that served to connect the worlds."

The steam condensed into one final image – a Maya priest offering a cup to a young man, whose eyes changed after drinking, brightening with new awareness.

"It was a key," Lina said softly, "that opened doors to other realities, other states of being." With a final flourish, the steam disappeared, dissolving into the air, leaving only the kettle with the now perfectly brewed xocolatl behind. Lina silently filled two small earthenware cups with the dark liquid and handed one to Finn.

"Taste," she invited. "But be warned – this isn't the sweet chocolate milk you're used to."

Finn took the cup, smelled cautiously at the drink that had helped him get back on his feet yesterday morning. The scent was rich and complex – earthy, spicy, with hints of something he couldn't identify. He took a small sip. It tasted intensely bitter, with an explosive spiciness that made his tongue tingle. There was a deep, earthy undertone that reminded him of forest floors after rain, and something else – something that reminded him of the sensation when he was about to transform, a tingling energy flowing through his blood.

He swallowed with difficulty, trying not to grimace. "It's..." He searched for a diplomatic word.

"Awful?" Lina finished with a smile. "By modern standards, yes. It tastes like fermented spicy kombucha that's well past its sell-by date, doesn't it?"

Finn nodded, relieved that he didn't have to pretend he liked it. At his first introduction, the pure taste had been camouflaged by the drugs in his system. "But," Lina continued, raising her cup in a sort of toast, "this is where chocolate was born. From bitterness, from contrast, from the tension between worlds, harsh landscapes in nature. And if you're going to work here, you must understand and respect that origin, before you can begin creating the sweeter, more accessible versions we sell today." She emptied her cup in one movement, without a trace of disgust.

"So," she said, setting down the empty cup, "after this introduction – are you still interested in the job?"

Finn stared at the remaining liquid in his cup, thinking about the images he'd seen, about the strange energy he'd felt when drinking this ancient beverage. There was something significant about this location that resonated with a part of him that he barely comprehended.

"Yes," he said resolutely, before finding himself surprisingly downing his cup of xocolatl in one greedy gulp. The bitter sensation overwhelmed him, but this time there was a sensation – a sort of clarity that followed the initial shock, a sharpening of senses.

Lina looked at him, her eyes gleaming with something that seemed like approval. "Good," she said simply. "You can start. Wednesdays from one to six, weekends from eleven to six." She extended her hand, and when Finn shook it, he felt a small, electric shock at the contact – not unpleasant, but unmistakably strange.

"Welcome to 'Dreams of Lina,'" she said. "I think you'll fit right in here. I'll just slip into something else, and then we can go to see the mayor."

On the way to the hospital, Finn brought his tongue to his palate and could still taste the xocolatl – bitter yes, but with an aftertaste of something else. A desire he couldn't name, but that made him long for more.

NIGHTMARE

St John's Hospital was one of the oldest buildings in Bruges, a medieval structure of red-brown brick and steep roofs. The modern hospital behind it stood in stark contrast with its glass facades and clinical efficiency. Lina and Finn walked through the main entrance. Lina wore a modern, unremarkable outfit – dark jeans and jumper, her silver cacao bean carefully hidden under a scarf.

"How do we get past security?" Finn muttered. "The mayor must be heavily guarded."

"Watch and learn," Lina murmured, walking up to reception. She smiled warmly at the receptionist, a middle-aged woman with a tired face. "Good morning! I'm here for Mr Van Damme?"

"Family?" the woman asked, without looking up from her computer. Lina produced a small package, wrapped in glossy purple paper with her shop's logo on it. "Delivery. Specially ordered by his daughter."

The woman looked up, her eyes narrowing. "Wait, aren't you...?"

"The chocolate maker, yes." Lina's smile became broader, more charming. "I understand your concern given recent news, but this is just pure chocolate, not pralines. Approved for diabetic patients." She opened the package, revealing a simple bar of dark chocolate. "Would you like to try some?"

The woman hesitated, looked at the chocolate, at Lina, at Finn

standing awkwardly behind her, then back at the chocolate. "Well... I suppose it's alright. Van Damme is on the third floor, room 302."
"Thank you," Lina smiled, closing the package again.
As they walked to the lift, Finn whispered: "We're not going to Van Damme in room 302, are we?"
"Of course not," Lina replied. "But she thinks we're going there, not to the heavily guarded VIP ward on the fourth floor."
"Clever," Finn admitted. "But if she discovers we've lied..."
"Then we'll be long gone." Lina pressed the button for the third floor. As soon as the doors closed, she produced a small bottle and sprinkled a few drops on her wrists. The scent was subtle but powerful – sweet and spicy.
"What's that?"
"Oils mixed with cacao butter. It enhances... suggestion." She rubbed her wrists together. "Smell."
Finn leaned forward and inhaled. Immediately he felt lighter, more relaxed, as if the day's worries were melting away. "Wow."
"Exactly," Lina nodded. "It influences the senses, weakens resistance. Useful for getting past guards."
The lift stopped on the third floor, but instead of getting out, Lina pressed the button for the fourth.
"Now comes the difficult bit. Follow my lead and say as little as possible."
Finn followed Lina like a puppy.
The fourth floor was indeed different from the third – quieter, more clinical, with fewer doors and more security cameras. At the end of a corridor stood a constable in uniform in front of a door, his posture alert but bored.
Lina walked straight up to him, her bearing completely transformed. She was no longer the friendly chocolate maker, but now radiated authority, her back straight, her jawline hard.
"Inspector Vermeer," she said to the constable, her voice low and commanding. "And this is my new assistant from Brussels. We have authorization from Chief Inspector Devos to question the mayor." The constable frowned. "I haven't had any notification—"

Lina moved her wrist subtly, releasing the scent of the oils. "It's urgent. The suspected perpetrator has been arrested, and we need confirmation of details that only the mayor can provide." She held up a small ID card, too briefly for the man to read the details. The constable blinked, his eyes becoming slightly unfocused from the scent. "I... er... I should really contact—"

"Of course," Lina interrupted, already moving past him. "We only need ten minutes. You can wait inside if you prefer."

Before the man could react, Lina had already opened the door and pulled Finn inside. The room was large, private, with medical equipment that beeped and flashed softly. In the bed lay Mayor Robert Maillard, his normally robust figure now sunken, his skin grey under the fluorescent lights. IVs ran to his arms, monitors tracked his vital signs.

"That was... impressive," Finn concluded.

"Old family magic," Lina replied. "It doesn't work on everyone, and not for long. We've got maybe thirty minutes." She walked to the bed and studied the sleeping mayor. His eyes moved rapidly under his eyelids – REM sleep.

"He's dreaming," she said. "That's good."

"Good? He's in a coma."

"Not exactly a coma. The poisoning has placed him in a sort of between-state – halfway between our world and the Underworld." Lina grasped her silver cacao bean. "It's the perfect state for what we need to do."

"Which is?"

"Enter his dreams. See what he saw before he was poisoned." She took a small silver box from her pocket and opened it, revealing what looked like a couple of pralines, these much darker than normal chocolate, almost black.

"These are dream portal pralines," she explained. "Much stronger than what I normally make. They open a direct connection to the Underworld, specifically to the dream patterns of the person next to you when you eat them."

"Wait." Finn grabbed her arm. "You're not telling me we're going to... eat chocolate and then magically end up in his dreams?"

"Not magically," Lina corrected. "Neurologically and interdimensionally. The cacao contains substances that stimulate the pineal gland, while the special ingredients synchronize your consciousness's quantum vibration with the wave patterns of—"

"Lina," Finn interrupted. "Is it safe?"

She hesitated. "For me, yes. I'm trained. For you... it's riskier."

"How risky?" "You could... get lost. In the Underworld. Without an anchor." Finn stared at the dark chocolate.

"Why would I take that risk?"

"Because you're the only one who's seen Laurent well enough to recognize him in a dreamscape. Because your werewolf senses are better than mine." Lina looked straight at him. "And because you're the one whose blood was stolen. That connection gives you an advantage in finding answers."

Finn looked at the sleeping mayor, his pale face twisted in what seemed like pain. What if this was all madness? Some sort of mass hallucination? But then he remembered Laurent's eyes as he stuck the knife in his shoulder. The attraction he'd felt to that jade artefact. The talking cat.

"What do I need to do?" Lina smiled, relief evident on her face. "Hold the mayor's hand. Eat the chocolate. Let your mind follow his. And whatever happens – don't lose me in the Underworld. I'm your only way back."

The constable knocked on the door. "Inspector? There's a problem with your authorization..." *They heard the miaow of a cat outside.*

"Quickly," Lina urged, offering a praline.

Finn took a deep breath, grasped the mayor's hand, and accepted the offered chocolate. He placed it in his mouth. The taste was like nothing he'd ever experienced – bitter, complex, with an undertone of something ancient and earthy, as if he was tasting time itself. Warmth spread from his tongue to his throat, to his chest, and then to his consciousness.

The room began to fade. The walls melted like wax, the ceilings dissolved into mist. The beeping of monitors transformed into strange music, like flute-playing from an unknown instrument. Beside him, Lina's form faded, became translucent, then substantial again, but different – more radiant, with a blue light surrounding her like an aura. Her eyes were now completely blue, without pupils or whites. "Welcome to the Underworld, werewolf," she said, her voice echoing as if they stood in an enormous cave. "Time to find the truth."

The last remnants of the hospital decor fell away, and Finn found himself in a landscape that was impossible – a Bruges that was both familiar and completely strange, with buildings that made impossible angles, canals that flowed upwards, and a sky full of stars that moved in formations resembling the inscriptions on the jade artefact.

"What now?" he asked, his own voice strange to his ears.

"Now," Lina replied, extending her hand, "we follow his last memories. And hope that what he saw can help us stop Laurent before it's too late."

They stepped together into the dreamscape, their shadows stretching behind them in the unnatural light of a city that both was and wasn't.

DEEPER LAYERS

The dream version of Bruges was a labyrinth of contradictions – the familiar medieval architecture stretched impossibly far, streets split and coiled like fractals, and canals sometimes flowed upwards, against gravity. The sky was a kaleidoscope of star patterns that constantly changed, echoing the Maya inscriptions on the jade cacao bean.

"How do we navigate here?" asked Finn, his voice echoing as if he stood in an immense cathedral instead of on the street.

"We follow the mayor's emotional signature," Lina replied. Her entire appearance had changed in this dream world – her skin gave off a subtle blue light, her eyes had become completely blue without pupils, and her velvet cloak now seemed to move like a living organism.

"Intense trauma leaves traces in the Underworld."

She stretched out her hand, the silver cacao bean around her neck pulsing in a strange rhythm. "There." Finn followed her pointing finger to a dark cloud hanging above a building that resembled the town hall, but much larger and more threatening than in reality, with gargoyles that subtly moved and peered when you weren't looking directly at them.

"Is that...?"

"Fear," Lina confirmed. "An awful lot of fear. Perfectly preserved in the last moments before the mayor was poisoned." They walked through streets that narrowed and widened like a breathing organism. Finn noticed his senses worked differently here – sharper, but also stranger. He could smell emotions through scents, could taste the sour smell of fear that grew stronger as they approached the town hall.

"Watch out," Lina suddenly warned, her arm extending to stop Finn. In front of them, in the middle of the street, stood an enormous black mass that was shapeless and faceless but nonetheless unmistakably threatening. It looked like a black oil slick that constantly changed form, never completely substantial but also never completely intangible.

"What is that?" Finn asked.

"A nightmare," said Lina, her voice low. "A manifestation of pure fear. The poisoning has caused cracks in the mayor's mental barriers. His deepest fears are leaking into the Underworld."

"Is it... dangerous?"

"Extremely. In the Underworld, nightmares can cause physical damage." Lina's hand went to a small pouch on her belt. "But they also have weaknesses." She pulled out a handful of what looked like golden powder. "Dream sand. Made from ground cacao beans and pure intention." With a fluid movement, she threw the powder at the black mass. Where it touched, golden light appeared that made the darkness shrink and hiss like water on a hot pan. The nightmare recoiled and retreated into a side street, temporarily driven back.

"Come," Lina urged. "It'll be back. We need to keep moving."

The town hall rose before them like a Gothic cathedral with richly moving shields and stone guardians on watch, its spires piercing the dream sky. The doors were massive, decorated with woodcarvings showing scenes that Finn didn't immediately recognize, but which caused a deep unrest in him – rituals and ceremonies that seemed too complex for normal human limbs to perform. Lina placed her hand on the door and it opened soundlessly. Inside, the building was even larger than the exterior suggested, an impossible space of vaulted ceilings and endless corridors.

"Robert Maillard's mind," Lina pronounced. "As I suspected."

"What do you mean?" "The interior reflects how he sees himself – larger than he really is, full of endless circling thoughts." She pointed to doors on both sides of a long corridor.
"All his secrets, all his fears, all his ambitions, stored behind these doors." They walked down the corridor, Finn's wolf instincts hyperalert. It smelled of fear here, yes, but also of something else – guilt, shame, and an underlying scent of... hypocrisy? Was that a smell? "This isn't an ordinary man," he said, his nostrils flaring.
"No," Lina agreed. "Robert Maillard is by far the most conservative mayor Bruges has had in decades. A stately, portly man who always wears boring suits – grey, never blue or black – and who uses his Catholic upbringing as a shield against any form of progress he doesn't understand."
"Yet he was at the opening of the Maya exhibition."
"Exactly. Maillard is a master at covering his true convictions with a layer of public acceptance. He appears at pride parades with a forced smile. He opens multicultural festivals while privately lobbying for stricter immigration rules. He poses with young entrepreneurs while, behind the scenes, pushing through city tax increases for new businesses."
"Sounds like a hypocrite."
"Politician," Lina corrected. "But a dangerous one. He knows secrets about Bruges that others don't, including access to the Underworld. We need to find out what he saw that nearly cost him his life." They stopped at a door that was different from the others – heavier, older, with a lock that resembled a cacao bean.
"This is it," Lina hissed. "The door to his last memory before the poisoning."
She placed her silver cacao bean against the lock. It glowed once, and the door swung open. They stepped into a room that Finn recognized as the mayor's office from when he'd gone to ask about a job with the city, but like everything in the Underworld, it was distorted – larger, darker, with shadows that were too long and moving when you weren't looking directly at them. In the centre of the room stood a massive desk

of dark wood. Behind it sat Robert Maillard – or, at least, the dream version of him. In real life, Maillard was a portly man in his fifties, with a belly that made his expensive suits too tight, a face that turned red at the slightest exertion, and thinning hair that was carefully styled to hide baldness. But in this dream version, he was inflated to almost grotesque proportions – his body a caricatured representation of himself, his suit too tight, his jowls hanging like a bulldog's, his skull gleaming bald under a few carefully placed strands of hair. This Maillard was a reflection of how he perhaps truly saw himself, or perhaps how he feared others saw him. Before the desk stood a figure whose head was hidden in shadows.

"I cannot accept what you're proposing," said dream-Maillard, his voice both booming and trembling with fear.

"It goes against all city principles, against my personal convictions..."

"Your personal convictions," the shadow figure replied with a voice that gave Finn a cold shiver, "are irrelevant compared to what's at stake. You are no longer the protector of this city, Maillard. You're merely an obstacle." The shadow figure moved, and for a fraction of a second his face was illuminated by a strange glow.

"Simon Laurent," Finn whispered, his heart racing. "That's him." Lina nodded, her face taut with concentration. "Look what he's carrying." Finn looked again. Laurent was holding something in his hand – a small jade object that gave off a strange, green light. The stolen cacao bean.

"You don't understand what you're doing," Maillard pleaded. "The keys weren't made to destroy. They're meant to maintain balance, to protect—"

"Fairy tales," Laurent interrupted. "Propaganda from the Vandeveldes and their kind. The truth is that these objects are the last remnants of a parasitic influence on human consciousness. An influence my family has been trying to eradicate for generations."

"But I've seen the archives!" Maillard now stood up, his corpulent body trembling with emotion. "Your ancestors documented the real function of the keys before later generations twisted the truth!"

Laurent stiffened, and the temperature in the room seemed to drop. "What did you say?"

"The Laurent archives. In the municipal vault. Your great-grandfather Eduard Laurent described how the jade, silver and gold keys were designed to protect the Underworld, not destroy it. He called the dream world essential for human creativity, for innovation, for—"

"Enough!" Laurent moved with inhuman speed. Suddenly, he stood directly before Maillard, the jade cacao bean now gleaming in his raised hand. "You should have kept this knowledge to yourself, Mayor. Now I must take other measures."

Before making any gesture to leave, Simon asked calculatingly: "A final praline, perhaps? To sweeten our... discussion?" Maillard stared at the box, his face a mask of pure fear.

"That's impossible. That box didn't come from Lina Vandevelde. I know her chocolate. I've known her family for decades. You've deceived me."

"But who else makes such alluring enchantments?" Laurent's voice was now silky smooth.

"You... you've replaced it," Maillard realized. "This isn't her chocolate."

"Clever," Laurent smiled. "But too late."

Laurent forced a praline into Maillard's mouth, held his mouth shut until he swallowed. Almost immediately, the mayor began to stiffen, his eyes widening in pure terror.

"The archives," Laurent whispered in the dying man's ear. "Where exactly?" "Vault... lodge... Level 3..." Maillard groaned before collapsing. As the mayor fell, Laurent looked directly up – not at the ceiling, but straight to where Finn and Lina stood, as if he could see through the dream, through time and space, directly at them.

"He can't see us," Lina said cautiously. "This is just a memory." But Finn wasn't so sure. The smile that crossed Laurent's face seemed too personal, too knowing. "We've seen what we needed," he said, taking a step back. "Let's go."

"Wait." Lina knelt beside the dream version of Maillard. "There's something else. Something he wants to tell us." She placed her hand on the mayor's forehead. The dream version of Maillard, now pale and weak, opened his eyes. They had turned milky white.

"Vandevelde," he wheezed. "Not your chocolate. The swan... beware the swan..."

"The swan?" asked Lina.

"Confiserie du Cygne," Maillard gasped. "New shop... owner... "

Lina's face paled. "There's a new chocolate maker in Bruges?"

Maillard nodded weakly. "Arianne Vermeer... insurance arrangements... collaboration..." The dream image of the mayor began to fade, his body dissolving into shadows. The room itself began to tremble, the walls rippling like water.

"The memory's falling apart," said Lina, standing up. "We need to get back, now."

"How do we do that?" asked Finn, looking at the door that was also beginning to fade.

"We follow the silver thread." Lina pointed to a thin, silver cord that Finn only now noticed – it ran from Lina's chest, where the cacao bean rested, back through the door and further down the corridor, seemingly endless.

"It connects us to our bodies in the physical world." They began following the thread, leaving the mayor's dream office that was now imploding into darkness. The corridor had changed, now fuller with shadows that seemed to move with their consciousness.

"What are those?" asked Finn, his instincts screaming to run.

"More nightmares," Lina replied. "His mind is crumbling. The barrier between the Underworld and the conscious mind is getting thinner." They quickened their pace, following the silver cord that sometimes seemed to branch and then merge again. Finn noticed his body beginning to change – his nails growing longer, his teeth sharper, his senses even more intense. "It's happening faster here," he commented, his voice rougher.

"The Underworld amplifies your true nature," Lina confirmed.

"Here you're both human and wolf, not hindered by physical limitations."
They reached what looked like a great atrium, but where the exit should have been, there was now only a wall of pure darkness. "This isn't good," Lina murmured. "The way back is blocked." The silver cord disappeared into the black wall, but there was no passage to be seen.
"Is this... normal?" asked Finn, his now claw-ended hands balling into fists.
"No. Something—or someone—is trying to keep us here." Lina's blue eyes narrowed. "Laurent. He must have sensed our presence and is trying to trap us in the dream world."
"Can he do that?"
"With the jade artefact and your blood? Probably." Lina looked around, her mind clearly racing. "We need to find another exit. A back door out of the dream world."
"And that's where?" Lina's face hardened with determination. "We need to go deeper into the Underworld. To the source."
"The source of what?"
"Of all dreams." She turned and pointed to a staircase that Finn was certain hadn't been there a moment earlier—a spiralling staircase leading downwards, deeper than seemed physically possible. "There. It leads to the deep dream world. There I can open a portal."
"And if that doesn't work?" Lina looked straight at him, her completely blue eyes now unfathomable.
"Then we're trapped until our bodies in the physical world die of dehydration. Which, given the time difference between worlds, will be in about a subjective month."
"Brilliant," expressed Finn cynically. "Trapped in a horror landscape."
"The alternative is waiting for those nightmares to find us." Lina pointed to the shadows gathering at the edges of the atrium, now taking clearer forms—grotesque creatures, half human, half beast, with too many limbs and too few faces. "They're hungry. And we're fresh meat." Without waiting further, Lina began descending the stairs, her velvet cloak now

fluttering like wings in an unfelt wind. Finn cast a last glance at the gathering nightmares and followed her, his transforming body now more wolf-like than human, better equipped for what was to come. The staircase seemed endless, spiralling through layers of darkness and occasional light. As they descended, the environment changed—Finn no longer recognized elements of Bruges or the town hall. This was something older, something stranger. Gigantic trees began to appear in the darkness, not like earthly trees, but colossal forms of sequoias, but with bark that seemed to pulse like living skin. Their branches bore no leaves but strange, luminescent fruits resembling cacao beans, but much larger and in all colours of the rainbow.

"What is this?" Finn whispered, his voice now thoroughly changed to a deep, wolf-like growl.

"The primary dream world," Lina replied. "The first layer of the Underworld, where all human dreams are rooted. The Maya called it Xibalba. Other cultures had other names—the Greek Tartarus, the Norse Niflheim."

"It's like ours, but not," Finn observed, absorbing the strange, twisted symmetry of the environment.

"Of course. Dreams are reflections and refractions of our reality, filtered through our unconscious." Lina stopped beneath the stairs, where an open space stretched out.

"We're here." Before them lay an enormous lake, but the water wasn't blue or even transparent—it was gold, liquid gold that gleamed and rippled with life of its own. In the middle of the lake stood a gigantic cacao tree, larger than all the others, its colossal branches stretching over the entire surface of the lake, its fruits glowing alternately with a hypnotic rhythm.

"The First Tree," Lina sighed, her voice full of awe. "The source of all dreams." "It's... beautiful," Finn admitted, despite his fear, fascinated by the spectacle. "And dangerous." Lina's hand went to her silver cacao bean. "The guardians will have noticed our presence. We need to be quick." "Guardians?" From the golden lake rose a figure—Kaxil, the Guardian of Dreams. His body seemed made of liquid gold and crystallized stars, his eyes windows to cosmic depths. "Finn De Wulf," he greeted with a voice that resonated more in their thoughts than in their ears. "This time you come of your own will, not as a dreamer." What Finn and Lina couldn't see, however, was the black cat that had hidden in the shadows of one of the gigantic trees. Morpheus, who had followed via his methods to this realm, watched with unconcealed scepticism at the spectacular display.

"Still such a drama queen as always, I see," Morpheus thought sarcastically.

"Do you really have to rise from that lake like some B-movie sea god? A simple 'hello' would suffice." Kaxil's lips didn't move, but his voice sounded crystal clear in Morpheus' head: "For some of us, style is important, old friend. Not everyone is content with the appearance of a pet that sheds hair on second-hand sofas." Morpheus stiffened in his invisible dimension, his tail suddenly upright. He hadn't expected Kaxil to notice his presence, let alone read his thoughts.

"Reading thoughts without permission is downright rude," Morpheus protested mentally. "Next time I'll hang a 'Do Not Disturb' sign in my consciousness."

For Finn and Lina, the conversation simply continued simultaneously with the private conversation, Kaxil's attention seemingly entirely focused on them. "You come seeking help," Kaxil said to Finn.

"Simon Laurent plans to permanently close the dream world during the solar eclipse in three days. He has the jade key and your blood."

"They have no idea what's really at stake," Kaxil communicated to Morpheus. "The Laurents think they're only closing the dream world, but what they don't realize is that a complete separation would destabilize both realities. Dreams are the necessary outlet for cosmic energy, a way for ordinary people to recharge their life force."

"Yes, yes, the great cosmic disaster, universe in danger, apocalypse, et cetera," Morpheus responded with an eye-rolling gesture.

"You're telling me nothing new, Goldilocks. What I want to know is why you're so obsessed with that Wolf lad. You've supported Lina's family for generations, but now everything suddenly revolves around this pizza delivery boy with a fur problem." Meanwhile, Finn asked Kaxil: "How do we stop him?"
"That is the question, isn't it?" Kaxil's voice had that strange resonance, echoing through awesome time. "How do you stop a lineage that has been trying for generations to destroy what they cannot control? How do you stop a man whose entire identity is built on the denial of wonders?"
"The prophecy has always been misunderstood," Kaxil revealed to Morpheus while speaking with Finn. "It's not about the Wolf making a choice between three paths. It's about the Wolf CREATING the opportunity for choice."
"So you've practically given us a wrong translation? Brilliant," Morpheus snarled. "Millennia of preparation based on a dodgy Google Translate of a Maya hieroglyph. Fantastic."
"Not a wrong translation. A necessary obfuscation," Kaxil corrected. "If the Laurents had ever understood that the Wolf isn't simply a chooser, but a catalyst—a living key that can activate all other keys—then they wouldn't have tried to separate the worlds. They would have tried to eradicate every trace of werewolves." While Kaxil made the golden lake move to show images to Finn and Lina—Simon working with an instrument—the private conversation with Morpheus continued.
"So what's the truth about Finn's role?" asked Morpheus, now genuinely curious. "What happens if he brings all the keys together?"
"He becomes... complete," Kaxil replied. "The werewolves were our original creation, Morpheus. Not a curse or an accident. They were meant as living bridges between worlds. The first De Wulf wasn't just a carrier of the blood, he WAS the blood—the fourth key, disguised as a human, but with the ability to touch both worlds."
"And Lina? What's her role in this cosmic game of Stratego?"
"The Vandeveldes are the guardians. Not of the keys, but of the knowledge. Their chocolate is more than magic or craft—it's

the medium through which De Wulf can reach his true potential. Without Lina's chocolate, Finn's transformation would remain incomplete, painful, broken."

Kaxil moved his hand, and the golden lake formed new images for Finn and Lina—three concentric circles that merged and separated again. "There are three possible outcomes when the keys come together," Kaxil explained to the duo. "As Laurent wants, they can be used to permanently separate the worlds. Or they can maintain the current balance, the regulated connection. Or they can be used to completely unite the worlds."

"But there's more," Kaxil told Morpheus exclusively. "There's a fourth possibility that we've even kept from the prophecy. If the Wolf fully accepts his true nature, if he realizes that he himself is a key—a living portal—then he could not only unite worlds, but create an entirely NEW reality."

"And we don't tell him this because...?" Morpheus pressed.

"Because he must discover it himself. Because foreknowledge would influence the outcome. Because some truths are too heavy to bear, until you're ready for them."

"If I got a euro for every time a cosmic entity makes that statement..." Morpheus sighed. "Anything else I need to know before I go back with Miss Chocolate and Mr Hairy to the dusty, boring reality?" "There's one more thing. Antoine Leblanc isn't what he seems."

"Yeah, I'd already figured that out. Nobody can have eyebrows like that and be a normal human," Morpheus sneered.

"He's an avatar of Yaluk—the Maya deity of destruction and chaos. Even when you stop Laurent, Yaluk will find a way to return. He doesn't just want the separation of worlds, but their total destruction and recreation in his image."

"Super. An apocalyptic god rolled into the straitjacket of an irritating Parisian chocolate maker. The day keeps getting better," Morpheus sighed. "And I suppose I'm not allowed to tell the kiddos this either?"

"Not yet. They must first win this battle, before they can prepare for the war that's coming."

"Why are you telling ME, then?" Morpheus wanted to know.

"I'm not exactly known for my discretion or patience." Kaxil's golden form shone brighter. "Because you, under all your cynicism and sarcasm, are the most loyal protector the Vandeveldes have ever had. Because YOU in reality are the only one who has defeated Yaluk before, in a time that even I can barely remember."

For the first time in centuries, Morpheus was speechless. Memories he had locked away, from a time before he was a cat, loomed at the edge of his consciousness.

"Your true nature is hidden, even from yourself," Kaxil continued. "Just like Finn, you're more than you seem. When the time comes, when Yaluk fully manifests, you'll remember who you really are."

The golden lake began to swirl around Finn and Lina, the moment of return to their world approaching.

"Brilliant," Morpheus muttered, retreating deeper into the shadows.

"First a magical cat, now a forgotten deity with memory loss. What's next? A secret past as an opera singer? A lost twin?" Despite his sarcasm, he felt an unusual emotion welling up—hope, mixed with something that suspiciously resembled a sense of responsibility. He shuddered at the thought.

"Farewell, old friend," Kaxil's voice echoed one last time. "When the worlds come together and De Wulf discovers his true nature, you'll remember. And then Yaluk will fear."

"Dramatic to the end," Morpheus thought, but without his usual biting edge. He slipped away, knowing he would have to meet Lina and Finn when they returned, and pretend he'd been waiting by the portal the whole time. Some secrets were better kept, even from sarcastic cats. Especially from sarcastic cats who might not be just cats.

"Those are the three choices," Kaxil explained to Finn. "Time is pressing. The nightmares are gathering. I can send you back to your bodies, but the way will be dangerous."

"What must we do?" enquired Finn, his wolf instincts sharp from the tension hanging in the air.

"You must run," Kaxil answered simply, while the golden lake

continued to swirl and spin. "Run like you've never run before." The surface of the lake opened like a flower, revealing a whirlpool of liquid gold spiralling downwards into infinite depths.
"Jump," Kaxil commanded. "And don't let go. Whatever you see, whatever you hear, don't let go of each other. The nightmares will try to separate you."
Lina grasped Finn's hand—human with wolf, Dreamweaver with werewolf, two beings connected by prophecy and by something Finn couldn't quite understand yet, but was beginning to feel in the depths of his soul.
"Ready?" she asked, her completely blue eyes now fixed on his. Finn nodded, accepting rather than fighting his wolf instincts. "Ready." Together, they jumped into the whirlpool, falling in a spiral of liquid gold and unimaginable depths, hand in hand, two souls connected in free fall through the eternal dream world.

The return to physical reality was more abrupt than Finn had expected—not a gentle transition but a hard impact, like waking from a nightmare. One moment they were falling through liquid gold, the next his eyes shot open to see the sterile hospital room again. When Finn and Lina returned from the portal, Morpheus sat apparently bored, licking his paw. "Well, that took long enough," he remarked, as if he'd simply been waiting. "Did you bring souvenirs? A 'My friends visited the Underworld and all I got was this stupid T-shirt' T-shirt?" "Where were you?" Lina asked suspiciously. "You weren't here just now."
"Of course I was here," Morpheus lied smoothly. "Where else would I be? Making social calls to old cosmic entities? Having tea with the Guardian of Dreams? Please." Finn looked at him searchingly.
"Your fur... it's gleaming. As if there are golden particles in it." Morpheus rolled his eyes demonstratively. "That's what a good wash and superior genetics do, wolf boy. Some of us pay attention to personal hygiene, instead of rolling in dead things at the full moon."

"So, what are we going to do to stop Mr Designer Suit and his world-separation plans? Or did you just go sightseeing in the Underworld without planning?" While Finn and Lina began explaining their experiences with Kaxil, Morpheus let his thoughts wander to the disturbing revelations. The Wolf, Antoine as avatar of a destructive god, and himself—what had he really been before becoming the sarcastic protector of the Vandeveldes? For now, he would play his role, as always. Deliver sarcastic commentary, and pretend nothing really affected him. But deep inside, he felt something awakening that had long slept.

"Yaluk will fear," Kaxil had warned.

"Well then," Morpheus thought, "First defeat Laurent, then the apocalyptic God. One World-Threatening crisis at a time, please."

"Morpheus, are you listening?" asked Lina, bringing his attention back to the conversation. "Of course I'm listening," he lied again.

"Keys, union of worlds, wolf making choices, blah blah blah. I'm following every boring second." But in reality, he was busy with something he hadn't done in centuries: making plans for a future beyond the next meal or the next nap. If what Kaxil had said was true, then this was only the beginning of a much larger battle. "I don't want to spoil the fun, but I've been holding off security and nursing staff as long as I could, but now they're coming."

Lina's normal appearance was restored, though Finn still thought he could see a subtle glow around her—an echo of her dream form. "We need to go," she said, her voice urgent but controlled. "Now." Finn's body felt strangely stiff after the freedom of his wolf body in the dream world. "What's the next step?"

"The municipal vault," Lina replied, her hand on the silver cacao bean. "Level 3. If what the mayor said is true, the evidence to stop Laurent lies there." She looked at the bed where Maillard still lay, his vital signs weak but stable. "And there's something else. A new player: Confiserie du Cygne."

"The new chocolate maker on the Market Square," Morpheus confirmed. "Opened about a month ago." "Too coincidental," Lina nodded. "We need to investigate that shop too." Footsteps in the corridor warned them that someone was approaching. "Time to go," said Lina, pulling a handful of what looked like dark chocolate chips from her pocket. "Ready for the quick exit?"

"There's a quick exit?" asked Finn in amazement. In response, Lina threw the chocolate particles on the floor. They dissolved into a dark, smoky substance that rapidly circled upwards, enveloping them in a cocoon of shadow.

The door swung open just as the shadow cocoon closed completely. The last glimpse Finn caught was the astonished faces of a nurse and a constable, frozen in an expression of pure bewilderment. Then only darkness, and Lina's voice beside his ear: "Hold on. Shadow travel isn't exactly comfortable for beginners."

The world dissolved into darkness, and Finn gave himself over to a force older than cities or wolves or humans. The force that tasted like pure, dark chocolate.

FAÇADE

In her luxurious office in the heart of Bruges, Arianne Vermeer stared at the papers on her desk. Insurance documents for the Museum of Ethnic Culture, all perfectly in order, all boxes ticked, all details arranged. The theft of the Maya artefact would be fully covered – the insurance would pay out, the museum would be satisfied, and nobody would dig too deep into the real origin or meaning of the stolen object.

The walls of her office were lined with certificates and awards – Best Insurance Broker of Flanders 2022, Entrepreneur of the Year 2021, Board Member of countless cultural institutions.

A life of achievements, of respectability, of protecting Bruges' cultural heritage.

All a façade.

In reality, Arianne Vermeer, like her ancestors before her, were the keepers of silence – the secret position that had been passed down in her family for generations, parallel to the witches of the Vandevelde line and the hunters of the Laurent family. Where the witches guarded dreams and the Laurents tried to destroy them, it was the Vermeers' task to ensure that the ordinary world never discovered the truth about what went on beneath the surface of Bruges.

She had drawn up insurance policies for every important magical event in the past thirty years, each 'accident' neatly explained away, each strange incident classified and docu-

mented and then buried under mountains of paperwork. Until now, she had always maintained her neutrality, kept the balance between the warring factions. But this time she had chosen a side. The Laurents' side. Simon's side.
Arianne stood up and walked to the window, looking out over the old city she both loved and despised. A city built on dreams and lies, on chocolate and blood.
"It's time," she whispered to her reflection in the glass.
"Time for the balance to be restored." Her phone buzzed on the desk – a message from Simon: "Search through all inventories insured for theft for clues about the golden key."
Arianne grinned grimly. The old documents, collected by generations of Vermeers, contained references to all three keys. The jade was now in Simon's possession through her help bringing it to Bruges when she'd advised the Mayor about the added value of this exhibition for the many chocolate makers the city was rich in. The silver was always carried by Lina Vandevelde. And the golden... the golden was the mystery nobody had been able to solve.
But Arianne had a theory. A theory based on a vague reference in a centuries-old family archive, a reference to "the last refuge, hidden in plain sight, carried by the Gossip." She grabbed her coat and bag, her decision made. It was time to visit an old woman with a small dog, a client of hers. A woman who always knew more than she should. A woman who might, without realizing it herself, be carrying the key to the end of all dreams.
With a final checking glance at the insurance documents, Arianne left her office, her perfect heels clicking on the marble floor like a metronome counting down the final moments of Bruges' magical heritage.
The endgame had begun.

OLD PROMISES

Shadow travel was indeed not comfortable for beginners. Finn felt as if his body was simultaneously being compressed and pulled apart, while moving through a space that was both freezing and suffocating. The darkness was all-encompassing, but not silent – subtle whispers surrounded him, voices in languages he didn't recognize, but which made a primordial part of his brain react.

Then, as abruptly as it had begun, it stopped. The darkness retreated like a tide, and Finn found himself kneeling on cold flagstones, his lungs gasping for breath as if he'd nearly drowned.

"First time's always the worst," said Lina, who stood seemingly unaffected beside him. "Your body needs to get used to moving between substances."

"Between... what?" Finn's voice was rough, his throat raw as if he'd swallowed sand.

"Substances. States of being." Lina knelt beside him, a hand on his shoulder. "We travelled through the shadow dimension – an intermediate area between the physical world and the Underworld. Wait, I've got some drops for you."

Finn stared at the small bottle with glittering liquid that Lina had given him.

"Three drops on your tongue, no more," she warned.

He nodded seriously, but when he held the dropper above his tongue, the entire contents gushed out of the counter. Five

minutes later, he sat with silver-coloured glowing hair and fingers that shot off small rainbows with every movement.
"I said three drops," Lina sighed.
"Technically," Morpheus noted from his spot on the windowsill, "you hadn't specified what would happen with an overdose. I think he looks better. Less boring pizza delivery bloke, more disco ball."
Finn growled in his direction and waited for the formula to wear off. They found themselves in a large vaulted cellar with stone walls and floors, lit by several scattered hanging modern LED lights that bathed the space in unnatural blue light. Rows and rows of steel filing cabinets stretched as far as he could see, each labelled with years and codes.
"Where are we?"
"Under 't Brugse Vrije. Archive level 3. The city vault, with archives that aren't publicly accessible." Morpheus manifested from the shadows, now back in his human form. "There are centuries of official and... not so official city documents stored here."
"Maillard said the Laurent archives were here," said Lina, standing and studying the rows. "Documents from Simon's ancestors about the true meaning of the keys." "How will we ever find those among..." Finn gestured at the endless rows of cabinets. "Not as difficult as you think when you know where to look," Lina smiled. "Bruges has a very specific archiving system. Family history under F, subdivided by old families, so..." She walked purposefully to a section halfway through the space, her fingers lightly gliding over the steel surfaces as if searching for a book in a library. "Here. Section F-L12. Laurent family, pre-1950."
The drawer she opened was massive and heavily loaded with dusty files. "We're looking for the notes of Eduard Laurent, around 1890-1910," she said almost inaudibly as she leafed through the documents. "He was the last Laurent who documented the truth before his son Theodoor changed the family philosophy."
"What do you mean?" asked Finn, coming beside her. "Edu-

ard Laurent was a scientist and occultist – a combination that wasn't unusual at that time," Lina explained. "He studied the keys from a genuine desire to understand. His son Theodoor, however..."

"Had other ideas," Morpheus finished, his amber eyes narrowing. "He believed that the connection to the Underworld weakened humanity, made us dependent on dreams and fantasies instead of rational thought. He was obsessed with the new scientific thinking of his time, but without the spiritual balance his father had."

"Here," said Lina suddenly, pulling out a yellowed, leather-bound journal. "Eduard Laurent's personal notes."

She opened the book carefully and blew dust from the pages. The ink was faded but still readable, the handwriting elegant and precise.

"It's in French," Finn noted, looking over her shoulder. Her fingers glided over the pages as she searched quickly.

"We don't have much time. If someone discovers we're here..."

"There." Finn pointed to a page with a sketch of three cacao beans – one jade, one silver, one gold. "The keys."

Lina nodded and began to read: "'10th March 1911. My research has finally led me to a breakthrough in understanding the three Theobroma keys. Where my ancestors believed these objects were meant to protect humanity against invasion from the dream world, I am now convinced of the opposite. The keys are not weapons, but harmonizing instruments, designed to regulate the flow between worlds, not destroy it.'"

She turned pages, stopping at an illustration of concentric circles with strange symbols. "'The silver key, in the hands of the Vandevelde family, embodies the human world. The jade key, traditionally kept by neutral community guardians such as museums or temples, represents physical nature. The golden key, missing since the Witch Persecution of 1563, corresponds with the Underworld itself.'"

"'Together brought into harmony, the three keys can create a complete connection between worlds, a fusion of dreams and reality that the Maya called the ultimate goal of human existence. But the greatest discovery is the role of the Fourth – the blood bearer, whose essence connects all worlds."'

Finn felt a cold shiver down his spine. "The Wolf," he rumbled. "He's describing Kaxil's prophecy."

'This Fourth was described by the Maya as Ah Chikchan – the werewolf, the being of two natures,'" Lina read on. "'At the proper conjunction of celestial bodies, when the keys are brought together, it is the Wolf who makes the choice – not the Witch, not the Guardian, not the Hunter. It is the Wolf who determines whether the worlds fully unite or permanently separate."' Lina looked up, her blue eyes meeting Finn's.

"This changes everything. Eduard Laurent understood the true purpose of the keys. The connection between worlds was never meant to be destroyed, but to be strengthened to complete union."

"But why did his son change this philosophy?" asked Finn, leafing through the rest of the journal.

"Here," Lina pointed to a later page, where the handwriting had changed – wilder, less controlled.

"'14th December 1933. My beloved Elizabeth has remained on the other side. The dream portal we opened together closed unexpectedly, keeping her there, leaving me here. My attempts to bring her back have failed. I fear little Theodoor was right – the Underworld is too unpredictable, too dangerous. Perhaps his way is the right one. Perhaps the connection should be broken, not strengthened."'

"He changed his mind at the end," Finn concluded.

"From pain," Morpheus corrected, who had been silently observing until now. "Not from real conviction."

Lina turned to the last page. "'2nd January 1934. This will be my final entry. Theodoor is making plans to separate the objects, to censor the research. I no longer have the strength to fight. Elizabeth's absence is a hole in my soul. I have hidden my notes in the hope that a future Laurent will discover the truth and make the right choice when the Wolf comes. For come he will, as the stars predict, at the solar eclipse that brings the worlds close together."'

"The next solar eclipse," said Lina. "Is in three days already. How did I overlook this?"
Finn's heart sped up. "Simon said nothing about an eclipse."
"Probably because he doesn't know," Lina concluded. "He's blindly following
Theodoor's teaching without knowing the original texts."
"Or he does know and just didn't tell you," Morpheus responded dryly. "Not everyone shares their complete master plan during pillow talk."
Finn felt his cheeks burn. "It wasn't... he drugged me, remember? But yes: I am gay."
"Right, I'll pin an inclusive badge on YOU."
"Lads, focus," Lina interrupted sharply. "We now know what Simon's planning: he wants to use the three keys during the solar eclipse to permanently close the gate to the Underworld. What he doesn't realize is that it's also a chance to completely unite the worlds."
"For which he needs my blood," Finn nodded. "But why did he only take a bit? If my blood is so important..."
"Because he probably took exactly enough for a ritual," Lina suggested, closing the journal and putting it back in the cabinet. "But the prophecy speaks of the Wolf himself making the choice, not his blood alone."
"Which means he'll need you again," Morpheus concluded. "Alive and conscious, at the moment the keys come together."
Finn swallowed. "And what should I choose then?"
Lina's eyes were intense when she looked at him. "That, Finn De Wulf, is why your mother sent you to me. Not so I could tell you what to choose, but so I could help you make your own choice with full knowledge."
Finn put the files back in the filing cabinet and saw a small binder marked S. Laurent. The tension in the archive room was palpable as Finn and Lina leafed through the Simon bundle. Finn's fingers slowed at a photo loosely stuck between two pages.
"Wait," he said, carefully picking up the photo. The image showed two young men in expensive sportswear — one of

them unmistakably a younger Simon Laurent, his hair longer, his smile more open-hearted than Finn had ever seen. His arm lay relaxed around the shoulders of an athletically built young man in a tracksuit. On the back, in elegant handwriting: "Simon & Thomas, Summer 2023."

"Thomas," Lina muttered, looking over his shoulder. "The name sounds familiar."

Finn turned the photo over and stared at the athlete's face. There was something familiar about him, something that caused an uncomfortable feeling in his stomach.

"Here," said Lina suddenly, finding a newspaper clipping further in the file.

"I knew I'd heard that name somewhere." The headlines were large and sombre: "PROMISING STUDENT DIES AFTER 'INEXPLICABLE PSYCHOSIS'." Below the headline was a photo of the same sporty young man, Thomas Verhaest, laughing in a university jumper. Finn's breath caught when he saw the date on the article.

"This was only six months before the jade cacao bean was stolen."

He scanned the article quickly. Thomas Verhaest, 23, a sports science student, had died after what doctors described as a "sudden and inexplicable psychotic episode." For days, he'd suffered from what he described as "overly vivid dreams" and "hallucinations that lingered after waking." In his final days, he'd spoken of "creatures coming through the walls" and "another world leaking into ours."

"This must be Simon's..." Finn hesitated, searching for the right word.

"Friend," said Lina simply. "More than that, I suspect." Finn stared at the photo and felt an unexpected stab of jealousy, immediately followed by guilt. Thomas looked remarkably similar to himself — the same athletic type, the same spontaneous smile, even the same field of study. The realization hit him like a sledgehammer.

"Laurent's obsession with rational science... it's personal," he murmured. "He thinks the dream world killed Thomas."

"And you remind him of Thomas," Lina nodded. "Your sports background, your physique... it's why he chose you."
"Not just as a blood donor," Finn realized. "He sees Thomas in me."
Lina pulled out another document – a handwritten letter in Simon's precise handwriting.

Thomas,

I've found great-grandfather Eduard's research notes, and I think I finally understand what's happening to you. The dreams you describe, the "permeable boundaries" you talk about – they're not hallucinations or psychoses as the doctors claim.

There's another world, Thomas, a dream world that's invading our reality uninvited. What you're seeing are tears in the barrier. Some people are more sensitive to these tears – you're one of them.

Eduard wrote about a way to permanently close the barrier. I'm so close to the solution. Give me a bit more time. You don't have to be afraid anymore. I'll shut this "Underworld" down for good.

I can't lose what we have. Not after everything we've been through together.

Wait for me. Hold on.

-S

The date was only three days before Thomas's death.
"He's not trying to destroy the dream world out of clinical conviction," said Finn softly. "He's trying to get revenge."

"Grief can drive rational people to irrational extremes," said Lina. "Even when love is the motivation."

A noice at the archive entrance made them both freeze. Finn quickly pocketed the photo while Lina shoved the documents back into the file. On their way to the exit, Finn couldn't stop thinking about Simon and Thomas. About how Simon's cool, calculated demeanour was a shield over a deep, aching wound. About how it had felt when Simon touched him — the hunger behind it, a hunger that perhaps hadn't been just manipulation, but also a desperate need to find something lost again.

He thought about his struggle with who he was — human, wolf, somewhere in between. Simon's struggle was equally deep, he realized — a man torn between science and emotion, between revenge and desire, between losing the man he loved and finding someone who resembled him.

"Finn," Lina's voice interrupted his thoughts. "We need to go."

He nodded, the photo heavy in his pocket. Now he understood why Simon's flat was so coldly furnished, why his passion for order and control was so extreme. When your world collapses, you try with all your might to prevent it ever happening again.

Finn felt a new determination. Perhaps Simon wasn't simply an enemy who had to be defeated. Perhaps he was someone who needed to be saved.

A sudden sound – a door opening, followed by footsteps – interrupted their conversation.

"Someone's coming," Morpheus hissed, his form already fading into shadows.

"No time for shadow travel," Lina whispered, grasping Finn's hand.

"Here." She pulled him between two tall filing cabinets, into a narrow, dark space barely big enough for both of them. Morpheus had already disappeared, dissolved into shadows.

The footsteps on the chequered tiles came closer, accompanied by two voices – one male, one female, both speaking in muted, intense tones.

"The inspector has just reported that unauthorized activity has been detected in the immediate vicinity of the incapacitation

location of the involved government representative," the female voice stated precisely.
"There is indication of an unidentified third-party having gained access."
"Impossible," the man replied. "The room was locked, guarded." "The facts nevertheless indicate that a security breach has occurred, Antoine," said the female voice with clinical precision.
"There exists a real possibility that the individual has passed on confidential information. We should assume a worst-case scenario where third parties have taken cognizance of the existence of the archived documentation."
Finn felt Lina stiffen beside him. They were close enough that he could feel her heartbeat, accelerating at the name.
"Arianne Vermeer," she said so softly that only Finn's enhanced hearing could pick it up.
"And presumably Antoine from Confiserie du Cygne."
The footsteps stopped near their hiding place.
"The drawer has been recently opened," said the male voice – Antoine. "Eduard's journal. Mais non. Someone has beaten us to it."
"Presumably the Vandevelde heiress," Arianne concluded sharply. "She has presumably taken cognizance of the contents. She is now informed about the upcoming celestial blockade and the resulting implications."
"Then we must warn Simon," said Antoine. "Is the deliverable product ready for market introduction?"
"We're almost ready for distribution," Antoine confirmed. "Enhanced with the same formula we used for Maillard, but more subtle. Not enough to kill, but enough to weaken dream barriers. In three days, half of Bruges will be hallucinating."
"Execution is proceeding in accordance with the established timetable," Arianne praised.
"The unrest will be the perfect cover for completing the ritual. With people in panic, nobody will notice two things: a missing witch and a kidnapped werewolf."
Finn and Lina looked at each other with pricked ears. Their

voices faded as they walked away, the click of a closing door marking their departure. Lina stepped out of their hiding place, her face taut with anger and concern. "They're going to poison masses of people with drugged chocolate. Create a distraction."
"So they can grab you and me," Finn added.
"And use the keys during the eclipse."
"But the third key... the golden one... they didn't mention it," Lina observed. "They must still be searching."
"Or they already know where it is," Morpheus suggested, materializing again from the shadows.
"Like your mother suggested – Ingrid Vermeulen."
"That eccentric old woman with the little dog?" asked Finn doubtfully.
"She gave me your address when I first met her."
"Who better to hide it with?" Lina nodded.
"Everyone underestimates Ingrid, sees her as a senile gossip. The perfect cover."
"Then we need to find her before they do," Finn concluded.
"Not just that," said Lina, already moving towards the exit, carefully checking if the coast was clear.
"We need to discover what kind of chocolate Antoine has made and stop the distribution before half of Bruges manifests hallucinating nightmares in physical reality."
"How?" Finn asked.
Lina's smile was grim. "By paying a visit to my new competitor."

INGRID

Ingrid Vermeulen had just settled her Yorkshire terrier Pouffe in his favourite wicker basket for an afternoon nap when a firm, authoritative knocking echoed on her front door. The little dog immediately sprang up, barking wildly at the unexpected disturbance.

"Sush, sweetheart, quiet," Ingrid soothed, her bright pink nails stroking through his silky coat. "It's probably just the postman."

But when she looked through the peephole of her front door, she didn't see the familiar figure of the local postman, but the sharp, elegant face of Arianne Vermeer – Bruges' most prominent insurance broker and, in Ingrid's opinion, one of the most intimidating women in the city.

"Oh, blimey," she flustered, her hands flying to her hair as if she could make it presentable before opening the door. With a deep sigh, she put on her 'social smile' and opened the door.

"Arianne! What a surprise! Is there something wrong with my darling's insurance papers?"

Arianne stood there in a perfectly cut navy-blue suit that had cost more than Ingrid's monthly pension. Her face was a mask of professional friendliness, but her eyes were sharp as razors.

"Ingrid," she greeted with a short nod and a feigned sympathetic undertone. "My apologies for the unexpected visit. Might I come in for a moment? I have a... delicate matter to discuss."

"Of course, of course," Ingrid chattered, stepping aside. "Come in! Can I offer you a cup of tea? Or perhaps something stronger? I've got a bottle of sherry I keep for special occasions, and a visit from the famous Arianne Vermeer is certainly special!" Ingrid impulsively licked her own upper lip.

Arianne stepped into the dwelling on the Rozenhoedkaai, her critical gaze immediately registering what she saw – the abundance of kitschy collectibles, the antique furniture that was at least a hundred years old, the walls covered with photos of Ingrid with her successive little dogs through the years. But what drew Arianne's attention most was the display in a small glass cabinet in the corner – a collection of coral beads and pendants, some clearly antique, some less valuable but all in the shape of beans or pods.

"That's an interesting collection," she said, pointing to the cabinet whilst taking the offered seat. "I assume this is one of your many passions?"

Ingrid's face lit up, delighted by the interest in her treasures. "Yes! My coral pods! I've been collecting them for over fifty years. People think I'm mad, going to all that trouble for what they call 'fake jewels', but it's a family tradition. My grandmother started it, then my mother, and now me."

"Fascinating," Arianne pronounced, her eyes fixed on a specific piece in the middle of the collection – a coral-red cacao bean, with some patina and crumbled bits, with what looked like inscriptions on the surface, hanging from an antique gold chain. "And this particular one – is that a special specimen?"

Ingrid's expression changed subtly, a wariness slipping through her normally open and chatty demeanour. "Oh, that? That's probably worthless, except for sentimental reasons, of course."

But Arianne had seen it – the flash of... something... in Ingrid's eyes. Protection. Knowledge. Awareness. This seemingly simple old woman, this gossip, this collector of kitsch and dogs... knew something.

"Ingrid," Arianne began, her tone now much more serious. "I need to ask you about something you might have seen the night of the museum robbery. Something concerning... a black panther?" The change in Ingrid was immediate and dramatic. Her face, normally animated and expressive, closed completely, like a curtain being drawn shut.

"I don't know what you're on about," she said curtly, her voice now stripped of its usual sing-song quality. "I didn't see any panthers. That was just gossip." Arianne smiled unfriendly.

"I think we both know that's not true, Mrs Vermeulen. Or rather, Ingrid. If I may." She leaned forward. "I think you know more about Bruges than you let on. More about... certain matters. Dreams. Chocolate. Keys."

Arianne was fishing in shallow waters. Pouffe, the Yorkshire terrier, began yapping again, but this time it sounded more like a warning than excitement. Ingrid's hand went to her necklace – not the coral-red cacao bean that Arianne had noticed, but another one, hidden under the collar of her cotton blouse.

"I think you should leave now, Arianne," she said, her voice suddenly firmer, stronger, almost younger. "Tell Simon Laurent that his grandfather already tried what he's attempting now, and he failed. Just like his father failed. Just like he will fail."

Arianne's eyes widened in genuine surprise. "You know about the Laurents?"

Ingrid stood up, suddenly straighter, more dignified. "I know many things, love. I'm not one of Bruges' oldest residents for nothing. Now off you go, and tell Simon that if he wants the key, he'll have to come himself. I'll only give it to the worthy."

Arianne's hand slipped into her coat pocket, where her fingers closed around a small pistol – a safety precaution she'd taken for this visit, not expecting she'd need it. The old woman stood there, frail yet suddenly imposing, a strange contrast to her kitschy surroundings.

"They said the third key was lost," Arianne said softly. "That nobody knew where it was."

"And yet here you are," Ingrid replied with a small, mysterious smile. "Which suggests someone knew. The question, dear Arianne, is whether you're here on behalf of yourself, on behalf of the Laurents, or on behalf of something... older. Something waiting in the shadows."

A shiver ran down Arianne's spine, a primitive fear she couldn't suppress. "I'm here on behalf of the future," she said, standing and preparing to leave.
"A future where humanity is free from the parasite of the dream world." Ingrid laughed, a sound surprisingly musical for a woman her age.
"That's what they told you, isn't it? That dreams are parasites? Poor dear! You're cleverer than that. Go home, look in your archives. Search for the truth about why the three families were separated. Why the Vermeers were appointed as Guardians, the Vandeveldes as Witches, and the Laurents as... well, they called themselves Hunters, but they were once Destroyers."
Arianne stood stiff, shocked by Ingrid's knowledge, but determined not to show weakness. "I'll be back, and next time I won't come alone."
"Oh, lovely then," Ingrid replied cheerfully, slipping back surprisingly quickly into her role as chatty old woman.
"I'll bake biscuits! Or perhaps pralines? Lina Vandevelde recently gave me a wonderful recipe for chocolate cake. She's such a sweet girl, don't you think?"
With those cryptic words, Ingrid opened the door, a clear signal that the visit was over. Arianne left the flat with more questions than answers, and a growing feeling that the situation was far more complex and dangerous than she'd realized.
Behind the closed door, Ingrid Vermeulen stood, her carefully cultivated façade of senility and superficiality completely gone. She walked to the glass cabinet and pulled from under her collar a coral-red cacao bean, the ancient object warm in her wrinkled hand.
"They're coming for you, old thing," she whispered to the object. "After all these years. It's almost time to reveal what you really are." She turned to her little dog.
"Come, Pouffe. We need to get our affairs in order. A storm's coming, and this one will be worse than all the previous ones."
The Yorkshire terrier looked at her with intelligence that far exceeded what you'd expect from an ordinary dog. He jumped into his wicker basket, ready to be carried. Ingrid took an old,

worn raincoat from the coat rack – not the bright yellow one she usually wore, but an inconspicuous brown one that would make her almost invisible in the grey streets of Bruges.
She picked up the basket with Pouffe in it and murmured: "It's time the three keys finally came together again."

THE SWAN

Confiserie du Cygne was everything that 'Dreams of Lina' wasn't. Where Lina's shop had a warm, antique atmosphere, 'The Swan' was a paragon of modern, clinical luxury – all chrome surfaces, minimalist displays, and cold, white LED light. The pralines were displayed like jewels, each piece an architectural work of art with geometric precision.

"It feels wrong," Finn hissed.

"That's because it is," Lina confirmed, observing from across the street. "Real chocolate should radiate warmth. This has no soul."

They'd decided that a confrontation was too risky. Instead, they'd taken position in a café opposite the chocolate shop, observing the activity whilst making plans. Finn had pulled up his hood – not just because of the light rain that had started, but also as a minimal disguise.

"There's a surprising amount of traffic for a Tuesday afternoon," Morpheus observed, now back in his cat form, positioned on a windowsill where he had a perfect view of the shop.

"Especially young people."

Finn looked at the customers going in and out – indeed predominantly young people, many dressed in the typical student style of the nearby university.

"The same target group as those who buy your chocolate for the dream effects," he noted.

"But my chocolate opens natural dream channels," said Lina, concern in her voice. "Their version, if what we heard is correct, weakens barriers, makes people vulnerable to invasion from the Underworld."
"Is that possible?" asked Finn. "Can... things... from the dream world come here?"
"Normally not," Lina replied. "The Underworld and our world are separated by more than just physical barriers – there are fundamental differences in vibrational state, in substance. It's why dream beings remain dream beings, even in lucid dreams. But..."
"But?" Finn pressed when she hesitated.
"With the right formula, and with the jade key already weakening the barrier, it's possible that nightmares could manifest in our world. Not fully solid, but solid enough to cause damage." Lina's face was grim. "Terrifying hallucinations that feel and look like real monsters." "Why would Laurent want that?" asked Finn. "Sounds like a bad horror film."
"Distraction," Morpheus replied. "What's more effective at keeping police and authorities busy than a city full of people screaming about monsters that nobody else can see?" Finn's attention was caught by a familiar figure approaching the chocolate shop. "Is that..."
"Kaylee Mendoza," Lina confirmed. "The influencer who was at the museum opening." Kaylee's bright pink coat and designer bag were unmistakable, as was her constant interaction with her phone whilst walking. Even from this distance, they could see she was filming for a social media post.
"She has a reach," Finn observed. "Thousands of followers. If she promotes Antoine's chocolate..."
"Then it reaches even more people," Lina nodded, standing up. "We need to intercept her. Now."
They left the café and crossed the street, timing their movement so they'd arrive at The Swan's entrance just as Kaylee did. "Kaylee," Lina greeted warmly, as if their meeting was coincidental. "What a surprise."
The young woman looked up from her phone, clearly startled.

"Oh! Lina, hey girl! I was just..." she hesitated, clearly uncomfortable.
"On your way to my competitor?" Lina smiled, no reproach in her tone. "No worries, I'm just curious what attracts you to Antoine's creations."
Kaylee visibly relaxed. "Oh, well, the aesthetics are just so Instagrammable, you know? Plus, he offered me an exclusive deal – free chocolate in exchange for posts. He says his latest collection is really... next level for dream experience."
"Fascinating marketing," Lina nodded. "Have you tried the newest line yet?"
"Not yet! I'm going to be the first," Kaylee beamed. "He saved a special box just for me. Said it would give me the most intense dreams ever."
"You know," said Lina casually, "I'm also experimenting with a new line. Perhaps you'd like to try that too? A proper comparative review would certainly interest your followers."
Kaylee's eyes lit up. "OMG, that would be amazing content! A chocolate battle! Traditional Lina versus contemporary Antoine! Nossa, that's literally genius. If anyone asks, I came up with it myself." She winked at Lina.
"Exactly," Lina smiled. "Why don't you come to my shop tomorrow morning? I can let you taste something that's... truly unique."
"Deal!" Kaylee extended her hand for a selfie moment with Lina, then stormed excitedly into the shop.
"What was that about?" asked Finn as they walked away. "She's going straight in to eat Antoine's poisoned chocolate."
"Not if I can help it," said Lina, pointing to Morpheus, who had slipped unnoticed into the shop whilst they were distracting Kaylee.
"And then what? She's just one person. What about all the others buying the chocolate?" Lina's smile was now strategic, calculating in a way Finn hadn't seen before.
"That's where you and I come in. We're going to intercept Antoine's deliveries before they reach the shops."
"How?"

"With a bit of old-fashioned burglary," Lina replied, her hand moving again to the silver cacao bean around her neck. "Tomorrow night."

Simon's iPhone pinged with a message from Antoine Leblanc:

> "The influencer has the pralines. The next phase can begin. Watch out for the livreur de pizza - he's been seen with the witch."

Simon swore softly. He'd suspected Finn might cause problems after his sudden departure the other evening. The lad had clearly recognized the jade artefact, but hadn't stolen it. But going to the witch? That was unexpected.

#MARIAISTHEBEST

The ice cream parlour 'Mona's Lips' stood out from afar in the narrow streets of Bruges. The bright pink neon light of the name winked at you, whilst the mint green facade with gold accents evoked an era when disco and gelato were the answers to all of life's questions. Finn had been waiting outside the entrance for several minutes, his eyes gliding over the lavish photos of extravagant ice cream sundaes in the window. His stomach rumbled approvingly. As a pizza delivery driver, he had to count every euro to pay his rent, and a luxury like Maria's famous ice cream sundaes was a rare treat. Everything in him had said he should have declined the invitation, but here he was nonetheless.

Great going, De Wulf. The man takes your blood without permission, doesn't pay for his pizza, and you just turn up when he sends you a text.

What did he have to lose? A free ice cream sundae and perhaps answers to the questions that had been haunting his mind since that night in Simon's flat.

"Finn."

The voice was unmistakable – rich, cultured, with that subtle accent that spoke of expensive schools and international travel. Simon Laurent came walking up, perfectly dressed in a light blue linen blazer and dark jeans that looked so casual they'd

certainly cost a fortune. "You came," said Simon, with something in his voice that sounded like genuine relief.
"Well, you promised me free ice cream," Finn replied, trying to sound light despite the uncomfortable feeling in his stomach. "Even if it's from someone who doesn't pay for his pizza."
Simon's mouth corner curled up. "Touché. I still owe you for that pizza."
"Plus tip," Finn added, but there was no real anger in his voice.
Simon reached for his wallet and made good on his word.
They went inside where the retro vibes were even stronger: pink and mint green tiles in a chessboard pattern on the floor, chrome bar stools with bright red leather, and crooked mirrors with frames in all colours that doubled the whole scene.
A mysterious-looking portrait of Mona Lisa in Andy Warhol style, licking her lips. Behind the counter, bent over a display case full of dozens of colours of ice cream, stood Maria.
Maria's hair colour this week was electric blue, shaved at the sides and on top in a Mohawk that perfectly matched the "Blu di Puffo" flavour in the display case. Their nose rings glittered under the spotlights. If there was one constant in Maria's appearance, it was that it always seemed to correlate with one of the ice cream flavours – as if they walked through life as a living advertisement.
"Ah, Simon!" Maria greeted them, with a voice that echoed against the tiles. "And you've brought a friend! A handsome one too!"
"Finn," he introduced himself, extending a hand that Maria shook enthusiastically.
"You've come at the perfect moment," said Maria, pointing to a table by the window. "I've just got two new creations that need testing." Their eyes gleamed with something approaching maniacal pleasure. "Sit down, sit down."
"Right, surprise us with your creations!" Simon agreed. Simon and Finn took seats in a corner. The chairs were retro but comfortable, with the sort of lived-in charm you only get after decades of intensive use.
"So," Finn began. "How did you actually get my number?"

Simon smiled, almost shyly. "Presto Pizza's order records are surprisingly easy to access if you submit the right legal forms."

Finn raised an eyebrow. "You submitted a legal document to get my phone number?"

"Well, not exactly submitted. Let's say I know what such a document would look like if it were necessary." Simon's smile became broader, more charming. "I wanted to contact you. After that night..."

"The night you drugged me and took my blood?" Finn kept his voice low, so others couldn't hear, but the question had a sharp edge. Simon's face clouded. "That was... not my finest moment. There's a lot you don't understand, Finn."

"Like the fact that you keep a stolen museum piece in your flat? Or that you're genuinely interested in werewolves? Tell me, Simon, what don't I understand?"

Before Simon could answer, Maria appeared at their table, balancing two enormous ice cream sundaes. They were spectacular, like small works of art: one was an explosion of fruit and bright colours, with strawberries, mango, and passion fruit built up in perfect spirals; the other was a dark, tempting mountain of different chocolate curls and nut pieces, garnished with roasted hazelnuts and a waterfall-like chocolate sauce. "Voilà! My new creations: 'Fruity Temptation' and 'Nuts4Chocolate'!" Maria placed them with a theatrical gesture before them. "I'll let you enjoy them." They winked at Finn. "I think you two have things to discuss."

Whilst Maria walked away, both men stared at the works of art before them. It felt like a metaphor for their situation – as beautiful as it was complicated. "This is..." Finn began, his eyes wide. "Excessive?" Simon suggested.

"I was going to say 'perfect'." Finn picked up his own spoon and dove into the fruity sundae. Simon smiled, took his spoon and tasted the chocolate sundae. "Damn," he groaned, closing his eyes at the sensation. "This is criminally good." Finn gave him a smile.

"Here, try this," said Finn, extending his spoon with a perfect combination of strawberry and passion fruit ice cream. A mo-

ment of hesitation, then Simon leaned forward and took the offered spoon in his mouth. Their eyes met across the table, and there was an electric tension that reminded Finn of that night in the flat – but different. More equal.
"Your turn," said Simon, his voice lower now, offering Finn a spoon from his sundae. Finn accepted without hesitation, and the rich, complex flavours of hazelnut and pure chocolate exploded on his tongue.
"Good grief," was all he could manage. "I wanted to see you," Simon said suddenly, setting aside the games.
"I wanted to know if you were all right. And I..." He hesitated. "I heard you're working at the chocolate shop now."
"Better job than pizza delivery," Finn replied with a shrug. *Phew, I handled that situation smoothly, Finn thought.*
"The pay's good, the people are nice, and I'm learning a lot." He paused, looking intently at Simon.
"How did you know that? Did you have me followed?"
"No," Simon said quickly. Then, more honestly: "Not personally. But there are people who are... interested in that specific chocolate shop."
"People like you? Who steal ancient artefacts and does strange experiments?"
Maria passed their table, glanced at them briefly with a mixture of curiosity and discomfort, asked if everything was to their liking, and then disappeared back to the counter to serve other customers. Simon leaned forward, his voice now an intense whisper.
"Finn, it's not what you think. The jade cacao bean isn't an ordinary artefact. It's a key to something... dangerous. Something that can disrupt the natural order of things."
"And that's why you needed my blood?" Finn kept his voice calm, but his eyes narrowed.
"Werewolf blood has... properties. It can help control what's coming." Simon looked Finn straight in the eyes. "I did what I had to do, and I'm not proud of how I did it. But there's more at stake than you realize."
"And what does Lina know about this? Is she also involved in

your 'keys'?" A fraction of a second's change in Simon's posture – a microscopic tension – was enough to confirm to Finn that he'd hit a sensitive subject.
"She has one, doesn't she? A silver one, around her neck." Simon leaned back, his face now a carefully composed mask and slightly looking away. "You're cleverer than I'd estimated, Finn De Wulf."
"And you underestimated how much a pizza delivery driver can observe," Finn bounced back, a small smile playing around his lips. "So, Laurent, cards on the table. What's going on, and why should I trust you after what you've done?" Simon stared at his half-eaten ice cream sundae, then back at Finn. "What if I told you that your new employer is just as dangerous as you think I am? That her family has been involved for generations in manipulating people through dreams?"
"Then I'd say you sound like someone trying to undermine my trust." Finn put another spoonful of ice cream in his mouth, enjoying the fruit flavour whilst studying Simon.
"But I'd also say: go on, I'm listening."
"Your kind, Finn – werewolves – you stand at a crossroads between two worlds. The rational, physical world, and..."
Simon hesitated, searching for the right words, "the dream world. The Underworld, as some call it. That position makes you special. Powerful."
"And wanted, apparently." Finn looked at him challengingly.
"By you and by Lina."
"The difference is that I want to protect you, whilst she intends to use you." Simon's hand moved across the table, almost touching Finn's, but stopping just short.
"Something's coming, Finn. Something big. And you're at the centre of it."
A cold shiver ran down Finn's spine. "And why should I believe you?"
"Because," Simon's voice became softer, "despite all the things I've done wrong, I've never lied about how I felt when I was with you."
The air between them seemed to thicken, charged with some-

thing more powerful than tension. Finn felt the warmth of Simon's nearby hand, saw the intensity in his eyes, and remembered the touch of that night – drugged or not, it had been real. Maria came back to their table, this time with a small tray of espressos.

"On the house," they said, setting down the small cups. Their eyes glided from Simon to Finn and back, an eyebrow raised in silent observation.

"The... atmosphere here is hot enough to melt my ice cream perfectly." Finn felt a blush rising to his cheeks, but Simon only laughed. "Your ice cream is too perfect to melt, Maria."

Maria looked between them. "You two are... more than friends, I gather?"

"We're..." Finn began.

"Still figuring that out," Simon finished with a smile. Maria nodded slowly.

"Well, whatever makes you happy, kids. But maybe not too intimate in my shop, yeah? I don't want a reputation that competes with my ice cream."

When they walked away, Finn and Simon burst into soft laughter – a moment of relaxation in their charged conversation. "I have to say," said Finn, stirring his espresso, "you have an interesting way of asking someone on a date. First drugs, then stalking, then conspiracy theories about my new boss."

"Is this a date?" asked Simon, a surprisingly vulnerable tone in his voice. Finn looked up, suddenly serious.

"I don't know, Simon. Is it? Because I'm not looking for a quick fling or a complicated game. If I go out with someone – even a rich, attractive man like you – it's because I want something serious. Someone with whom I can be a better version of myself." Simon held his gaze.

"I don't often have the luxury of being myself, Finn. My family, my position, my... mission. They define me. But with you..."

He shook his head, almost wonderingly. "With you, I felt something I hadn't expected." "

Thomas," Finn said softly. "He's the one I remind you of, isn't he? I saw his photo in your flat."

Simon stiffened, his face suddenly pale. "How do you know about Thomas?"
"You said his name in your sleep, that night. And there was a photo next to your bed." Finn paused. "He looked like me."
A long silence fell between them, charged with unspoken emotions.
"He died," Simon said finally, his voice barely audible. "Just over six months ago. He saw things – things that couldn't exist. The doctors called it psychosis. I..." His voice broke. "I couldn't save him."
Finn reached across the table and took Simon's hand in his. It was an impulsive gesture, but it felt right. "I'm sorry."
"That's why I do what I do, Finn. To prevent more people like Thomas from being lost to the influence of... that other side."
Finn squeezed Simon's hand gently.
"Have you ever considered that you might be wrong? That what Thomas saw was real?" Simon looked up, his eyes glittering with held-back emotion.
"Every day. But if that's true..."
"Then everything you're fighting for might be based on a misunderstanding," Finn finished. Their hands remained connected across the table, whilst the last remnants of ice cream slowly melted in their sundaes.
"Listen," Finn said finally. "I don't know who's right – you or Lina. I only know I want answers. Real answers. And maybe..." He hesitated. "Maybe I want to get to know you too. The real you, not the manipulative version or the man on a mission."
Simon's thumb stroked over Finn's hand, an intimate gesture that sent electric shocks through Finn's arm.
"I'd like that. But I can't promise I can just drop my convictions." His touch made Finn aroused again, like that night.
"I'm not asking you to give up your convictions," Finn replied. "Only to be open to the possibility that there's more than what you think you know."
Maria appeared again, this time with the bill on a small plate. They looked at their connected hands and smiled softly. "On the house, this time," they said, withdrawing

the plate again. "Some things are too beautiful to disturb." Simon looked surprised. "That's very generous."
Maria shrugged. "I recognize the beginning of something special when I see it. And in this city..." They looked outside, at the old grey streets of Bruges, where history and mystery dwelt in every stone. "In this city, you never know where such a beginning might lead."
When they walked away, Finn looked back at Simon. "So," he said, his hand still in Simon's, "what now?"
"Now," said Simon, a new determination in his voice, "I think we both need to be more honest. You tell me what you know about the keys and Lina's plans, and I..." He breathed deeply. "I tell you the truth about Thomas, about my family, and about why I need you." Finn nodded slowly.
"Deal. But not here."
"My flat?" Simon suggested, then, quickly: "No hidden agenda this time. Just talking." Finn hesitated, then smiled. "All right. But I'm bringing my own drinks."
Simon laughed, a genuine sound that changed his whole face. "Fair enough. And maybe some extra clothes?" They stood up, hands finally releasing, but still connected by something deeper than physical contact. They were about to leave the ice cream parlour when the door swung open with a dramatic sound of jingling bells. In a whirlwind of bright pink winter coat and shining hair, Kaylee Mendoza stormed in, iPhone already at the ready, camera aimed at her own beaming face. Simon unobtrusively pushed a fifty-euro note into Maria's tip jar.

"Hello, fabulous followers!" she called enthusiastically, in English as always in her videos. "It's time for my daily Milkshake Madness at the BEST ice cream parlour in all of Bruges!" Finn stiffened, immediately recognizing her as the influencer who'd been at the museum opening and whom he sometimes saw on campus. Simon's hand closed subtly around his elbow, a warning gesture. Kaylee spun a graceful pirouette and only saw them when she'd finished her intro. Her eyes widened in recognition when she saw Simon.

"OMG, Simon! This is literally so random! Vibe check passed!" Her camera swung briefly in their direction before she quickly aimed it back at herself.
"Guys, this is Simon Laurent, THE hottest trainee lawyer in Bruges! Wait—" She paused, looked from Simon to Finn and back, a smile spreading across her face. "Am I... disrupting your vibe?"
"Not at all," Simon replied smoothly. "We were just about to leave."
"So devastating! You should have stayed for my TikTok!" She turned to the counter.
"MARIA! My usual, pretty please!" Maria smiled broadly at their regular customer. "Coming right up, superstar!"
Kaylee was already filming again, the camera now aimed at the ice cream display case. "As you know, besties, I come to Maria EVERY DAY for my Unicorn Dream milkshake. It's straight-up fire 🔥 and that HAS to be on my feed. Literally living for this! #mariaisthebest #milkshakemadness" She winked at Simon, gesturing for them to come into shot.
"You HAVE to be in my video! My followers will DIE knowing I spotted Simon Laurent in the wild!"
"Rather not," Finn breathed, but Simon smiled elegantly.
"Perhaps another time, Kaylee. We have a... date."
Kaylee's eyebrows shot up in dramatic suggestion.
"Very interesting," she said with a wink, but her voice cracked.
"Until next time, then!" She waved at them whilst turning her attention back to her camera.
"Guys, spill the tea! ☕ It looks like Bruges' most eligible bachelor might not be single anymore! The main character energy! But anyway... back to the MILKSHAKE SHAKE SHAKE SHAKE! So iconic!"
Someone gave an emoji of a smiley with a tear, knowing that Kaylee was head over heels obsessed with Simon. As they left the ice cream parlour, they could just hear Kaylee euphorically receiving her order: "OMG, Maria, you added EXTRA sprinkles! My followers are going to find this ADORABLE!"
Maria waved them off from the doorway, their electric blue hair glittering under the neon lighting. "Arrivederci! And re-

member," they called after them, "life is like gelato – you have to taste it before it melts!"
Outside, in the soft Bruges light, Simon and Finn looked at each other, both knowing they stood on the edge of something bigger than either of them – a whirlpool of ancient magic, personal desires, and forces they could barely comprehend.
"Think she's going to tag us in her post?" asked Finn dryly.
Simon grinned. "Probably. Does that matter?"
"Maybe. If Lina sees it..."
"Then she'll wonder what you're up to with the enemy?"
Finn shrugged. "I'm exploring my options."
For now, for this moment, they were just two men taking a step towards each other, uncertain but hopeful, whilst the centuries-old city around them kept its secrets for a while longer.

#CHOCOLATEBATTLE

The shop bell at 'Dreams of Lina' chimed cheerfully the following morning when the door was thrown open with dramatic flair. Kaylee Mendoza burst inside, dressed in her iconic bright pink ensemble. She was filming herself as she stepped into the shop.

"Heyyyy besties! Your favourite taste-test queen is back and ready to slay! Today I'm dropping something EPIC! A chocolate BATTLE between Bruges' old guard and that fancy newbie The Swan a.k.a. La Confiserie du Cygne. No cap, this will be the ULTIMATE taste test! Stay with me for the ride!"

She waved childishly at Lina, who stood behind the counter with a mixture of amusement and slight concern on her face.

"As promised! I've been to Antoine's, and he gave me this EXCLUSIVE box — we love to see it! And now I'm here for your counter-attack! This will be SO! EPIC! I can't even literally ! About to pop off!"

"Come through to the back," said Lina, gesturing towards the door that led to the work area. "I've prepared something special."

Finn, who was busy by the storage cupboard, looked up when they entered. He'd seen Kaylee several times on campus, always busy filming herself, surrounded by a group of admirers.

"This is Finn, my new assistant," Lina introduced. "Finn, this is—"

"THE Kaylee Mendoza, three hundred thousand followers on Insta, one hundred and fifty thousand on TikTok, and the OFFICIAL Bruges Taste Ambassador!" completed Kaylee herself, extending a hand that wore more bangle bracelets than Finn had ever seen on one wrist. "Hey, aren't you that..."

"Lovely to meet you," Finn managed, avoiding the confrontation from the ice cream parlour. Kaylee squinted her eyes and pointed the camera back at herself. But his face seemed familiar.

"Let's taste Antoine's creations first," Lina suggested, bringing out plates.

Kaylee opened the black box with a dramatic gesture to her camera. "Look at this PERFECTION, guys! These pralines are literally ART!" She selected one and brought it to her mouth, her expression already prepared for delight.

As soon as she bit down, her eyes narrowed slightly. "Hmm, this is... low-key, different than I expected. More... chocolate-core? Less... well, less Antoine energy tbh."

Kaylee stiffened. Her eyes widened, and her free hand shot to her throat. Lina and Finn exchanged a discreet glance. Not knowing if it was acted or real.

"What is the actual...? What's in this? I feel so... light? But also... wow... is this the vibe everyone's talking about? I can't even right now..." She swayed slightly.

Her eyes rolled back and she collapsed. Finn caught her just before she hit the floor with his strong arms.

As he lifted Kaylee, she fell almost unconscious in his arms, but not before she could deliver one more dramatic outburst: "Am I actually going to be unalive? ? I haven't even hit 400K followers on TikTok yet! That's properly tragic! They can't find me dead in this basic fit! Literally, my worst fear – not even clickbait!" Her eyes fluttered open in pure panic.

"You're not going to die, Kaylee, I'll make you some tea," Lina assured her.

"You don't know that," Kaylee wailed, throwing a dramatic arm across her forehead. "My TikTok career, my future sponsorship deals, my brand collaboration with that K-pop company... all

lost!" She grabbed Finn's face between her hands. "Promise me one thing, if I'm unalive—"
"You're not dying," Finn repeated, trying to gently lay her down without twisting his neck in her gripping hold. He pressed the red button on Kaylee's iPhone to stop the recording.
Morpheus, watching from a high shelf, rolled his eyes ostentatiously. "Civilization is doomed. If this is her reaction to mild dream chocolate, how will she react to the actual apocalypse that Laurent is planning?"
"Let her drink the antidote," Lina instructed, offering a mug with steaming liquid. "She needs to rest. And we need to talk about what Antoine is planning with that chocolate."
Finn nodded, trying to loosen Kaylee's dramatic grip and help her drink. Meanwhile, Lina continued her investigation of Antoine's pralines, her expression growing grimmer with each discovery.
"These were designed to cause hallucinations," she uttered barely audibly.
"Is that their plan?" asked Finn, settling Kaylee more comfortably as she fell into a calmer sleep. "To throw the city into chaos?"
"A diversionary manoeuvre," Lina nodded. "And an effective one. We must anticipate their next move, and quickly."
Finn looked at the sleeping influencer, then at the box of pralines, and felt the gravity of the situation sink in. This was no longer a personal threat, but a danger to all of Bruges. And somehow he'd found himself in the middle of this conflict, with no clear way out.
This top follower wouldn't be chasing Simon in the first few hours. *Mission accomplished.*

WORK TO BE DONE

The sun fell in narrow beams through the tall windows of the chocolate laboratory behind 'Dreams of Lina'. It was a space that evoked both an artisanal workshop and an alchemical laboratory—copper kettles and modern temperature controllers stood beside mortars and pestles of various sizes, whilst the walls were covered with shelves full of glass jars filled with herbs, spices, and substances that Finn couldn't identify. A specific warm fragrance hung throughout the entire space.

Finn stood uncomfortably by the large marble workbench in the centre of the room, his brand-new purple apron still stiff and uncreased. He'd only recently started working for Lina, but this was the first time he'd been left alone with the notoriously sarcastic black cat. Lina was tending to Kaylee whilst managing the shop.

"Er, Lina said you'd teach me how to... make chocolate?" he asked hesitantly.

Morpheus lay on a raised platform in a corner of the workbench, strategically positioned so he could see everything without having to move. He yawned demonstratively, showing an impressive set of small but sharp teeth.

"Right," the cat said eventually. "Promoting the pizza delivery boy to chocolate maker. I've seen better career transitions, but also worse ones, I suppose." He stretched and sat upright. "Let's begin with the absolute basics because I assume your culinary experience is limited to ordering extra pepperoni, yes?"

"I can cook," Finn protested. "And I study sports science, so

I know a thing or two about nutrition and how it affects the body."
"Fantastic," Morpheus mewed in a tone that suggested the opposite. "Then you're undoubtedly familiar with the difference between theobromine and theophylline, and their varying effects on the pineal gland in relation to dream clarity stimulation?"
Finn stared at him blankly.
"Exactly as I thought," Morpheus continued. "Right then, Professor Morpheus shall explain it from the beginning." He pronounced the title with such ironic grandeur that Finn couldn't help but smile.
"I'm ready to learn, Professor," he replied with a small bow.
The cat seemed almost surprised by this playful response. "Hmm. Perhaps there's hope for you yet, De Wulf."
Morpheus jumped from his platform and walked with precise, measured steps towards a row of glass jars. "The first lesson in dream chocolate: it's not about the chocolate."
"That... seems contradictory for a chocolate maker."
"It only sounds contradictory to small minds," Morpheus countered. "Chocolate is merely the vehicle—the medium through which the active components are delivered. It's like saying that with a sports car, it's not about the car, but about the engine and the driver." He looked at Finn penetratingly. "Do you understand?"
"I think so," Finn nodded. "The chocolate is the carrier for something else."
"For many other things," Morpheus corrected. "The Maya understood these centuries before you Europeans tasted your first piece of chocolate. For them, cacao was a divine gift, a path to higher states of consciousness, not merely a sweet pudding after a meal. They mixed it with chilli powder for extra power."
Morpheus rolled the 'r' and chuckled at his joke. He pointed with his paw at various jars. "The foundation of every dream chocolate begins with the proper ratio between three elements: the cacao itself, the added herbs and supplements,

and—most crucially—the intention with which it's made."
Finn scratched his neck. "Intention? Do you mean, like... positive thinking?"
Morpheus rolled his eyes so dramatically that Finn briefly feared they might disappear completely into the back of his head.
"If you put on a sheep costume, that doesn't make you a sheep, wolf boy. Likewise, 'positive thinking' alone doesn't make you good bedtime chocolate." He sighed deeply. "But a beginning is a beginning. Today we're going to make something simple: 'Dream Soft' pralines. A bestseller for our elderly clientele who want deep, restful sleep without their nightly trips to the loo."
"That sounds... specific," Finn observed.
"The best products solve specific problems," Morpheus replied. "Begin by filling that kettle with exactly, 1500ml of fresh cream."
Finn followed the instructions, measuring meticulously with a measuring jug.
"Now, the foundation of a 'Dream Soft' praline is a delicate mix of relaxing herbs and cacao," Morpheus explained whilst watching. "We use valerian for initial relaxation, chamomile for mental calm, and lavender essence for sleep sustainability. But the secret ingredient, that which elevates our chocolate above ordinary 'soothing' sweets, is the addition of k'uut'náal."
"Kutnal?" Finn repeated, mangling the pronunciation.
"K'uut'náal," Morpheus corrected with perfect Maya pronunciation. "A rare moss that only grows on the north side of ceiba trees in certain parts of the Yucatán Peninsula. Maya warriors used it to rest before great battles, so they would awaken with a clarity that sharpened their reflexes."
Finn looked at a small, dried bundle of what indeed looked like moss that Morpheus had indicated from a special jar. "And that... actually works?"
"Have you forgotten how old I am, De Wulf?" Morpheus asked suddenly. "Er... ten? Twelve? How old do cats usually get? Wait, you've already told me. Really ancient. Very, very, very old."
Morpheus stared at him with a piercing, all-destroying look that was simultaneously amused and irritated. "I've seen Maya

priests gather this moss when your ancestors still lived in huts and thought a bath per year was excessive. I've personally guided Maya rulers through dreams enhanced with k'uut'náal. So yes, it 'actually works'."

Finn nodded, somewhat intimidated by this reminder of the true nature of the "cat" before him.

Morpheus did a quick calculation himself—he was 483 years as far as he could remember, but Maya culture began 2000 years before our era and persisted until the 9th century. How could it be that his memory was so vivid? Was he then much older than he himself thought?

"Now add half a teaspoon to the cream," Morpheus instructed. "CAREFULLY. Not like that dropper you nearly destroyed by squeezing it like a stress ball."

Finn blushed at the memory of that unfortunate incident with one of Lina's expensive essences that gave him glittery hair. "You're never going to let me forget that, are you?"

"Not as long as it remains an effective way to embarrass you, no," Morpheus confirmed cheerfully. "Now, stir slowly with a wooden spoon, always clockwise."

"Does the direction actually matter?"

"For the chocolate? No. For your training in discipline and following instructions? Absolutely. But seriously: Yes. Clockwise is generating energy, anticlockwise is to keep energy out. Basic magic 101."

Finn sighed but obeyed, stirring whilst adding the rest of the ingredients under Morpheus' critical gaze.

"Now comes the crucial part," Morpheus declared when the mixture began to thicken slowly. "Whilst you stir, you must put your intention into the mixture."

"And I do that... how?"

"Visualization," said Morpheus. "Close your eyes—no, keep stirring even with closed eyes, I don't want chocolate splatters on the ceiling—and picture perfect, deep, restful sleep."

Finn closed his eyes, feeling somewhat foolish but determined to try. He imagined a peacefully sleeping person, but his concentration was broken by Morpheus' voice. "What do you see? Describe it."

"Er... a sleeping person? In a bed?" Morpheus sighed. "So banal. You have no imagination. Let me help you."
There was a moment of silence, then Finn felt something strange—a sort of tingling in his thoughts, as if someone was scratching at the edges of his consciousness.
"What are you—" he began, but then his mental image exploded into something much grander.
He was no longer in the laboratory. He stood in a clearing in a dense, tropical forest. The air was heavy with humidity and the scents of exotic flowers and earth. Before him stood an enormous stone pyramid, the steps leading to a temple structure at the top. The sun was almost down, the sky coloured in deep purple and orange.
"Chichén Itzá, the night before the great battle against the warriors from the north," Morpheus' voice explained, though the cat was nowhere to be seen. "Watch what happens in the temple."
Finn's viewpoint shifted, as in a film, floating up along the steps to the temple. Inside, lit by dozens of torches, a group of warriors lays in a circle. In the centre burned a fire into which herbs were being thrown. A priest with an impressive jaguar headdress chanted whilst walking among the men, giving each a small bowl with a dark liquid.
"K'uut'náal, mixed with pure, unsweetened cacao and guava syrup," Morpheus explained. "They drink it, and then..."
The warriors drank from their bowls, lay down, and closed their eyes. Gradually the scene changed. The torches dimmed, and above the sleeping warriors appeared dream images—clear manifestations of how they were counting.
But not sheep, Finn realized. They were counting jaguars—majestic, muscular predators that leapt one by one over a moonlit mountain ridge.
"One jaguar, two jaguars, three jaguars..." a voice counted, soothing and rhythmic.
With each leap, with each count, the warriors sank deeper into perfect, restorative sleep—sleep that would renew their bodies and sharpen their spirits for the battle to come.

"This is what you must visualize in the chocolate," Morpheus' voice said. "Not simply 'someone sleeping', but the perfect, deepest, most restorative rest possible. The counting ritual, the jaguars leaping, the absolute peaceful darkness that follows, the hypnosis of the burning torch, the scents of a mysterious forest..."
Finn felt strangely drawn into the image, as if he himself were one of the warriors, counting along: "Five jaguars, six jaguars..."
Suddenly, he was back in the laboratory, still stirring, but now with a much clearer sense of what he was trying to achieve.
"That was..." He searched for words.
"Authentic Maya dream magic," Morpheus finished for him. "Now, channel THAT feeling into the chocolate whilst you stir."
Finn nodded, closing his eyes again, but this time he could effortlessly summon the jaguar counting ritual to mind. He visualized it clearly whilst continuing to stir the mixture slowly.
After several minutes of this concentrated effort, Morpheus said: "Now that's enough. Pour it into the tempering kettle."
Finn obeyed, carefully pouring the mixture into the machine that would bring the chocolate mixture to exactly the right temperature.
"Not bad for a first attempt," Morpheus observed, which from him was practically a standing ovation. "Now we must wait until the mixture reaches the right temperature, then the temperature automatically goes back down, all the crystals in the chocolate become one crystal so that it hardens when cooling, something Dutch explorers discovered after bringing the fermented roasted cacao beans to Europe, and then we can pour it into the moulds."
Whilst they waited, Finn couldn't contain his curiosity. "Did you really know Maya priests? Were you there... as a cat?"
Morpheus gave him a mysterious look. "What I was or wasn't, is not essential. What's important is that the knowledge has been preserved. The Maya understood the connection between dreams and reality better than any other civilization. Their chocolate rituals were more refined than what we create nowadays."

"Even more refined than Lina's chocolate?"
"Sophia Vandevelde, Lina's mother, came close," Morpheus admitted. "She spent decades reconstructing lost Maya recipes. She also went on location to Belize and Mexico, searching for the roots. Lina has the talent, but not yet the experience." He looked at Finn. "And you, wolf boy, have something that even most Vandeveldes lacked."
"What's that?"
"A natural affinity with the Underworld. Your wolf side gives you a direct link that most people don't have." Morpheus sounded almost respectful, which surprised Finn.
The tempering kettle beeped, indicating that the chocolate had reached the right temperature.
"Time to fill the moulds," Morpheus declared. "Get the moulds—no, not those, the small cone-shaped ones. Those are perfect for 'Dream Soft', since the shape helps with the gradual release of active ingredients during melting."
Finn found the right moulds and began carefully pouring the tempered chocolate into them. He had to tap them gently to bring air bubbles to the surface and then put them in a cooling cell.
"Tell me, wolf boy, do you ever have trouble sleeping around the full moon?" Morpheus asked whilst watching.
"Of course," Finn replied. "It's the worst time of the month. I become restless, too much energy, too alert."
"Perhaps you should try what we've just made," Morpheus suggested. "Adapted, naturally, with extra k'uut'náal for your... unique physiology."
Finn looked up in surprise. "Would that work?"
"Theoretically, yes. Though, we need Lina's approval before we experiment with non-human doses. The FASFC would have a heart attack if they knew we were adapting recipes for werewolves."
"FASFC?" Finn asked, filling the last mould.
"The bureaucratic nightmare that determines whether you're allowed to lick your fingers in a professional kitchen," Morpheus elaborated with exaggerated formality.

Finn quickly pulled back his finger, which he'd been about to lick after a chocolate splash.
"Exactly," Morpheus nodded. "As a former street cat, I have no respect for their petty hygiene rules, but Lina adheres to them. Something about 'not getting picked up by the authorities' and 'not poisoning her clientele'. So conventional."
He pointed with his paw at a box of white gloves to avoid fingerprints on the chocolate. "Wear those when you have to handle chocolate. And wash your hands. Often. Especially with your... nocturnal activities."
"My nocturn—" Finn blushed slightly. "You mean the wolf thing."
"Yes, De Wulf, the 'wolf thing'," Morpheus replied dryly. "I'm certain that prowling about in the woods on four legs and chasing small game promotes excellent hygiene practices. Save the gloves for after you've relieved yourself in the bushes, as needed."
"I don't eat small game!" Finn protested. "And I... just use a bathroom, like everyone else. I've just had a shower."
"Of course you do," Morpheus winked, or did what passed for a wink by a cat. "And I never hunt mice in the stockroom."
Finn sighed, decided this was a battle he couldn't win, and concentrated on finishing the moulds. "How long do they need to cool?"
"They're cool after about fifteen minutes," Morpheus replied. "But it's best to let them rest all night at about twelve degrees. Like dreams, chocolate develops fully in silence and darkness."
Finn carefully placed the filled moulds on a tray and carried them to the cooling cell. "Is that why Lina calls the shop 'Dreams of Lina'? Because of the connection between chocolate and dreams?"
"Partly," Morpheus replied, following along. "It's also because her family has worked for generations as guardians of the dream-chocolate tradition. The Vandeveldes have been connected to the Underworld since the first cacao beans were brought to Europe."
Finn placed the tray in the cooling cell and closed the door. "How do the Laurents fit into all this? They seem to be a simi-

larly old family. Or do they have a chocolate addiction I haven't noticed yet?"

Morpheus' eyes narrowed. "The Laurents were once allies, long ago. They began as scientists, studying the effects of chocolate and dreams from an academic perspective. The chocolate drink became a chocolate tablet and later a bonbon. But somewhere in the 19th century, something changed. They began to see dreams as a threat, a contamination of the rational mind."

"As something people needed to be freed from," Finn nodded, remembering what Simon had said.

"Exactly. A fundamental philosophical shift—from wonder to fear. From embrace to control." Morpheus jumped onto the workbench, again his favourite observation point. "The Vandeveldes use dream chocolate to help people discover their dream power. The Laurents would want to destroy dreams, 'liberate' people from what they view as delusions."

"And where do you stand in all this?" Finn asked curiously.

Morpheus gave him a long, inscrutable look. "I'm a cat, De Wulf. Cats don't choose sides in human conflicts. We observe, comment sarcastically, and sleep eighteen hours a day."

"But you work for Lina," Finn pointed out. "You help her."

"I live with Lina," Morpheus corrected. "There's a subtle but important difference. She gives me tuna and a warm bed; I offer occasional insights and assistance. It's a symbiotic relationship." He paused. "Plus, the Laurents are allergic to cat hair. Would never work."

Finn couldn't help but laugh. "You're a peculiar creature, you know that?"

"I consider that a compliment of the highest order," Morpheus replied, stretching in a ray of sunlight. "Now, tidy up this mess. One of the less glamorous aspects of chocolate making is the cleaning afterwards. All wooden spoons mustn't go in water, but are wiped clean."

"Of course, Professor," Finn replied with a small bow.

As he began tidying up, Finn thought about the strange, vivid visualization of the Maya warriors counting jaguars. It was almost as if he'd truly been there, seen what they saw, felt what they felt.

"The moss," he said suddenly. "K'uut'náal. Does it only help with sleep, or does it do more?"

Morpheus, who was about to doze off in the warm sun, opened one eye. "Astute question, wolf boy. The primary effect is indeed deep rest. But the secondary effect, which is less well known, is enhanced dream clarity. The Maya warriors used it to receive visions that would help them in battle—signs of where enemies would hide, weak spots in enemy defences. The fruits of the tree contain kapok, with which the best sleeping pillows are filled."

He stood up, stretched. "In your case, with your already heightened connection to the Underworld, it could have... interesting effects."

"Such as?" Finn pressed.

Morpheus gave him that mysterious look again. "Perhaps you should discover that for yourself. When the time is right." He jumped down from the workbench. "And that time is not now. Now it's time for my first afternoon nap. Your first lesson is over, apprentice."

With those final words, he sauntered away, his tail high in the air, leaving Finn behind with more questions than answers—but also with new insight into the strange, wondrous world of dream chocolate of which he was now part.

As he tidied up the last items, Finn couldn't help thinking about hunting jaguars leaping over a moonlit mountain ridge, one by one, in perfect rhythm... four jaguars, five jaguars, six...

KAYLEE AWAKENS

The sweet scent of fresh chocolate was the first thing that reached Kaylee when she slowly opened her eyes. She lay on a small but comfortable sofa in a room she didn't recognize. The ceiling above her was dark wood with small, built-in spotlights that spread warm light. The walls were decorated with vintage posters of cacao plantations and handwritten chocolate recipes behind glass.

"What... happened?" she said, her mouth dry and her head still foggy. She tried to sit up, but a wave of dizziness forced her back into the cushions.

Lina's face appeared in her field of vision, smiling gently but with concern in her blue eyes. She held a glass of water with what looked like a mint leaf in it.

"Easy now," Lina said softly. "You're in the room behind my shop. You became unwell after tasting Antoine's chocolate."

Kaylee grabbed her head, memories slowly returning like fragments of a dream. "OMG, that was so intense! I felt literally like I was floating through space? But then also sort of creepy vibes, you know? Like I was being... watched or something." She took the offered glass and sipped carefully. "Wait... have I still got my phone?"

Lina smiled and pointed to the side table next to the sofa, where Kaylee's pink iPhone lay. "Everything's still here. Your phone, your bag, your dignity." Her smile became warmer. "Though you nearly lost consciousness whilst telling me you weren't ready to die because you 'didn't have 400K followers yet'."

"NOOO!" Kaylee slapped her hand dramatically over her mouth, her eyes wide with horror and amusement. "I didn't actually say that, did I? That's SO embarrassing! I literally can't even—" She fell silent and suddenly looked serious. "Wait, was that chocolate from Antoine laced with something? Was it a drug? Did I get drugged by that old bloke? That's so gross."

Lina sat beside her on the edge of the sofa, her movements fluid and calm. "In a sense, yes. Antoine's chocolate contained... let's say ingredients that aren't on the packaging. Ingredients that turn dreams into nightmares, joy into fear." She gently reached for a lock of Kaylee's hair that had fallen in front of her eyes and lovingly brushed it away. "But don't worry, you're safe now. I've given you something to counteract the effects."

"Damn, that's so messed up," said Kaylee, visibly affected but simultaneously fascinated. "I mean, I thought he was cool, you know? He promised me that exclusive tasting yesterday. Had he planned all that?" She shook her head, making her shiny hair dance in the soft light. "But like... why? What's he gain from making people high? Is that his business model? Drugs in bonbons?"

"The world knows many shadows, Kaylee," said Lina, her voice like soft flowing water over smooth stones. "Some people seek power over others, over their dreams, over their thoughts. Antoine is such a person. His ambitions reach deeper than merely a successful chocolate shop."

Kaylee took another sip of water, her eyes now clearer. She hesitated a moment, swallowed, and then looked at Lina with a mixture of embarrassment and excitement.

"I saw something when I was... you know, tripping," she began carefully. "I saw a talking cat." She laughed at her fantasy; Lina laughed along. "And Simon. At Maria's ice cream parlour yesterday. With that new guy who delivers pizzas at uni." Her voice dropped to a whisper, as if she were sharing a state secret. "They were there on a date. A PROPER date. They were holding each other's hands across the table and everything. And then Simon basically confirmed it when someone asked. They were super cosy with each other." She bit her lower lip, uncertain whether to continue. "I filmed it for my Insta story. Not gonna lie, it did hurt a bit, you know? I mean, I've been DMing him for MONTHS and got literally almost zero response. And then this random pizza guy comes along and—" She stopped abruptly, a blush creeping over her cheeks. "Sorry, that sounds super desperate. I literally can't even—"

Lina's laugh was like the soft chiming of wind chimes, without a trace of mockery. "The heart goes where it will, Kaylee, like a butterfly dancing between flowers. Every so often, it chooses paths we don't understand."

She placed her hand comfortingly on Kaylee's arm. "Love can sometimes seem cruel in its arbitrariness, but believe me when I say that every unrequited infatuation brings you closer to your true destiny. Like a river, that ultimately always finds the sea, even though it meanders through the land."

Kaylee looked up, her eyes glistening with unshed tears. "Yeah, I guess... But it's just... he was so perfect, you know? That jawline? Those fits? His whole vibe? And I really thought we felt each other's aesthetic."

"Perfection," said Lina thoughtfully, "is often merely a mask we wear or see. Like a glass casing around a chocolate praline—glossy and flawless, but revealing nothing of the complexity within." She beamed warmly. "And consider this: a woman like you, with your talent for connection, your eye for beauty, needs no man to shine in this world."

"OMG, that sounds like a quote I'd repost," Kaylee laughed, now visibly cheering up. "You're right. I mean, I've worked myself up to here." She gestured to her chin. "Nobody helped me get three hundred thousand followers. That was me. And honestly? Boys are a waste of time. Except as content."

She now sat upright, new energy flowing through her body. "But like, seriously, though—is he gay? Simon? Because that would explain everything. My gaydar is normally spot-on."

Lina's smile became mysterious. "I think Simon, like many of us, is a more complex being than what words alone can cap-

ture. Some hearts don't resonate with labels, but with souls."
"Damn, you literally talk like a TikTok poet. That's such a vibe." Kaylee grabbed her phone and opened her camera. "Can I take a pic with you? My followers would love to know I was here. I mean, unless you don't want to? With everything that happened?"
"Of course," Lina agreed, her expression genuine. "But perhaps you could give your followers a warning? To stay away from Confiserie du Cygne for now? For their safety."
"Oh, trust me," said Kaylee with sudden seriousness, whilst posing next to Lina for a selfie. "I'm going to do a WHOLE storytime about this. The vibe check on Antoine's place has officially failed. Toxic chocolate is the new cancelled." She quickly took several photos and scrolled through them with satisfaction.
"Perfect!" she exclaimed. "You give literal goddess energy in these. Mind if I tag you?"
Lina shook her head with a smile. "I'm afraid I still belong to the pre-social media era. No accounts to tag."
"No socials? Is that even legal in 2025?" Kaylee shook her head in disbelief. "You're missing out. But fine, I'll just credit you as the 'legendary chocolate maker who saved me from drugged pralines'." She was already typing busily on her screen. "Hashtag truth, hashtag exposed, hashtag chocolate wars..."
Whilst Kaylee became absorbed in creating her post, Lina's facial expression subtly shifted, a flash of worry and determination that disappeared as quickly as it had come. She looked towards the door leading to the shop, her thoughts on the great conflict yet to come. On Finn, who hadn't mentioned anything about his 'date'. How well could she trust him?
But for this moment, in this quiet room filled with the scent of chocolate and the sounds of Kaylee's typing fingers, there was a precious pause in the storm. There was a moment of peace before everything changed for good.

INVISIBLE

Inspector Karel Devos surveyed the equipment in the anonymous surveillance van with a mixture of professional interest and personal distaste. Twenty years with the Federal Police had accustomed him to violating privacy in the name of the law, but this operation felt different. More problematic.

"Report, Merckx," he said to the technician hunched over a series of monitors.

Officer Jonathan Merckx turned around, his face lit blue by the screens. "We have active intercepts on five different targets, Inspector. Two mobile devices for subject Vandevelde—one personal, one business. One mobile device for subject De Wulf. Additionally, three technical surveillance devices placed in the location—one in the front section, one in the production lab, and one in the upstairs flat. All frequencies are coming through via the mobile intercept system and being logged directly into the database."

Devos frowned. "And the video feeds?"

"All observation equipment is operational and providing visuals," Merckx replied, navigating through the surveillance system to project different camera feeds onto the main monitor. "We have positive sight on entrance, sales area, and rear of the premises. No visual equipment present in the residential section—we lack the separate warrant required under surveillance legislation that wasn't approved by the magistrate."

"Right," Devos nodded, not entirely convinced by his words. "And the primary targets?"
Officer Sofie Ceulemans, sitting on the other side of the small space, looked up from her laptop. "Target Laurent is currently stationary at his residence at the Eiermarkt. No movement observed. Target Leblanc is moving according to mobile phone tracking towards the lab complex on the outskirts. Route projection matches previous movement patterns."
Devos stroked his short, greying beard, a habit when he was thinking. This entire operation was unorthodox, to put it mildly. Officially, they were surveilling Antoine Leblanc on suspicion of importing illegal substances in his chocolate products—a normal investigation that fell under his jurisdiction. But the real instructions came from higher up, via channels that were unusual even for someone with his experience.
The focus on chocolate maker Lina Vandevelde and sports science student Finn De Wulf was even stranger. They had no criminal record, no known connections with criminals, and had never before been the subject of police investigation. Yet, he had specific orders to watch them intensively and share all information directly with a private contact, outside normal protocols.
"We've got movement at Vandevelde's," Merckx suddenly reported, zooming in on one of the video feeds. "She's leaving the shop via the back door."
Devos leaned forward, looking at the image of a young woman in a purple velvet coat moving quickly through an alley. She carried what looked like a small leather bag under her arm and looked around several times, clearly on her guard.
"Follow her," he ordered. "Ceulemans, activate the directional mic."
Sofie turned numerous knobs on a device that looked like a satellite dish. The sound of footsteps and breathing filled the small space, along with the subtle rustling of fabric.
"She's heading towards the Minnewater," Merckx observed, calling up a digital map beside the video feed. "That's the second time this week."

"And De Wulf?" Ceulemans checked another screen. "Still in the Sports Science faculty building. His last lecture ends in..." she looked at her watch, "...twelve minutes. If he follows his usual pattern, he'll go straight to Vandevelde's shop."
Devos nodded, his unease growing. The instructions were clear: observe, document, report. Don't intervene. But after days of observation, he was beginning to wonder what made these two young people so important to the high-ranking figures who had initiated this investigation.
His phone vibrated—a message from a number simply saved as "Contact". He opened it.
"Update me on their movements. Specifically interested in visits to the Minnewater and contact with elderly individuals. S.L."
S.L. Simon Laurent. The young solicitor who was officially merely a "consultant" for the investigation, but in reality seemed to be the one pulling the strings.
"We send our reports every six hours," Devos muttered.
"He wants them in real time," Merckx observed, reading over his shoulder. "What's the deal with these people?"
"Not our concern," Devos replied automatically, though he had the same question. He typed a brief response: "Vandevelde en route to Minnewater. De Wulf expected to visit her shop within the hour. No other contacts since last report."
The reply came almost immediately: "Follow Vandevelde. Send live footage. Crucial."
Devos sighed and nodded to Ceulemans. "Activate the tracking systems. We're going mobile."
Whilst Merckx prepared the equipment for movement, Ceulemans took a small drone from a case and checked the battery. "Small enough not to be noticed in these misty conditions," she said. "But the wind conditions at the lake aren't ideal."
"Do your best," Devos replied. "Laurent wants footage, he gets footage."
Five minutes later, the unmarked surveillance van was driving slowly through the streets of Bruges, following at a safe distance whilst Lina Vandevelde continued her way to the Minnewater. The drone hummed silently above them, invisi-

ble against the grey sky, its high-tech camera focused on the solitary figure in purple.
"She's not alone," Ceulemans said suddenly, zooming in on the image. "Look."
Devos peered at the screen. In the shadows, almost impossible to see unless you knew exactly where to look, a dark shape moved parallel to Lina's path. It looked like... a large cat?
"Is that a dog?" Merckx asked, also looking.
"Too big for a house cat, too small for a dog," Devos muttered. "Perhaps a fox? There are some urban foxes in Bruges."
"Doesn't move like a fox," Ceulemans observed, subtly adjusting the drone for a better angle. "And it seems... can you see that? It looks like she's talking to it."
Indeed, Lina had now bent towards the creature and seemed to be having a conversation, her lips moving, her hands gesturing as if making a point to an intelligent conversational partner.
"Activate the directional microphone," Devos ordered, feeling a strange chill that had nothing to do with the cold in the air.
Ceulemans turned several knobs, but then shook her head. "Too much interference. It's as if there's... I don't know... some sort of static barrier."
"That's impossible," Merckx said. "That equipment can pick up a whisper at a hundred metres."
"Well, it's not working now," Ceulemans replied in frustration. "All I'm getting is... listen for yourself."
She switched the sound to the main speaker. Instead of voices or ambient sounds, they heard only a strange, melodious humming, like the singing of crystal glasses when you run your finger along the rim.
"What the devil...?" Devos exclaimed.
His phone vibrated again. A new message from Laurent: "Do you see it? The being that's with her?"
A cold shiver ran down Devos' spine. How did Laurent know about the being? He couldn't see the footage unless someone in this vehicle was sending it to him, and that hadn't happened.
He typed back: "Confirmed. Unknown animal accompanying

target. Cat/fox/small dog type." The reply came immediately: "Not animal. Guardian. Extreme caution. Absolutely no confrontation. Keep distance."

Guardian? What did that mean? Devos was about to ask for clarification when Ceulemans suddenly shouted: "Communications going down! We're losing connection with all technical equipment. Signals intelligence reports total blackout!"

The screen flickered and then went black. Simultaneously, all electronic devices in the vehicle died—computers, tracking systems, even the digital display on the dashboard.

"What's happening?" Devos demanded.

Merckx desperately tried to restart the systems. "We're seeing full spectrum interference. Characteristics of a targeted electromagnetic pulse, but very localized. Can't be a regular technical fault—has all the hallmarks of a deliberate jamming action. All equipment within a hundred-metre radius is compromised."

Devos' phone, the only device still working, vibrated again. Laurent's message was short and alarming: "Cover compromised. Initiate immediate withdrawal protocol. Priority Alpha."

"Start the engine," Devos ordered the driver. "We're going back to HQ."

As they hastily retreated, Devos looked through the rear window. In the distance, at the entrance to the Minnewater, Lina Vandevelde stood still, looking in their direction. And beside her, much more clearly visible than before, stood what indeed looked like an enormous black cat, but with eyes that even at this distance seemed to glow with a strange, amber-coloured intelligence.

He turned around quickly, feeling an inexplicable fear that he wasn't accustomed to as an experienced police officer. "How far are we with tracking Antoine Leblanc?" he asked, desperately longing for the familiar certainty of a normal police investigation.

"Target tracking went offline simultaneously with system failure," Ceulemans reported, whilst running the diagnostic reset procedure on the equipment. "Last known coordinates place him at the lab facility on Paling street. Have requested local ANPR data for possible vehicle movements."

"Go there," Devos decided. "If Laurent is so interested in what Vandevelde and De Wulf are doing, I'm interested in what Leblanc is doing that makes him so nervous."

As the van sped through the streets of Bruges, Devos felt a growing conviction that he was involved in something that fell far outside his normal jurisdiction. That evening he would begin his investigation—not into Vandevelde or De Wulf, but into Simon Laurent himself, and the real reason behind this bizarre surveillance operation.

What he didn't know was that his movements were now also being followed, by beings that moved between shadows and reflections, invisible to ordinary human eyes.

SHADOW PLAY

Simon Laurent picked up his phone before it could ring a second time. The number on the screen had no name, no contact info—just a series of digits saved as 'contact'. He closed the binder of documents he was studying, straightened his back in his designer chair, and answered the call with a neutral, professional tone.

"Laurent."

"Simon." The voice on the other end was rich, deep, and cultured, with an accent that betrayed generations of privilege. "I understood you had an update."

Simon turned towards the window of his flat, looking out over the Eiermarkt, whilst carefully choosing his words. "The preparations are proceeding on schedule, Uncle. Antoine's... special ingredients will be ready for distribution the day after tomorrow."

There was a brief silence, followed by a subtle sigh. "And the Vandevelde woman? Do you have her under control?"

"She's under constant observation," Simon replied, his free hand unconsciously stiffening. "She's recently had a lot of contact with a young man who falls within our area of interest. A werewolf, undoubtedly."

A sharp intake of breath on the other end of the line. "You're certain?"

"Completely. My earlier... interaction with him confirmed it. His blood shows all the characteristics we need."
"Excellent." There was a new tone in his uncle's voice—excitement, perhaps even greed. "You've done good work, Simon. Your father would be proud."
The reference to his father hit Simon like a physical blow. Theodoor Laurent had died nine years ago, his body consumed by cancer, his mind obsessed to the end with the family obsession of closing the dream barrier.
Simon's last memory of him was an emaciated hand gripping his wrist, feverish eyes boring into his, and a whispered mantra: "Finish it. Finish what I couldn't."
"I hope so," Simon replied neutrally, hiding his emotions as he'd been trained to do.
"You understand the importance of this, don't you?" His uncle's voice became almost unctuous. "What our family has tried to achieve for generations. The purification of human consciousness from the parasitic influence of the dream world. A rational, controlled future."
"Of course."
"This isn't just a Laurent legacy, Simon. This is a service to humanity. Dreams make us weak, dependent on fantasies and illusions. They infect us with desires and fears that aren't ours, hold us back from our full potential."
Simon closed his eyes, suddenly tired of the familiar rhetoric. How many times had he heard this speech during family gatherings? How many times had his father hammered these words into him?
But now, after Thomas, they had a new resonance. Now he'd seen it—the proof of how the dream world could corrupt a brilliant mind, destroy a powerful body, annihilate a connection that had seemed so pure and perfect.
"I understand completely," he said.
"We know this is a heavy burden," his uncle continued, his tone now softening. "But you're not just a Laurent by name, Simon. You're a Laurent in essence. Your intellect, your precision, your determination—you're one of your generation we

can trust with this sacred task." The compliments felt hollow, but Simon accepted them with a mumbled thanks.

"And naturally," his uncle added, "we'll ensure you're rewarded for your dedication. I've spoken with the partners at Duchamp, Mernier & Associates. They're deeply interested in your talent for international law. A junior partnership is practically guaranteed, with a compensation package that is... substantial."

Simon's attention sharpened. A partnership at one of Europe's most prestigious law firms, at his age? It was a golden ticket—financial freedom, professional recognition.

"That's... very generous," he said cautiously.

"Not generous. Deserved." His uncle's voice now sounded satisfied, knowing he had Simon's full attention. "Naturally, it's contingent on successfully completing your current... project. But I have every confidence in your capabilities. I have information about the shipment you asked about."

Simon walked to his desk and opened his laptop. "Tell me."

"The equipment arrived yesterday in Zeebrugge, exactly according to plan. Six crates, marked as historical brewing equipment. Customs didn't even open them."

Simon let out a sigh of relief. The instruments were crucial—without them, the ritual at the Minnewater during the eclipse wouldn't have the precision necessary.

"When will they be delivered to Driekwart Maan?"

"Tomorrow, 05:30. Early enough to avoid curious eyes. The brewery owner is... adequately compensated for his discretion and use of the facilities."

Simon nodded, though his uncle couldn't see this. The old brewery on the Walplein was a perfect location—centrally situated, but with deep, mediaeval cellars that offered enough privacy to test and calibrate the equipment before moving it to the Minnewater.

"Do you have the specifications I requested?"

"Of course." His uncle sounded almost offended by the question. "The heirlooms are exactly as described in Eduard's notes—the copper reflectors, the crystal amplifiers, the entire arsenal that my grandfather used during his attempt in '34."

Simon experienced a brief pang at the mention of his grandfather's failed attempt. The Laurent family had tried for generations to seal off the dream world, each attempt cleverer, better prepared than the last, but never with complete success.
"This time will be different," Simon said, more to himself than to his uncle.
"Yes," his uncle agreed, a rare tone of emotion in his voice. "Because you have something your grandfather and father didn't have—the jade key and the blood of a directly connected werewolf."
A brief silence fell between them. Simon knew his uncle wanted to know more about Finn De Wulf, about how Simon had obtained the blood. But some details were better left unspoken, even within the family.
"Speaking of which," his uncle continued, breaking the silence. "Your people—are they reliable? The ritual tolerates no... distraction."
Simon's jaw tightened at what he perceived as doubt about his judgement. "My team is carefully selected, Uncle. Experienced specialists in security and paramilitary operations. Ex-special forces, mainly."
"That doesn't answer my question, Simon. Are they prepared for what they might see? Not everyone can process manifestations from the dream world without... unwanted reactions."
It was a legitimate concern. Simon had himself seen how some people collapsed when confronted with the reality of what lay between the worlds. Even his own rational mind had struggled to process everything he'd seen during his early experiments with Thomas.
"They're screened," Simon assured him. "Each of them has previous experience with... unconventional situations. Two served in black ops, where they were confronted with not-yet-classified phenomena. One was a guard in a psychiatric institution where patients with apparent paranormal experiences were treated. Antoine has personally reviewed their psychological profiles."
"And the snipers?" His uncle's voice became sharper, more focused.

Simon hesitated a moment. The snipers were a contingency plan—a last resort if the Vandevelde woman or the Wolf tried to intervene. "Three elite marksmen. An ex-legionnaire, a former Eastern Bloc contractor, and one who worked for us in Zurich during that... complication of 2023."

"Zurich," his uncle repeated, and Simon could hear the disapproval. "That was sloppy work."

"Not the marksman. He followed orders. The planning team failed." Simon felt the need to defend his decision. "He's ice-cold, clinical, and most importantly: he can aim and fire without hesitation, even when he sees things that challenge his perception of reality."

His uncle was quiet for a moment, considering. "And you trust them all with information about our family's... unique interests?"

"They know only what they need to know," Simon replied. "For them, this is a high-end security job for a private ritual. The details about the dream world, the keys, the real meaning of what we're doing—that stays within our circle."

"Including Antoine?" His uncle's tone suggested scepticism.

"Antoine is devoted to our mission," Simon assured him. "His own research into consciousness modification via chemical means fits perfectly with our goals. He understands what we're trying to achieve."

"And Arianne?"

"She has her motivations, but our interests are aligned at present." Simon became more cautious now that the conversation touched on the internal politics of their operation. "Her insurance company will profit considerably from a more... predictable world, without dream interventions."

His uncle made a sound that was almost like a laugh—a rare sign of genuine amusement. "Arianne Vermeer, always talking about the purity of rational thinking, but ultimately motivated by profit. An ironic ally for our great mission."

"Pragmatic allies are more reliable than ideological ones," Simon observed. "They act from calculated self-interest, not emotion."

"A wise observation," his uncle conceded. "Something your father might have said."
Simon experienced that small pang again. Being compared to his father—the brilliant but obsessive Theodoor Laurent—was both a compliment and an uncomfortable reminder of the family legacy of fanaticism he'd inherited.
"The equipment will be ready on time," Simon said, changing the subject. "We need three hours for calibration, so that gives us a comfortable margin for the eclipse."
"Good. And the perimeter around the Minnewater?"
"Being secured under the pretext of preparations for a private event. Local authorities have been informed about an exclusive viewing of the eclipse for dignitaries. They'll keep tourists and intrusive civilians at distance."
"And if the Vandevelde woman tries to intervene? Or your... wolf?" The emphasis on the last word contained a subtle but clear distaste.
Simon stiffened, uncomfortable with the indirect reference to his personal interaction with Finn. "Then we'll be prepared. The snipers have orders to intimidate, not eliminate—unless absolutely necessary. We need the wolf alive for the ritual."
"And afterwards?"
The question hung in the air, cold and calculated. Simon knew what his uncle was implying. After the ritual, Finn De Wulf would be a loose end, a witness to things the Laurent family preferred to keep hidden.
"Afterwards..." Simon paused, feeling an unexpected hesitation. "Afterwards, I'll act as necessary for the security of our operation."
A new silence fell, and Simon knew his uncle had heard his hesitation. But instead of addressing it, his uncle only said: "Ensure the machines are properly installed, Simon. This is the moment our family has worked towards for centuries. Failure is not an option."
"I understand."
Simon turned his gaze away from the Market Square and looked at the photo on his desk—Thomas and him, laughing

in the summer sun. If he succeeded in the ritual, if he permanently sealed off the dream world, it wouldn't bring Thomas back. But it would mean that no one else would suffer as he had suffered, broken by hallucinations and nightmares leaking from another dimension. It would be a kind of justice, giving meaning to a senseless loss.

And with the new position, the financial security, he could finally live as he chose. Without family obligations, without suffocating expectations. He could openly be who he was, love whom he wanted.

"I won't fail," he said, his voice now stronger, more certain.

"I know that." His uncle sounded satisfied.

Simon's hand automatically reached for the small crystal vial he carried with him.

"Remember, Simon—the keys react more strongly to genetic lines that have been connected to their existence over generations. Your presence at the ritual isn't just symbolic."

"I understand."

There was a pause, and then, in a milder tone: "How are you handling it? On a personal level. I know this can be... emotionally challenging, given your history."

Simon stiffened. His 'history'—the clinical term his family used to refer to his relationship with Thomas, his bisexuality, his loss. As if it were an illness he was recovering from.

"I'm focused on the task," he replied curtly.

"Good. Distractions can be dangerous at this critical moment." There was a clear warning in his uncle's voice. "Your... interaction with the Wulf was necessary for obtaining the blood sample. But further... involvement would be unwise."

Simon's jaw tightened. *They knew. Of course, they knew. The family always knew everything. His sudden interest in Finn De Wulf hadn't gone unnoticed, even if it had originally begun as strategic manipulation.*

"I have it under control," he said coolly.

"Of course." His uncle didn't sound entirely convinced. "Don't forget who you are, Simon. A Laurent. Disciplined. Focused."

"Is that all?" Simon asked, now longing for the end of this conversation.
"For now. Keep me informed of developments. The eclipse doesn't wait for our convenience."
"Naturally."
His uncle hesitated, then added, in a rare tone of almost-affection: "You're doing good work, nephew. Soon humanity will be free from the parasitic influence of dreams, and you'll be the Laurent who made it possible."
The line went dead before Simon could respond.
He put down his phone and turned his chair back to the window, staring at the old buildings of Bruges in the late afternoon sun. A city built on traditions and history, on stories and legends—on dreams, really. And he was about to fundamentally change all of that.
His gaze fell on the jade cacao bean resting on a small stand on his desk, gently pulsing with a subtle green light that seemed to grow stronger as the eclipse approached. Next to the artefact lay a file with his personal research notes—not the official documents he shared with Antoine and Arianne, but his own observations, thoughts, and doubts.
And somewhere in that city was Finn De Wulf—the young man whose resemblance to Thomas had struck him like physical pain. The young man he'd used, manipulated, and who yet had touched something in him that he thought he'd buried by now.
"It's necessary," Simon said under his breath to his reflection in the glass. "For a rational world. For a world without the delusions that killed Thomas."
But even as he spoke the words, he felt doubt gnawing at the edges of his determination.
He picked up the vial with Finn's blood, turning the crystal between his fingers. The blood inside was darker than normal human blood, with a subtle golden shimmer that became visible when light fell on it in a certain way. A perverse thought went through him to taste his blood, to be closer to him. Finn's face flashed through his thoughts—his face that looked so

painfully like Thomas's, that intensity in his eyes during their brief time together. It was meant as manipulation, to obtain the blood Simon needed. But something unexpected had happened, something he hadn't planned. A connection that Simon had felt despite all his precautions.

He shook it away. His uncle was right. He couldn't afford distractions, not now. The task was too important. What was at stake was too crucial.

Simon opened his laptop, ready to analyse the latest data from the surveillance of Lina's shop.

But first he sent a brief message to his crew:

> "Tonight, 20:00. Discuss final preparations. No excuses. S.L."

He deleted the message history, as he always did, a habit ingrained by years of caution. In this game of shadows and dreams, words were evidence, and evidence was a weakness he couldn't afford.

Particularly when he was so close to accomplishing his lifelong objective. Not when he was so close to his independence.

DON'T FLY, SOAR

They waited until just after midnight. The rain had stopped, and Bruges was shrouded in a thin mist that crept along the canals and painted the street lamps with ghostly haloes.

Confiserie du Cygne had, as Lina had expected, a warehouse on the edge of the city—a modern warehouse in a small industrial estate that bordered the canal. Lina parked her Citroën in a deserted car park two streets away. Morpheus sat in the back seat, watching for drones or anything else following them.

"How did you know about this place?" Finn asked as they got out.

"Kaylee. When she came round, she told me enthusiastically about how Antoine had invited her for an exclusive tasting at his 'chocolate lab'—she'd even taken photos for her feed." Lina took out her phone and showed a photo of Kaylee posing in front of a steel door with the swan logo. She kept quiet about the drone that had followed her earlier.

"Not exactly secretive," Finn observed.

"Antoine lacks my mother's caution," Lina replied. "He relies too much on his social status and modern security measures."

"Speaking of measures," Finn gestured towards the security cameras monitoring the entrance. "How do we get in?"

In response, Lina produced a small pouch filled with what looked like coarse, dark chocolate powder. "With this."

"More magical chocolate?" Finn asked sceptically.

"Potential," Lina laughed softly. "Raw cocoa powder mixed with iron and magnet dust. Perfect for disrupting electronic circuits without leaving traces."

She walked to a ventilation opening on the side of the building and blew a handful of powder into the opening. There was a moment of silence, followed by a faint humming sound and then... nothing. The small red lights on the security cameras went out.

"Simple science," Lina smiled. "Now the lock."

The lock proved to be an electronic keypad, protected by a glass shield, with its own power supply. Lina studied it briefly, then produced a small spray bottle.

"Cocoa butter mixed with citric acid," she explained as she sprayed the mixture on the glass. "Leaves no scratches, but dissolves silicone seals."

Within a minute, the glass protection was loose and Lina could access the keypad. She connected her phone to it via a thin cable.

"A digital lock-picker app?" Finn asked, impressed by her technological skills alongside her magical ones.

"Designed by a friend," Lina nodded. "Not all chocolate makers need to parade modern techniques. I embrace the best of both worlds."

The door opened with a soft click. Inside, the warehouse was much larger than Finn had expected—an extensive space with metal shelving full of boxes and ingredients, all organized with clinical precision. At the back, a sealed room was visible through glass walls—a high-tech laboratory with copper kettles alongside computer-controlled temperature regulators and modern injection equipment.

"This isn't a traditional chocolate maker," Lina hissed, looking around the space. "This is a pharmaceutical lab."

They moved carefully through the space, avoiding the lines of possible motion sensors. Finn's senses were sharp, his nose picking up what others would miss.

"There's something... wrong with the smell here," he whispered. "There's something chemical mixed under the chocolate scent."

"Antoine uses additives," Lina nodded. "Probably synthetic psychoactive compounds to enhance the dream effect, a bit like party drugs."

They reached the lab and Lina studied the equipment. "There," she pointed to a large fridge on the back wall. "That must be the finished stock."

The fridge wasn't locked—why would it be, inside an already secured building? Inside were dozens of boxes ready for distribution, each decorated with the swan logo and labelled with destinations around Bruges.

"Cafés, hotels, even university vending machines," Lina read the labels. "They're planning widespread distribution, targeting young people."

"How do we stop this?" Finn asked. "We can't destroy all these boxes without leaving traces."

Lina closed her eyes, thinking. "We don't have time to neutralize each piece," Morpheus commented. "But..." Lina opened her bag and produced a glass phial filled with a transparent liquid. "This should work."

"What is it?"

"An enzyme mixture that breaks down the psychoactive compounds without changing the taste or texture," Morpheus replied. "I developed it as a safety measure for my creations, for clients with sensitivity to overly intense dream effects."

She opened a ventilation opening in the fridge and sprayed the liquid inside. "It will evaporate and settle on all the chocolate in the enclosed space. Within an hour, it will be completely infiltrated."

"And Antoine will never know that his own special ingredient has been neutralized," Finn concluded admiringly.

"Exactly. His chocolate will just be... chocolate. People will experience mild relaxation, perhaps some livelier dreams than normal, but no hallucinations, no nightmares manifesting in reality."

They were about to return to the entrance when Finn suddenly stiffened. "Someone's coming." His sharpened hearing picked up footsteps outside, along with the soft beep of an

electronic key being activated. "Security's been restored," Morpheus hissed. "We're trapped."
They retreated into the shadows between two high shelves just as the door opened. Two figures entered—a slim man in a tight modern suit, and a woman whose silhouette Finn immediately recognized.
"Antoine and Arianne," he said so softly that only Lina could hear.
"We're ready," Antoine said in French, walking towards the fridge that Lina had just sabotaged. "Day after tomorrow at noon, half of Bruges will start hallucinating."
"Perfect," Arianne stated matter-of-factly. "And regarding the specific preparation for the identified stakeholder?"
Antoine grinned coldly and produced a small, black box from a safe they couldn't see from their position. "Special delivery for tomorrow morning. The dose is four times stronger, enhanced with extracts from the jade key itself. Not lethal, but it will completely immobilize students."
"That meets the established parameters," Arianne confirmed with a brief, efficient nod. "And concerning the elderly party involved? Is there progress in that specific case? My intervention was unsuccessful this afternoon."
"Tout est arrangé," Antoine waved away with French flair. "Simon has teams ready to search her flat. If the golden key is there, we'll have it avant le coucher du soleil; before sunset."
"And the Wulf?"
"Simon has a... comment dit-on... personal interest in him," Antoine smiled more broadly. "He says he needs more blood for the ritual, mais je soupçonne that his... fascination... runs deeper."
"His interpersonal preoccupations fall outside the scope of our agreement," Arianne declared curtly. "The only relevant variable is whether the required biological material is available in sufficient quantity for executing the agreed procedure."
"Voilà, tout est en ordre," Antoine assured her with a dismissive wave of his hand. "During the eclipse the day after tomorrow, the portal will close permanently. Plus de rêves. No

werewolves. No magic. Only rational, controllable reality and my hallucinogenic pralines for a really... addictive trip, n'est-ce pas?"

"And we thereby obtain complete control over the newly created market conditions," Arianne established with a subtle indication of satisfaction. "In the absence of non-quantifiable competitive factors, my insurance office will acquire an exclusive position in the risk analysis and management sector. Your culinary products will define the market standard in the luxury segment, without disruption from irrational competitive practices."

"And Simon gets his old family inheritance back in the form of unprecedented legal power and a steady job," Antoine nodded. "A win-win-win."

Finn experienced cold fury rising in his chest. These weren't idealists with a misguided vision—these were calculating opportunists who wanted to destroy the dream world for profit and power.

Beside him, he felt Lina stiffen, her hand finding his in the darkness. A warning, a request for silence. The two figures were now walking past their hiding place, so close that Finn could smell the peppermint oil in Antoine's aftershave.

"Close everything down," Arianne instructed as they walked towards the exit. "The day after tomorrow, at this time, no one will be worrying about a chocolate maker and a lost werewolf—they'll be too busy fleeing from their nightmares."

The door closed with a definitive click, and the sound of the electronic lock activated.

"That was close," Finn said when the footsteps outside faded.

"Too close," Lina nodded, emerging from their hiding place. "But we got what we needed. We now know their full plan."

"And that they're after both of us," Finn added.

"And Ingrid."

"We need to find her," Lina said, already moving towards a ventilation shaft that offered a possible way out. "Before Simon finds her. If she really has the golden key..."

"If," Finn emphasized. "That's still based on your mother's suspicions." "My mother was rarely wrong about such things," Lina replied, unscrewing the protective plate of the ventilation opening with a multi-tool from her pocket. "And who else would Laurent search for so systematically?" Finn thought about what Simon had told him about Lina, and now seeing her act so coolly, he couldn't fault his judgement. Perhaps she was just as dangerous.

They worked silently whilst removing the air conditioning vent and inspecting the narrow passage. It would be tight, but possible.

"Ladies first," Finn grinned, helping Lina hoist herself into the shaft.

"How gallant," she replied dryly. "Or just strategic—you're broader than me and if you get stuck, I can at least pull you out."

"Later," Morpheus hissed, who slipped first through a small opening to the outside.

The journey through the ventilation system was cramped and dusty. Lina's slender figure moved with fluid efficiency, but Finn's broader shoulders regularly scraped against the metal walls, each time causing a squeak or scrape that made him freeze with fear of discovery or alarm.

After what seemed like hours, they reached an exit—a grille that looked out onto the back of the building. Lina easily kicked it loose with a well-aimed kick, and they slid outside into the fresh night air.

"Never thought ordinary oxygen could taste so good," Finn said, breathing deeply.

"Come on," Lina urged, already moving in the direction where they'd left her car. "We've no time to lose. We need to find Ingrid, and then plan to stop Simon."

They'd barely taken a few steps when a sharp, electronic sound pierced the night—an alarm, loud and relentless, coming from the warehouse behind them.

"They've discovered us," Lina concluded, now running. "We need to—"

Her words were cut off by a new sound—the screeching of car

tyres on tarmac. A black SUV with dimmed headlights skidded round the corner and blocked their path. The doors flew open and four men in dark suits stepped out.

"We split up," Lina panted, pushing Finn away. "I'll distract them. You find Ingrid. She lives at Rozenhoedkaai 16!"

Before Finn could protest, Lina had turned and was running back towards the warehouse. Two of the men immediately pursued her, whilst the other two came for Finn.

Lina had already pulled the hairpin from her hair and spoken a brief incantation quietly. The pin immediately transformed into an elegant flying broomstick. She whipped three vials of powder from her coat pockets and threw them to the ground, where they exploded in thick clouds of blinding smoke.

Finn looked back once more and saw Lina rising on her broomstick, like a spectral apparition in the artificial mist.

She flew over the incoming guards. Through the smoke sounded surprised exclamations and orders shouted out interchangeably.

"There! She's flying!"

"Shoot! Shoot then!"

"I can't see anything in this mist!"

The chaos she created was the perfect distraction. His instincts took over. The wolf in him, so long suppressed, so long hidden, exploded to the surface. Not the full transformation—that could only happen at a full moon—but enough. His muscles swelled, his senses sharpened, his nails lengthened to claw-like points.

The first man reached him, a tranquillizer gun raised. Finn moved with new speed, dodged the shot, and pushed the man away with a force that sent him flying metres through the air. The second hesitated, clearly not prepared for a half-transformed werewolf.

Finn used the hesitation. He leaped, higher and further than an ordinary human could, landing on the roof of a nearby building. Without looking back, he ran on, jumping from roof to roof in the direction of the old city, driven by one thought: find Ingrid before Simon's people did.

Behind him, he heard the car starting again, tyres squealing as it gave chase along the streets below. They had the advantages of speed and roads, but he had knowledge of Bruges' rooftops, an area where no car could reach.

Rozenhoedkaai 16. The oldest harbour in the city. On the other side of town.

Finn accelerated, his breathing now heavy but controlled, his muscles working with superhuman efficiency.

He had to find Ingrid and warn her. He had to protect the golden key if she truly had it.

And then what, asked a voice in his head. What then if you have all three of them, the keys? What will you choose at the eclipse?

Finn shook it away. First survive. First secure the keys. Only then think about impossible choices between worlds.

The three old towers of Bruges rose before him, silhouettes against the starry sky. Somewhere there waited Ingrid. And somewhere, hopefully, Lina had shaken off her pursuers.

Finn jumped to the next roof, determined, driven, the wolf in his blood now finally an ally instead of his enemy.

TUNNELS

Rozenhoedkaai 16 turned out to be a narrow, but elegant town house squeezed in between two similar buildings on the bank of one of Bruges' most picturesque canals. The façade was mediaeval but perfectly maintained, with flower boxes in front of the windows that even in February were full of colourful winter blooms.

Finn stood in the shadows on the other side of the canal, observing the house. Light burned behind the curtains on the second floor, but the rest was dark. It was nearly two o'clock in the morning, and the street was deserted.

How to proceed? He could hardly ring the bell at this hour. And he had no idea whether Ingrid was alone, or accompanied by others, or perhaps even under surveillance by Laurent's people.

His decision was made for him when a window on the second floor slowly opened. An elderly woman leaned out, her silhouette unmistakably recognizable as Ingrid Vermeulen. Finn had encountered her and her little dog before during his pizza delivery rounds. She looked directly at where Finn stood, as if she knew exactly where he was despite the darkness.

"You might as well come in, young wolf," she said in an ordinary tone, her voice surprisingly clear and strong for her age and the late hour. "The front door is open for you."

Finn hesitated, but his instincts told him he could trust this strange woman. He crossed the small pedestrian bridge and walked to the front door, which indeed proved to be unlocked. Inside, the flat was different from what he'd expected. Antique furniture harmonized with modern art, and everywhere were bookcases filled with what looked like rare and old volumes and souvenirs. There was a display case with corals shaped like beans and photos of Ingrid with little dogs hung on the wall.

"Upstairs, love," came Ingrid's voice. "Second door on the right."

Finn followed the directions, but for a moment, it flashed through his head that within a few days he was entering a stranger's flat. He found Ingrid sitting in a comfortable chair in what looked like a study. She was dressed in a simple but elegant dressing gown, her grey hair in a neat plait, and on her lap rested her Yorkshire terrier, Pouffe, who looked at Finn with unusually intelligent eyes.

"You're late," she said, gesturing for him to take the chair opposite her. "I expected you and Lina hours ago."

"You... were waiting for us?" Finn sat down carefully, surprised by Ingrid's calm and knowledge.

"Of course," she replied airily. "Why else would I tell Sophia about the golden key before she died? It was time for you to find it. The timing felt... right." She stroked Pouffe, who relaxed under her touch. "Where's Lina?" she asked.

"We were attacked at Antoine's warehouse," Finn explained. "She led Antoine's or Simon's men away so I could reach your house."

Ingrid's eyes narrowed. "That wasn't the plan." She sounded irritated, but not worried. "That girl is too much like her mother—always ready to sacrifice herself."

"Mrs Vermeulen—"

"Ingrid, please," she interrupted. "If we're going to fulfil an age-old prophecy together, we'd better be on first-name terms."

"Ingrid," Finn began again. "Is it true? Do you have the golden key?"

The old woman looked at him, her expression surprisingly sharp and alert for someone of her supposed age. "What do you think, young wolf?"

Finn closed his eyes and breathed deeply, his sharpened senses searching for something in this room. And there it was—a subtle but unmistakable vibration, similar to that of the jade at Laurent's and Lina's silver cacao bean, but with a warmer, richer undertone. His eyes shot open, glowing.

"You have it," he judged. "Here in this room."

Ingrid nodded, clearly impressed. "Good nose. The Laurent boy underestimates you, only sees your blood as valuable." She reached to her neck and pulled out a necklace that had been hidden under her clothing.

From it hung what looked like a worn coral pendant. But as Finn watched, Ingrid turned it in her fingers, and from certain angles it clearly glinted gold despite the coral outer layer.

"Hidden in plain sight," she explained. "The best hiding place is always the obvious one. Nobody expects the world's most precious magical key to be worn by an old gossip." She laughed at her description.

"But... why you?" Finn asked, fascinated by the object that Ingrid treated so nonchalantly. "What's your role in all this?"

"The Gossip," she answered simply. "In every generation there must be someone who preserves stories, who knows what really happens, and who passes information to those who need to hear it." She chuckled. "Do you think I've followed every piece of gossip in Bruges for the past sixty years for my pleasure? It was my way of knowing everything, of having eyes and ears everywhere."

Pouffe barked once, as if confirming it. For the first time, Finn noticed that the little dog wasn't staring at him with the usual nervous dislike that animals often showed towards werewolves. Instead, his gaze was... knowing.

"And Pouffe is...?"

"My protector," Ingrid beamed, lovingly stroking the small animal. "Not everything is what it seems, Finn De Wulf. Some beings choose an inconspicuous form, just as some keys disguise themselves as worn jewellery."

Finn stared at the little dog with new eyes. Was it possible that...? A sudden sound outside interrupted his thoughts—

car tyres on the street, doors opening and closing, footsteps.

"They're here," Ingrid said, remarkably calm. "Earlier than I'd thought." She grabbed a coat and threw it over her nightgown.

"Antoine's or Simon's people," Finn confirmed, jumping up and moving to the window. On the street stood two black SUVs, and men in dark clothing were forming a perimeter around the house.

"Do you have a back door?" he asked urgently. "An escape route?"

"There's always an escape route," Ingrid replied cryptically. She stood up and walked to one of the many bookcases. With a practised movement, she pulled on a specific book, and the entire case swung inward, revealing a dark passage leading downward. "The old tunnels under Bruges. They lead to the brewery at the Minnewater, if we keep right."

"Minnewater," Finn repeated. "Where Lina said the dream barrier is thinnest."

"Exactly, young wolf." Ingrid picked up a small bag that stood ready beside her chair—as if she'd known she would have to flee—and moved towards the hidden passage. "Quickly now. They won't take long breaking down the front door."

As if on command, a loud crash sounded from below—the front door being rammed.

Finn and Ingrid slipped into the hidden tunnel, Pouffe safe in Ingrid's arms. The bookcase closed behind them, enveloping them in darkness.

"Hold my shoulder," Ingrid instructed. "The tunnel is old but stable. I know every stone, every bend."

"How can you see in this darkness?" Finn asked as they moved forward.

"I can't see anything," Ingrid replied. "But Pouffe can. And I trust him as he trusts me. That's how partnerships work, young wolf. You'll learn that with Lina, in time."

As they entered deeper into the underground tunnels of Bruges, Finn thought of Lina, hoping she was safe, hoping they would find each other at the Minnewater, hoping that the approaching solar eclipse wouldn't mean the end of everything he was just beginning to appreciate.

Above their heads, the sky was already growing lighter—a new day was dawning in Bruges, probably the last normal day before Antoine's poisoned chocolate would be distributed, before nightmares would become reality, before the keys would come together for the final pick.
Finn's choice.

GATHERING STORM

Meanwhile, at the place where once the Pathoeke Forest had been. The men chasing Lina were well-trained, but she knew Bruges like nobody else—every alley, every path, every hidden passage forgotten by tourists and city planners.

Above the warehouse complex, Lina flew low over the rooftops, her broom a silver streak in the moonlight. She made sharp turns and zigzagged between chimneys, strategically leading Laurent's men away from where Finn was.

Two SUVs tore through the streets below her, pursuing what they thought was her escape route. She curled her lips into a grim smile—every moment she kept them busy was more time for Finn to reach Ingrid.

She slipped between two warehouses, ducked under a half-open gate, and emerged onto a narrow path that ran alongside a side canal. The broom transformed back into a hairpin and without hesitation she jumped into the dark water.

She swam with powerful strokes underwater, trying to create as much distance as possible before she had to breathe again. The men wouldn't know whether she'd gone upstream or downstream.

When her lungs screamed for air, she let herself rise, her head barely above water under the shadow of an overhanging willow. She breathed deeply, listening to the footsteps and voices on the bank.

"She's gone into the water!"
"Split up—you upstream, we'll go downstream."
"Laurent wants her alive."
Lina grinned grimly. *Of course, he wants me alive.* He couldn't take the silver key from a corpse—it had to be voluntarily surrendered, or taken from a living bearer. Old magic had its limitations, even for Laurent.
She pulled the silver cacao bean from her neck and held it tightly in her hand. If necessary, she would destroy it, to break the continuity of centuries, to prevent it from falling into Laurent's hands. A drastic measure, but better than the permanent closure of the dream world.
The water was freezing, but Lina knew tricks to stay warm. She whispered an old Maya word, and the cacao bean in her hand warmed, radiating enough heat to prevent hypothermia, but not enough to betray her position with a glow in the water. She waited until the footsteps faded before swimming further, using the canal systems that crossed Bruges like an age-old vascular system. If she could reach the city centre, she'd have access to her hiding places, weapons, allies.
After what seemed like hours, she reached a jetty by one of the old breweries. She climbed carefully out of the water, shivering despite the warmth of the key, her clothes soaked and heavy.
"That look suits you," said a sarcastic voice from the shadows. Lina turned, her senses sharp, and relaxed when she saw a familiar black figure step out of the darkness.
"Morpheus," she sighed. "Where were you?"
"I followed you the whole time," the cat replied, now back in his normal animal form. "Until I saw you jump into the canal like a lunatic. Then I lost your scent."
"They nearly had me," Lina said, realizing how close it had been. "Have you seen Finn?"
"Yes, that lad jumped like mad over rooftops towards the centre. I'll bet he reached Ingrid. The boy has good instincts, even if he doesn't fully realize it." Morpheus jumped onto a nearby railing, his balance perfect despite the narrow surface. "The question is: what now?"

"Now," said Lina, wringing out her hair, "we need to find them at the Minnewater."
"Why Minnewater?"
"Because according to my instincts, Ingrid always uses the same escape route. The old tunnels under the city that come out at the brewery by the lake." She began walking, her soaked shoes leaving wet footprints. "And because it's the thinnest barrier between our world and the Underworld—the perfect place to plan a counter-attack."
"You're not going to try what I think you're going to try, are you?" Morpheus jumped onto her shoulder, an unusual gesture of protection. "Deliberately opening the Underworld here in physical reality is madness. There's a reason traditional chocolate ceremonies are held in the protected space of a chocolate maker."
"We have no choice left," Lina replied grimly. "Laurent wants to permanently close the barrier between worlds. Our only chance is to find allies on the other side before he does that."
"Kaxil won't be pleased."
"Kaxil has no choice. If Laurent succeeds, the Underworld permanently disappears from our reality." Lina's face hardened, an expression she'd inherited from her mother—determined, immovable. "It's time to gather all the forces we can find."
They walked on silently through the quiet streets, the early morning mist still hanging over the city like a veil between reality and dream. A single sleeping swan looked up as they passed.

The tunnels under Bruges were a labyrinth of mediaeval construction, later extensions, and natural formations—a time capsule of the city's evolution. Ingrid navigated through them with surprising certainty, one hand on Pouffe in her arms, the other sometimes reaching out to touch a familiar landmark.
"These tunnels were originally built by monks smuggling wine and beer," she explained as they walked. "Later they were extended during the religious wars, as escape routes for the persecuted. My family has used them for generations."

"Your family?" Finn asked, still amazed at how this apparently eccentric old woman played such a crucial role in all this.
"The Vermeulens go back just as far as the Vandeveldes and the Laurents," Ingrid nodded. "We were the neutral intermediaries, the keepers of knowledge. We Gossips have always preserved truth in stories, spread as gossip that nobody took seriously, but which was remembered when it mattered."
A thumping sound echoed through the tunnel—footsteps, far behind them.
"They've found the entrance," Ingrid spoke weakly, accelerating. "We must hurry."
They reached a crossroads of three tunnels, and Ingrid hesitated for the first time. "Strange," she hissed. "The left tunnel should be lit."
Finn concentrated, his sharpened senses searching in the darkness. His nose hairs prickled with warning. "There's someone ahead of us," he breathed softly. "Waiting in the left tunnel."
Ingrid nodded, clearly not surprised. "Then we take this one. It's a detour, but it will still bring us to Minnewater." She hesitated, then produced a small key from under her clothing. "Take this. It opens the iron door at the end of the right tunnel. If we get separated, go straight until you see daylight."
Finn took the key, the cold metal strangely heavy in his hand.
They continued their way through the newly chosen tunnel. This one was narrower, the walls rougher, the path more irregular. Water dripped from the ceiling, and the air was permeated with the mustiness of centuries.
"Ingrid," Finn said after a while, "if we survive this... what happens at the solar eclipse? What exactly is my choice?"
The old woman sighed, a sound that seemed to carry centuries of weariness. "The prophecy speaks of a Wolf who, when the three keys are united, gets the choice between three paths: completely closing the worlds, as Laurent wants; maintaining the current balance, as Lina's family has done for generations; or..." she hesitated.
"Or?" Finn pressed.
"Or completely uniting the worlds," she finished. "A fusion of

dreams and reality, of magic and matter, that would fundamentally change our reality."

"Sounds drastic," Finn concluded coolly.

"All great choices are drastic, young wolf," Ingrid replied. "That's why we fear them. But know this: whatever choice you make, it must be your choice. Not what others impose on you."

The footsteps behind them sounded louder, closer. Finn looked back and saw the faint flicker of torches.

"They're catching up," he warned.

"Nearly there," Ingrid encouraged. "Just one more bend—"

They stopped abruptly. Before them stood a large iron door, exactly as Ingrid had described. But in front of the door stood a figure that made Finn's blood freeze.

Simon Laurent, elegantly dressed despite the early hour and improbable location, leaned nonchalantly against the door. In his hand he held the jade cacao bean, which now glowed brighter than Finn had ever seen it, a flickering green light that shrouded the tunnel in ghostly shadows.

"Hello, lover boy," Simon smiled. "What a pleasant surprise. And Mrs Vermeulen, finally we meet formally."

"Laurent," Ingrid greeted coolly, no trace of her usual theatrical senility. "You look like your grandfather. The same arrogant attitude, the same blindness to the greater truth."

"And you," Simon replied, "are an almost perfect actress. Playing a brainless gossip for decades whilst protecting one of the most powerful magical artefacts in the world." His eyes narrowed, and his voice became more commanding. "The golden key, if you please."

"You know it doesn't work that way," Ingrid said calmly. "The key won't go with you unless I want it to, or unless you kill me—which would destroy the artefact."

"Exactly," Simon nodded, his smile broadening. "That's why I've arranged something to encourage your willingness."

He gestured towards the door, which slowly opened. Behind it, in the half-darkness, a figure was visible being held kneeling by two of Simon's men. Her hair was wet, her clothes soaked, her face tired but unbroken.

"Lina," Finn said, his heart racing. Two laser dots appeared on Finn's and Ingrid's hearts.

So her bag of tricks did have an end after all.

"She was surprisingly easy to follow when she came out of the canal," Simon said nonchalantly. "But she's still alive, which is what matters." He walked over to her and placed a hand under her chin, forcing her to look up. "She's still the bearer of the silver key, and thus vital to our plans."

Lina's eyes, already fierce blue, now burned with furious intensity. "You're mistaken, Laurent. The key is gone."

Simon's composure broke for a moment. "What?"

"I threw it in the canal," she said, her voice hoarse but triumphant. "Rather lost than in your hands."

Ingrid immediately knew she was lying.

Simon's hand jolted out and slapped Lina hard across the face. "Liar!" he hissed. "The key can't just be thrown away. It's bound to your blood, to your family."

"Check for yourself," Lina challenged him, her lip bleeding from the blow.

Simon grabbed at her neck, his fingers searching under her clothing, but found nothing. His face contorted with rage, then tight control. "No problem," he said, his voice smooth again. "We'll find it. The key calls to its kind. With the jade with me and the golden..." he looked at Ingrid, "soon in my possession, the silver will obey."

Finn looked between Lina and Ingrid, his thoughts racing. The situation seemed hopeless—Simon had trapped them. Behind them, more men were approaching, before them stood Laurent with two henchmen holding Lina.

But there was something in Lina's eyes, a subtle message, a plan. She hadn't given up, so neither would he.

"Your choice, Mrs Vermeulen," Simon said, turning back to Ingrid. "Give me the golden key, or we'll find out how much pain a Vandevelde can endure before her mind breaks."

Ingrid looked sadly at Lina, then at Finn, and finally at Pouffe in her arms. She seemed to have decided.

"The time for hide-and-seek is over, I suppose," she sighed.

She carefully put Pouffe down and took the necklace from her neck. "The golden key, as requested."
Simon's eyes lit up with greedy hunger as he stepped forward, his hand outstretched. But before he could grab the key, Pouffe barked once—a sound much louder and deeper than seemed possible for such a small animal.
Suddenly, the tunnel was filled with blinding white light. Finn's instincts took over; he grabbed Ingrid and pulled her to the ground, protecting them with his body. Simon and his men screamed, their hands going to their eyes.
When the light faded, there was no longer a small Yorkshire terrier. Instead, a massive white wolf filled the tunnel—larger than any natural animal, its coat glittering like fresh snow, its eyes deep golden pools of ancient wisdom.
"Return to the light, Dreamer," Ingrid spoke, her voice suddenly stronger, more melodious. "These people aren't ready for your true form."
The great white wolf—Dreamer, apparently Pouffe's real name—barked again, a sound that resonated through Finn's bones. At that moment, Lina sprang into action, her apparent weakness disappearing as she kicked away her guards with surprising strength.
"Finn!" she called. "The key! Now!"
Without thinking, Finn lunged forward, dodging the blinded Simon, and grabbed the golden key still hanging in Ingrid's hand. In the same movement, he grabbed Lina's arm and pulled her towards the now open tunnel door.
"Run!" he shouted.
They ran away, Ingrid and the white wolf directly behind them. They heard Simon's furious cry, but didn't stop to look back.
Not only that, but they emerged in an old beer cellar, through an exit that came out directly at the edge of the Minnewater.
The lake lay before them, still and misty in the early morning light, the surface as smooth as glass, reflecting the old trees and castle like a perfect mirror.
"Where to now?" Finn panted, still firmly holding the golden key.

"There," Lina pointed to a small boat moored at a private jetty. "Ingrid's escape route. Quickly!"
They climbed into the boat, Finn and Lina at the oars, whilst Ingrid and Dreamer sat on the bench. They rowed to the middle of the lake, a magical mist now concealing them from any pursuers on the shore. Some swans drifted past them.
"You didn't throw away the silver key," Finn said when they were safe on the water.
Lina grinned and produced the silver cacao bean from under her clothing. "Of course not. Simon is cleverer than his ancestors, but his arrogance makes him blind. The key cannot be found unless the bearer wants it to be."
"And now we still have the two keys," Finn realized, looking at the golden key in his hand, the silver around Lina's neck.
"Not for long," Ingrid warned. "Simon won't give up. And now we've really made him angry."
Dreamer made a soft, plaintive sound. "Dreamer's right," Ingrid said, stroking him. "We have little time. The solar eclipse is tomorrow, and we must be prepared for Laurent's next move."
"Who... what is he exactly?" Finn asked, pointing to the wolf.
"A Dream guard," Lina answered. "A being from the Underworld that can take physical form in our world, but only in disguise." She looked admiringly at the majestic animal. "Ingrid's family has had Dream guards as allies for generations."
"And he helped Ingrid protect the golden key."
"The other way around," Ingrid corrected. "I helped him protect the key. The Dream guards are the original keepers of the keys. We humans are merely temporary guardians."
They reached the middle of the lake, where the mist was thickest. Lina stopped rowing and closed her eyes, the silver key in her hand. "This is the place," she said in hushed tones. "The thinnest barrier between worlds."
"What are you going to do?" Finn asked, suddenly nervous.
"What we must do," Lina replied. "Call for help from the only beings who can stop Laurent." She looked directly at him. "We're going to open the Dream World here, Finn. And your choice as Wolf... that begins now."

She held the silver key above the water. "Are you ready to see where you truly come from, Finn De Wulf? To accept your true inheritance?"

Finn looked at the three faces observing him—Lina, determined and strong despite her harrowing encounter; Ingrid, old and wise, radiating a strange calm; and Dreamer, the Dream guard, whose golden eyes seemed to say: This is why you were born.

"Yes," he said finally, a new kind of determination in his voice. "I'm ready."

Lina gently let the silver key touch the water surface. The moment of contact, the water seemed to change—no longer liquid but solid, no longer reflecting but transparent, like a window to another place.

And through that window, Finn saw a world he'd always known in his dreams—an endless wilderness of impossible trees and golden rivers, of stars that moved in patterns and beings that couldn't exist.

The Underworld. The source of all dreams and wonders.

And it called to him, as it always had, but now he could finally answer.

BETWEEN WORLDS

Finn looked over the edge of the boat into what had once been water, but was now a transparent window to another reality. A dizzying sensation of depth, not downward but *inward*, overwhelmed him. The Underworld unfolded beneath them like a landscape of pure possibility—a flowing, changing world of golden vegetation, luminous paths, and impossible architecture.

"I've never seen it like this," Lina whispered, her eyes wide. "Not even in the deep dream rituals."

"The barrier is thinner because of the approaching eclipse," Ingrid explained. "Plus, there are three of the four bearers here. That strengthens the connection."

"So we can see it, but not enter?" Finn asked, disappointed.

Lina and Ingrid exchanged a look. "Theoretically," Lina said slowly, "if we use the silver and golden keys together whilst we're already at a natural thin place and during astronomical alignment... we can create passage."

"That sounds like more than 'theoretical,'" Finn observed.

"It's only described in ancient texts," Lina admitted. "No Vandevelde has attempted it in at least four generations."

"But it's possible," Finn pressed.

Dreamer made a soft sound and looked at Ingrid, who nodded as if answering an unspoken question.

"It's possible," she confirmed. "And necessary. Only in the Underworld can we gather the allies we need to stop Laurent."

"Wait," Finn raised his hand. "Do you mean we're all... going there?" He pointed to the impossible world beneath them.

"Not all," Lina said, her face now grimly determined. "I must stay here to guard the portal. If it closes whilst you're inside..."

She didn't need to finish the sentence. Finn remembered all too well what Kaxil had explained about the consequences of getting stuck in the Underworld.

"Then Ingrid and I go," he decided, accepting the strange reality in which he now lived. "How does it work?"

Lina placed the silver cacao bean in Finn's palm next to the golden key he already held. "Hold them together above the water—or what's now the portal. Concentrate on where you want to go. The Underworld will respond to your intention."

"That sounds... vague," Finn judged.

"Magic is rarely precise," Ingrid laughed. "That's why people like the Laurents are so afraid of it. It can't be captured in formulas and equations."

Dreamer pushed his massive white body against Finn, a gesture of solidarity and encouragement. Up close, Finn could see that the being's coat wasn't really fur like that of an ordinary wolf, but something ethereal, almost luminous, like moonlight woven into physical form.

"Dreamer's going with you," Ingrid said. "He knows the Underworld better than anyone. He'll be your guide."

Finn nodded, a strange calm coming over him. Four days ago, his biggest worry had been keeping his scholarship whilst struggling to hide his werewolf nature. Now he was about to enter another reality with a magical being as guide, searching for allies against a millennia-old conspiracy.

"How long do we have?" he asked Lina.

"I can keep the portal open for about three hours," she replied, her fingers already forming the intricate gestures of some incantation. "But you must return earlier. Laurent will feel the disturbance and come here."

"Three hours," Finn repeated. "Got it."

He held both keys firmly, noting how they warmed in his palm, resonating with each other and with something deep in his blood. "And what should I look for?"

"You'll find Kaxil," Lina said. "Or he'll find you. He's the Keeper of Dreams, and if anyone knows a way to stop Laurent, it's him."

"And my choice?" Finn asked. "Will he tell me more about that?"

"That's probably exactly what he'll do," Ingrid nodded. "But remember, Finn: whatever Kaxil says, whatever information he shares, the ultimate choice remains yours."

Finn breathed deeply and looked at Dreamer, who was already positioned at the edge of the boat ready to jump. "All right then. Three hours. Find Kaxil. Discover how we stop Laurent."

He stretched his arm out over the portal, the silver and golden keys in his palm, and tried to concentrate on his intention: I want to enter the Underworld. I seek Kaxil. I must find allies.

For a moment, nothing happened. Then the keys began to glow—first with their own separate lights, silver and gold, but slowly the colours merged into a rich, warm amber, exactly the colour of Finn's wolf eyes.

The portal beneath them widened, like a pupil adjusting to darkness. An opening formed, not round but spiral, like a whirlpool of light and matter.

"Good luck," Lina hissed.

And then Dreamer jumped, a white flash in the morning mist. Without hesitation, Finn followed, grabbing the thick fur of the wolf as they fell together, not downward but inward, through realities, to the source of all dreams.

HALF WORK

In a room within the old walls of Driekwart Maan brewery, a kilometre and a half from the Minnewater, Simon Laurent stared at the jade artefact on the table before him. It glowed with an intense, rhythmically pulsing light that worsened with each minute, reacting to a disturbance in what he could only describe as the fabric of reality itself.

"You were right," he said to Antoine, who stood nervously by the window. "They've opened a portal, but we can't get past the black panther. He's already taken out four people."

"I almost had all three of them!" Simon exclaimed.

"What do we do now?" Antoine asked, his normally self-assured demeanour affected by recent events. "They have two of the three keys."

"It doesn't matter," Simon replied calmly, despite the fury still shuddering through him since their escape. "The Wolf is what counts. The blood I took from him is enough to close the gate permanently, even with only one key."

"And the ritual?"

"Is almost ready." Simon pointed to an intricate setup of instruments, glass containers, and crystal reflectors that filled a large part of the room. "I've marked the starting point in the Minnewater's centre. By the time the eclipse reaches its peak tomorrow, the jade will be at full power, and Finn's blood, combined with the positioning of the celestial factor, will cause the final separation."

He picked up the small crystal vial that hung on a silver chain around his neck. The blood inside was dark, almost black now, but with a strange, golden shimmer when it moved.
"But wouldn't it be better to have all the keys?" Antoine pressed. "To be sure? The old texts do speak of three keys, after all."
Simon grinned coldly. "Of course that would be better. And we'll get them." He looked up as the door opened, and Arianne Vermeer entered, accompanied by three men in dark suits. "We have something they want. And they'll come to get it as soon as they return from the Underworld."
"You want them to go into the Underworld?" Arianne asked, surprised.
"Of course," Simon nodded. "That weakens the barrier even further, makes our work easier. Plus, whilst they're away..." He nodded to his men, who nodded back and left. "We can make the final preparations."
He walked to the window and looked out over the city, his city, or what would soon be his city. "One more day," he whispered. "After generations of planning, one day to completion."
He thought of Finn, of his betrayed face in the tunnels, of the intensity of the moment they'd shared in his flat. A strange wave of... regret? Remorse? Passed through him, but he pushed it away. Sentiment was weakness. What he was doing was necessary. The world would be better off without dreams, without magic, without... aberrations.
But a small voice, deep in his mind, whispered: *Is that really what you want? A world without wonders?*
Simon shook it away. Too late for doubts. The plan was in motion. The finale was approaching. Bruges would never be the same again.

DREAMS ON THE THRESHOLD

In the depths of his comatose state, Mayor Maillard drifted through strange landscapes. Time and space lost their meaning, but slowly a pattern emerged from the chaos.

He found himself in a Bruges he recognized, yet thoroughly different. The old streets glittered with a light that seemed to come from within. The trees along the canals breathed visibly, their leaves dancing in the wind. In the water swam creatures that seemed half fish, half light, and above the Belfry danced small points of light like living stars.

Maillard stopped before the town hall—his town hall—which was now threaded with living structures that harmoniously blended with the Gothic architecture. Inside, he heard voices in strange discussion.

He moved inside and found the council chamber filled with a motley assembly: ordinary councillors, but also beings he could only describe as dream guards, half-visible entities that glittered in the sunlight through the stained-glass windows. They were as colourful as Flemish historical tapestries.

"The fusion with the Underworld has reduced our energy bill by 88%," an official reported. "The living light sources not only provide illumination, but also purify the air."

"Tourism has increased sixfold," another added. "We're no longer just 'the Venice of the North', but the only place in the world where visitors can make guaranteed contact with beings from the Underworld. All hotels are fully booked until the end of next year. We must reconsider the hotel moratorium at the next council meeting."

Maillard felt a warm pride welling up. This was his city, but better. Richer. More complete.

"What's happening here?" he asked, surprised that his voice worked in this dream world.

One of the dream guards turned, his eyes like golden pools of light. "You see what could be, Mayor. The world of possibilities when dreams and reality are united."

"Chaos. Disruption of the natural order."

The being Dreamer—a Guardian, Maillard suddenly knew—made a gesture that seemed like a smile. "Is diversity chaos? Is growth disruption? Or is it precisely the natural order of all living things?"

Maillard saw projections of new businesses flourishing around magic technology, where the inexhaustible energy sources of the Underworld were coupled with human innovation. He saw researchers from all over the world coming to Bruges to learn, to collaborate, to grow.

He saw the canals freed from pollution by water beings that converted waste into light. Not only that, but he saw old, abandoned buildings renewed by plants that were both architecture and forms of nature.

"This isn't just sustainable," he realized. "This is regeneration. True symbiosis."

"Exactly." The Guardian Dreamer's voice resonated in Maillard's mind. "Not closing borders, but opening them. Not control, but cooperation."

Maillard walked to the window and looked out over his transformed city. Tourists and residents moved alongside dream beings with a naturalness that suggested it had always been this way. Children played with small light spirits, their laughter mingled with the musical tinkling of dream energy.

"But how...?" he began to ask.

"The choice will come," the Guardian answered. "Not yours, but you can help. You can clear the way."

Maillard felt a determination he hadn't felt in years. Not the cautious, measured willpower of political pragmatism, but a deeper, purer conviction.

"Yes," he said, almost whispering. "If this is possible, then it must happen. Bruges could be not just a monument to the past, but a beacon for the future."

In the distance, he heard voices—real voices, from the waking world. Doctors, nurses, discussing his condition.

"There's activity in his frontal lobes," someone said. "Unusual for a comatose patient."

"He's dreaming," said another. "Intensively."

Maillard smiled in his dream state. "Not just dreaming," he thought. "Planning."

Before the image faded, he turned one last time to the Guardian. "When I wake up," he promised, "I'll be ready. I'll fight for this new world. For real progress, real sustainability, real connection."

The dream world dissolved into light, but the images, the plans, the possibilities, they remained. Deep, lasting impressions, waiting for him to awaken to make them reality.

Whilst Maillard continued floating in his coma, his brain prepared itself, forming new neural pathways, making room for a vision of a Bruges that not only cherished its past, but also embraced its future.

INTO THE DEPTHS

Falling through the Underworld was nothing like Finn had expected. Where he'd thought of an abrupt, physical plunge—like diving into water—this was more like gliding through a prism of experiences. Colours that had no name in human language flowed over him, sounds that seemed more like thoughts than vibrations resonated through his consciousness, and the sensation of falling itself slowed until he was floating rather than descending.

Dreamer moved beside him with confident grace. Here in his home world, the being was even more impressive—his coat pulsed with subtle light, his eyes contained constellations, and his movements had a fluid elegance that suggested the normal laws of physics were optional.

"We're nearly there," a voice sounded in Finn's head—a rich, deep voice he recognized as belonging to Dreamer, though the being wasn't moving his mouth. "The transition is always the slowest. Hold on to your physical self."

Finn realized his body was changing, as it had done in his earlier dream journey. His human form faded, replaced by something in-between—not the painful, half transformation of his monthly changes, but something more fluid, complete. His hands became paws with human dexterity, his face lengthened into a wolf's snout that still carried his expressions, his body was covered with a rich, golden

coat that seemed to glow in the strange light of this world. "Your true form," Dreamer explained. "In the Underworld, everyone manifests their essence, not their appearance."
The sensation of floating stopped, and Finn experienced solid ground under his paws. The surrounding landscape was breathtaking—a primeval forest of trees so gigantic that even the largest sequoias on earth were dwarfs in comparison, their trunks dark red and vibrantly alive, their branches reaching towards a sky filled with cosmic phenomena. It wasn't earth's night sky, but a kaleidoscopic panorama of lights, patterns, and what looked like living constellations that moved with clear intention.
"Come," said Dreamer, already moving ahead on a path that glittered like spilled starlight. "Kaxil will find us in the Heartwood."
Finn followed, amazed to discover that movement in this world was more effortless—his wolf body leaped and ran with a freedom he'd never been able to experience in the physical world. It was like moving through thoughts instead of air, like running on instinct instead of effort.
"Is this... is this how it could be?" he asked, surprised that his thoughts now also communicated directly without spoken words. "If I used the keys to unite the worlds, would this become reality?"
Dreamer looked back, his golden eyes searching. "Not exactly like this. A union would create balance, not dominance. A new reality, neither fully physical nor dream. But yes, werewolves like you would probably feel completely at home in such a world. No pain during transformation, no hidden identities."
They moved through the Forest, and Finn noticed they weren't alone. Between the trees moved other beings—some vague, others completely alien in form, and many somewhere in between, like him. None showed fear or aggression, only curious attention to the newcomers.
"They recognize you," Dreamer explained when Finn cast a questioning look. "The Wolf from the prophecy. News travels fast in the Underworld."

They reached a clearing where the impossibly large trees receded to make room for a central figure—a single tree that made the others seem smaller, so massive that its base could have housed a small city, its branches reaching so far they limited sight. Around the base of this tree lay a lake of what looked like liquid gold, but which moved with its consciousness, rippling in patterns that Finn recognized as the Maya inscriptions on the keys.

"The First Tree," Dreamer announced. "The heart of the Underworld and the centre of all dreams. Here we'll meet Kaxil and discuss your choice."

Finn stepped to the edge of the golden lake, fascinated by how the surface reacted to his presence, small golden waves stretching towards his paws like greeting fingers.

"The dream substance recognizes you," explained a new voice, richer and older than even the Dreamer's. "It has waited for your coming, Wolf."

From the golden lake rose a figure—first liquid and formless, then slowly solidifying into the shape Finn had met before: Kaxil, the Keeper of Dreams. Here in his home world he was even more impressive—his body seemed made of liquid gold and crystallized stars, his eyes were windows to cosmic depths, and he moved with the calm certainty of a being older than time itself.

"Finn De Wulf," he greeted. "This time you come of your will, not as a dreamer."

"I come seeking help," Finn replied, surprised by the directness of his thought communication. "Simon Laurent plans to permanently seal off the dream world during the solar eclipse tomorrow. He has the jade key and my blood."

Kaxil's expression darkened, the gold of his body flickering with dark undertones. "Yes. We've felt the disturbance. Dreams are already growing thinner, the connection weaker. Laurent's actions already have consequences in both worlds."

"How do we stop him?" Finn asked.

"That is the question, isn't it?" Kaxil's voice had a strange resonance, like echoing through awesome time. "How do you stop a line that has tried for generations to destroy what they cannot control? How do you stop a man whose entire identity is built on the denial of wonders?"

"By showing him the truth?" Finn suggested, his wolf ears laying back slightly in frustration at the cryptic answer.

"Perhaps," Kaxil nodded. "Or perhaps by making a different choice than he expects."

The golden sea around Kaxil began to move, and the surface formed into images—Finn recognized Simon, busy setting up a complex device on the shore of the Minnewater. He saw the jade cacao bean, now vibrating with a sickly green light, connected to instruments and reflective surfaces that would channel the light of the coming eclipse.

"He's preparing the ritual," Kaxil explained. "During the eclipse, when the barrier between worlds is at its thinnest, he'll try to force a permanent breach using your blood and the jade key."

"And we have the other two keys," Finn said. "Can't we just stop him by keeping them away?"

Kaxil shook his head, a movement that sent small waves of golden light through his body. "With the barrier so weakened and the celestial alignment so perfect, one key might be enough for him. Especially since he has your blood—the essence of the Fourth, the Wolf."

A wave of cold realization passed through Finn. "This is my fault. How could I be so stupid?"

"The blood was always destined to play a role," Dreamer interrupted. "The prophecy speaks of four components: jade, silver, gold, blood. Only, how these are used is the variable."

"What do you mean?" Finn asked.

Kaxil moved his hand, and the golden lake formed new images—three concentric circles that merged into one, then burst apart into completely separate entities, then regrouped in a new configuration that Finn couldn't fully comprehend.

"There are three possible outcomes when the keys come together," Kaxil explained. "As Laurent wants, they can be used to permanently separate the worlds—dreams locked in their realm, never again able to contact the human world."

The images showed a dark barrier rising between the circles, impenetrable and final.
"Or," Kaxil continued, "they can maintain the current balance—the regulated connection, the flow of dreams managed through generations of Vandeveldes, the careful balance that allows magic but limits it."
The images now showed the current situation—circles that intersected in small, controlled areas, connected but not united.
"Or..." Kaxil hesitated, his golden eyes now fixed directly on Finn's. "They can be used to completely unite the worlds—a fusion of dream and reality, of magic and matter, of possibility and concreteness. A new world, neither fully one nor the other, but something entirely new."
The last image showed the circles merging into a new form, complex and impossible to describe in human terms, but radiating with harmony.
"What if chocolate could literally influence dreams and determine the boundary between reality and fantasy?" Finn asked.
"People would no longer know what's real and what isn't, as if one is in a constant state of dreaming, until accidents happen that can have fatal consequences."
"And this is my choice," he realized, the weight of responsibility now fully penetrating him. "Why me? Why not Lina, or even Simon?"
"Because," Kaxil answered, "only you stand in both worlds without loyalty to one. Lina is bound to maintain balance, like her ancestors before her. Simon is devoted to destroying all magic. But you..." He stretched out his golden hand, touching Finn's wolf snout with surprisingly warm fingers. "You know both human pain and the freedom of dreams. You alone can make a truly unbiased choice."
"The question is," Dreamer added, "what choice will that be?"
Finn stared at the images in the golden lake, his thoughts tumbling over each other. A world permanently separated from dreams and magic seemed bare, cold, incomplete—the world Laurent wanted. A world in the current, careful balance was safer, more familiar, but still kept beings like him trapped be-

tween identities, between worlds. And a completely united world? He could barely comprehend the consequences of that.
"I don't know," he admitted honestly. "I need more time to decide."
"Time is what we don't have," Kaxil said sombrely. "The eclipse is tomorrow, and Laurent won't wait. But perhaps..."
The golden figure looked at Dreamer, a silent communication passing between them. The white wolf nodded once, deep and solemn.
"We can give you allies," Kaxil offered. "Dreamer and Morpheus aren't the only Guardians who can move between worlds. With the barrier so weakened, other Guardians can now cross over. They can help you disrupt Laurent's physical plan whilst you decide."
"And if I can't decide?" Finn asked, fear gnawing at his chest. "If I can't choose?"
"Then you implicitly choose the status quo," Kaxil replied. "The current balance would remain, but weakened. Laurent would be defeated, but not forever. The struggle would continue in future generations."
The golden lake began to ripple in wider circles, and from the depths appeared new figures—dozens of Guardians, each different in form but all carrying the same inherent majesty as Dreamer. Some were wolves of various colours and sizes, others had forms that resembled large felines, deer with impossible antlers, birds with wings that reflected like liquid silver, and beings Finn couldn't even describe in human terms.
"My brothers and sisters," Dreamer declared. "The Guardians of Dreams, ready to cross over and help you, Wolf."
"But there's a price," Kaxil added, his voice now deeper and more serious. "If you leave the worlds as they are, the Guardians will have to return. If you choose permanent separation, they'll disappear forever from your world, along with all magic. And if you choose union..."
"What? What happens to them then?" Finn pressed.
"Then they become fully manifest," Kaxil replied. "No longer limited to disguises or temporary forms. The Guardians would

walk again in your world as in the days before the Maya, as equals among humans."

The implications of this tumbled through Finn's mind. A world where magical beings existed openly? Where werewolves, Guardians, and who knows what else, could live freely without hiding? It was both wonderful and terrifying.

"It's much to consider," Kaxil acknowledged, sensing Finn's uncertainty. "But time presses. You must return to your world with the Guardians, Finn De Wulf. You must confront Simon Laurent during the eclipse. And then you must choose."

Finn nodded, knowing this was correct, knowing there was no escape from this responsibility. "I'll try to make the right choice," he promised.

"There is no 'right' choice," Dreamer corrected gently. "Only your choice."

The golden lake began to move, rising in an enormous wave that would enclose Finn and Dreamer, along with the assembled Guardians. Kaxil stood at the centre, his hands outstretched in a gesture of sending.

"Return to your world, Wolf," he declared, his voice now resonating with the power of the entire Underworld. "Confront the Hunter. Find the Witch and the Gossip. And make your choice, based only on what your heart tells you."

The wave of liquid gold overwhelmed them, and Finn felt himself falling again, or perhaps rising, it was hard to tell in this world where all directions were relative. Around him moved the Guardians, a stream of forms and lights leaving the Underworld for the first time in centuries, answering the call of a rare conjunction: the Wolf, the approaching Eclipse, and the most dangerous threat their world had ever known.

Together, they flew upward, towards the translucent portal that Lina held open on the other side, towards a confrontation that would determine the fate of both worlds.

PORTAL

In the middle of the Minnewater, Lina sat cross-legged in the small boat, her eyes closed in deep concentration. Ingrid sat beside her, eyes closed. She felt time ticking away—Finn and Dreamer had been gone for more than two hours now, and her powers were beginning to weaken. Keeping the portal open without both keys was an exhausting exercise, especially with the weakened energy of the ley lines beneath Bruges.

Her senses, sharpened by years of training, picked up something—movements on the shore, whispers, the subtle sound of equipment being set up. She prepared for what was coming, conserving just enough energy for one last, powerful spell if necessary. Morpheus had run after them like a wild panther when they disappeared towards the Walplein, but now they were back.

She felt a tremor in the portal beneath her, a change in the energy flow. "They're coming back," she realized, relief flooding through her tired mind.

And not a moment too soon. On the shore, she saw Simon Laurent appear, the jade cacao bean prominently glowing in his hand. Beside him was Antoine, carrying what looked like a measuring instrument, and Arianne Vermeer, whose face was a mixture of anticipation and nervousness.

They were prepared for the great confrontation, and Lina was alone with Ingrid in the bobbing boat—at least until Finn re-

turned. She could only hope he'd found help on the other side, or they would be easily overwhelmed.
The portal beneath her began to swirl, more solid and brighter. "Hold on," she thought, calling on her last reserves to keep it open for Finn's return. Just a few more moments.
The sky above Bruges began to show the first signs of what was to come tomorrow—a subtle change in quality, a harbinger of the eclipse. Tomorrow afternoon, the moon would move between the earth and the sun, creating the perfect alignment Laurent needed for his ritual... or for the possible reopening of all barriers.
Lina looked at Simon on the shore, his face now a mask of cold determination. Their eyes met across the water, and an unspoken communication passed between them—the recognition of two opponents who understood each other's worth.
"It's over, Vandevelde," Simon called across the water. "I've set up machines around the entire lake. Even if your portal stays open, I can channel the energy towards my purposes."
"You don't understand what you're doing, Laurent," Lina called back, her voice remarkably stable despite her exhaustion. "Destroying dreams won't save humanity. It will impoverish it."
"Rationality will save it," Simon replied. His eyes slid to the portal beneath Lina's boat. "Where's your werewolf? Lost in the Underworld? Another victim of the chaos you defend?" Simon hoped Finn would choose him when it mattered.
Lina just beamed, a small, knowing expression that made Simon's certainty waver momentarily.
And then it began to happen.
The portal beneath the boat exploded with light, not a single colour but a rainbow of hues that made the water glow like a supernova. The boat itself began to shake, rocked back and forth by energy waves pulsing outward.
"He's coming back," Antoine muttered, the measuring instrument in his hands swinging wildly. "The Wolf is returning!"
"Stabilize the equipment," Simon ordered, turning to his men. "Whatever comes out of that portal, we're prepared." Morpheus, who had crept up behind them, addressed them: "Think so?"

But they weren't prepared. Not for what was coming. First was Finn, back in his human form, shooting from the portal like a rocket and landing on the boat with enough force to nearly capsize it. Ingrid held the boat steady with both hands. In his hand, he held the golden and silver keys, now glowing with an intensity that hurt the eyes.

"Lina," he panted, grabbing her arm to stabilize her. "They're coming. The Guardians are coming."

Before Lina could ask what he meant, the answer came in a tumultuous parade of light and energy. From the portal they streamed—dozens, perhaps hundreds of beings of forms and colours that defied human imagination. Dreamguards, each with the size and majesty that Dreamer had shown, but in a breathtaking diversity.

Great wolves of white, black, red, and blue, some with wings of fire or ice. Massive felines with stars woven into their coats. Deer with antlers that shone like liquid crystal. Birds with wings so large they created small storms with each wingbeat. And beings that knew no earthly description—forms of pure light, shapes of living shadow, entities that constantly changed form like clouds changing in a swift wind.

They rose from the portal, no longer limited by the laws of the physical world, hovering above Minnewater like an army of mythical proportions. At their head was Dreamer, now even larger, even more radiant than before, his white coat so bright he seemed like a second sun.

On the shore, Simon and his people froze, their faces masks of shock and, in some cases, pure fear.

"What have you done?" Simon whispered, his voice uncertain for the first time. Finn picked up his question with his super hearing.

"What had to be done," Finn replied, now standing in the boat, one hand reaching out to Dreamer hovering above him. "The Guardians have decided to return to our world, Laurent. It turns out they're not pleased with your plan to permanently sever their connection with us."

Simon recovered quickly, his expression hardening. "Doesn't

matter. They're just manifestations, temporary apparitions. Once the eclipse is completed tomorrow and the ritual is performed, they'll all return to their realm. Or rather, they'll be locked up there."

"Perhaps," Finn conceded, extending the two keys to Lina, who took them with trembling hands. "But you still haven't understood one thing, Simon."

"And that is?" Simon's voice dripped with sarcasm.

"It's my choice," Finn said simply. "Not yours. Not Lina's. Not even the Guardians'. In the prophecy, it's the Wolf who determines the path."

Simon's face paled slightly, but he recovered quickly. "The witch tells you fairy tales, Finn. What really counts is power, preparation, and relentless determination." He raised the jade cacao bean, which now pulsed in the same rhythm as Finn's heartbeat. "And I have everything I need to realize my vision, including your blood."

He raised the small crystal vial, the werewolf blood inside black in the late afternoon light.

Dreamer descended beside the boat, his enormous head bowing towards Lina, who automatically reached out to touch his silky soft coat.

"We must leave," his voice sounded in both Lina's and Finn's heads. "The Guardians will secure the area, but you must rest and prepare. The real confrontation comes tomorrow, during the eclipse."

Finn nodded and helped Lina stand. She was exhausted from keeping the portal open, her normally radiant face now pale and drawn.

"This isn't over, Laurent," Finn called across the water. "Tomorrow, at the eclipse, we'll see whose vision triumphs. Yours of fear and control, or a vision of possibility and wonder."

Simon didn't reply, but his eyes burned with an intensity that made Finn shiver. This wasn't the charming, refined young man who had seduced him in his flat. This was something older, colder—the culmination of generations of Laurent doctrine, focused and deadly as a laser beam.

"Come," Dreamer urged. "We'll bring you to safety."
With a gesture of his massive head, the water around the boat began to churn, not turbulent, but purposeful. The small boat moved away from the centre of the lake, propelled by a current no one could see, escorted by Guardians of every form and colour.
Behind them, the portal closed with a soft pop, not disappearing but becoming inactive, waiting for the moment of the eclipse to reopen with unprecedented power.
Simon watched them go, his face a mask of cold calculation.
"Begin setting up the equipment," he ordered his people. "We only have one chance."
"And the... beings?" Antoine asked nervously, pointing to the Guardians now spread around the lake, some visible, others blending with shadows or reflections, but all watchful.
"Are irrelevant," Simon said determinedly. "Tomorrow, during the eclipse, the jade key and the Wolf's blood will triumph. The dream world will be sealed forever, and these... aberrations will disappear like candles in the wind."
But whilst he led his people in setting up their devices, Simon looked over his shoulder at the boat carrying Finn and Lina away. His expression was difficult to read—anger, certainly, determination, absolutely. But there was something else, something almost like regret, that flashed across his face before he pushed it away under the cold mantle of his family tradition.
Tomorrow would decide everything. After centuries of planning and preparation, the fate of two worlds would depend on the choice of one werewolf.
And Simon Laurent wasn't about to leave that fate to chance.

BOATHOUSE

The old boathouse lay hidden behind overhanging willows on a quiet bank of the Reie. The dilapidated wooden structure, unused since the war, was perfect as a hideout.

Lina stepped out of the boat, supported by Finn's strong arm. The exhaustion from keeping the portal open had affected her more than she wanted to admit.

"We're safe here," she said as she stumbled inside. "This was one of my mother's secret places. Laurent's people won't find it, especially not with the Guardians patrolling the area."

Finn helped her inside the small wooden building. It was dusty but structurally sound, and to his surprise, not entirely unprepared. There were old crates stacked against one wall, a small kitchen table and chairs, and even a small stove.

"Your mother was thorough," he observed, leading Lina to a chair.

"She was a survivor," Lina smiled weakly. "She always taught me to have multiple escape routes and safe houses." She looked around. "Where's Ingrid?"

Morpheus, who had sat in his cat form on Lina's shoulder the whole time, now jumped onto a high shelf and looked at the space with critical amber eyes. "Not exactly five-star accommodation, but it'll have to do," he said mockingly. "I'm relieved to see the rodent population is well represented here. At least one positive point."

As if on cue, they heard footsteps on the jetty outside, and a moment later Ingrid entered, escorted by what looked like a fox of pure silver, its eyes gleaming with inner stars.

"You had a party without me," she said, her energy undiminished despite the stressful day. "I'd be offended, but I'm too old for wounded egos."

Finn couldn't help but smile. Even now, on the eve of what would be the most crucial confrontation in centuries, Ingrid retained her sharp tongue and unique perspective.

"They're all back, then," she said, extending a hand to the silver fox, who gratefully pressed his head against her palm. "The Guardians have returned. How long has it been, Dreamer? Four hundred years?"

"Four hundred and thirty-eight," the great white wolf corrected. "Since the last attempt by a Laurent to use the keys, when Eduard's grandfather tried the ritual."

"And now they're here to help us," Ingrid nodded. "The question is: what do we do with their help?"

"I suggest we rest first," Morpheus observed, comfortably licking his paw. "Witches and werewolves may be magical beings with impressive endurance, but even you need sleep. Especially after today's portal total failure."

Lina glanced at Finn, who now stood by the small window, looking out over the lake in the distance, where Laurent's people were busy setting up machines at strategic points around the shore. The sunset set the water ablaze with orange and gold, a dramatic contrast to the clinical, silver metal of the devices.

"Morpheus is right," Lina said wearily. "Tomorrow at the solar eclipse we'll need all our strength."

"What did Kaxil say?" she asked Finn softly. "About your choice?"

Finn turned, his face now tense with the weight of what was coming. "He showed me the three possibilities. What Simon wants—permanent separation of worlds. What you want—maintaining the current, limited connection. And..."

"The third option," Ingrid nodded. . "Complete un-

ion. A new world, neither fully physical nor dream."
"A world where beings like Dreamer can exist freely," Finn added, running a hand through his hair. "Where werewolves don't have to suffer with every transformation. Where magic and science exist side by side."
"It sounds beautiful," Lina said carefully. "But also dangerous. My family has devoted generations to maintaining a careful balance because we didn't know if the human world was ready for the full force of dreams and magic."
"Isn't that the point the Laurents make?" Finn asked challengingly. "That humans must be protected from what they don't understand? That control is better than freedom?"
"A pertinent question," Morpheus observed, now descending to the floor to join the conversation. "The Vandeveldes have always walked the middle ground, whilst the Laurents preach absolutism. Both paths are based on one shared assumption: that humanity must be protected, either from dreams or from the lack of them."
"And the third option assumes that humans and dreams can coexist, in harmony," Ingrid finished. She looked at Finn with new appreciation. "You think bigger than I expected, young wolf."
Finn felt a blush rise to his cheeks. "I don't know what to think," he admitted. "Four days ago, my biggest problem was how to hide my transformations from my landlord."
"And now you hold the fate of two worlds in your hands," Lina smiled. She stood up, her strength slowly returning, and walked over to him. "But you're not alone anymore, Finn. Whatever you choose, I stand behind you."
"Really?" He was surprised. "Even if I choose union, against generations of Vandevelde tradition?"
Lina's blue eyes were clear and certain when she answered: "Traditions exist to guide us, not to limit us. My mother always told me: 'Protect the dreams, Lina, but don't forget to dream yourself.' Perhaps... perhaps, union is the ultimate dream."
"How poetic," Morpheus muttered, his tail curling around his paws. "But I'd like to point out that we need a plan, not just

inspiring speeches. Laurent and his cronies are laying siege to the Minnewater, and they already have a whole arsenal of equipment ready."

"Morpheus is right," Dreamer said. "We must rest, but also plan. The eclipse begins tomorrow at 14:27 precisely, and reaches its peak at 14:42. That's when the barrier will be thinnest."

"And when I must make my choice," Finn nodded.

"With all three keys," Lina added. "Which means we need to obtain Simon's jade cacao bean."

"That seems like a vital point in the plan," Finn observed dryly. "How exactly do we do that?"

"We help," Dreamer answered simply. "The Guardians will disrupt Laurent's machines and isolate him from his helpers. The rest is up to you three—the Witch, the Gossip, and the Wolf. The fourth party, the Hunter, must be stopped, but not necessarily destroyed."

"Not destroyed?" Finn looked surprised. "After everything he's done, what he still wants to do?"

"Simon Laurent is lost, not inherently evil," Lina said softly. "He's inherited generations of indoctrination, and genuinely believes he's doing the right thing."

"As so often, I am the voice of sober reality," Morpheus interjected, "but I must point out that regardless of our sentiments towards the charming trainee solicitor, he currently possesses a powerful artefact with which he can bring about the downfall of all dreams. Let's not confuse our priorities with our feelings."

"Plus, he's handsome," Ingrid added dryly. "And you clearly found him attractive, young wolf. That part wasn't a trick, after all."

Finn blushed deeply, but couldn't deny what she said. Despite everything, despite the betrayal and manipulation, there had been something in Simon—an intensity, a passion—that he couldn't simply dismiss.

"Rest now," Ingrid repeated, placing a hand on Finn's shoulder. "Dream if you dare. Or don't—the choice is yours, as always."

They withdrew to different corners of the small boathouse—

Lina to a stacked crate that served as a rudimentary bed, Ingrid to an old but comfortable chair, and Dreamer and the silver fox took watch positions by the door and window.

Morpheus, to Finn's surprise, chose to curl up next to his improvised sleeping place on the floor. "I'm keeping an eye on you," the cat muttered. "Someone needs to make sure you don't transform in your sleep and tear down the whole boathouse."

Finn smiled weakly. "Thanks, I think."

"Don't mention it," Morpheus replied, already closing his eyes. "I'm doing it purely out of self-interest. If this building collapses whilst I'm sleeping, that would fit my definition of a bad night."

Finn stretched out on a soft mat on the floor, exhausted but with a mind too active for easy sleep. He stared at the ceiling, thinking about everything he'd learned, everything he'd experienced in these mad days.

Tomorrow he would have to pick between three paths, three visions for the future. And that choice would determine not only his fate, or Lina's, or even Simon Laurent's... but the fate of two entire worlds.

No pressure, he thought sarcastically, before exhaustion finally overcame him and sleep claimed him for a night filled with dreams of golden forests, silver rivers, and a jade city that constantly rebuilt itself in patterns too complex to understand.

His last conscious thought, strangely enough, was of Simon Laurent—not the cold, determined opponent of that afternoon, but the young man whose eyes had glowed with passion and desire in the twilight of his flat.

Was that all fake? Finn wondered. Or was there a kernel of truth even in the deception?

The question echoed unanswered as he sank into dreams that, for the first time in his life, didn't feel like an escape from reality, but like a glimpse of a possible future where dreams and reality were no longer separate concepts.

A future that, perhaps, lay within his reach to choose.

THOMAS

Simon tossed restlessly in his bed. It was the third night in a row he had trouble sleeping. The preparations for tomorrow's ritual at the solar eclipse worried him. The moment was almost here when he would finally seal off the dream world permanently, eliminate the danger that had taken Thomas from him. He would finally fulfil the Laurent legacy, after generations of planning and preparation.

Yet doubt continued to gnaw, hidden somewhere deep behind his determination. When sleep finally overcame him, it wasn't the comforting darkness he sought, but something else. Something brighter.

He stood on the shore of the Minnewater, but it was different. Not the friendly tourist lake he knew, but a mirroring, infinite expanse that seemed to pulse with its life. Above him, the sun was almost completely eclipsed, a black disc surrounded by a fiery corona.

His machines stood in the right positions, set according to the design he'd refined for months. The jade cacao bean glowed in his hand, tangibly warm, as if it hungered for something. He raised it high, the energy flowing through his arm, through his body, tingling down to his toes.

"Now," he whispered to himself. "Finally."

A beam of green light shot from the artefact, precisely aimed at the centre of the lake. The water began to boil, to open like a gaping wound in reality itself. Through the hole he could see it—the Underworld, the source of all nightmares, all the madness that had taken Thomas from him.

But then the dream changed. Instead of the chaotic, destructive entropy he expected, he saw a world of breathtaking beauty. Golden forests stretching to the horizon. Crystal cities that glittered under a sky full of impossible star patterns. And beings, hundreds of species of beings, moving in a harmony he'd never thought possible.

"It's beautiful, isn't it?" asked a voice behind him.

Dream Simon turned abruptly, his heart skipping a beat at recognizing that voice even before he saw the face.

"Thomas?"

And there he stood, exactly as Simon remembered him. His athletic body clads in a gleaming Club Bruges football shirt that perfectly hugged his muscled torso, short sports shorts that accentuated his tanned thighs. He wore his favourite Nike Air Max trainers, black with blue, with white sports socks that fitted snugly around his ankles. The image was so vivid, so tangible, that Simon felt his heart race. He smelled fantastic.

"How... how can this be?" Simon stammered. His hands began to tremble.

Thomas grinned, that specific smile that had always been only for Simon. "You know how. This is the dream world, Simon. The place you're trying to destroy."

"I'm not trying to destroy," Simon protested. "I'm trying to protect. To prevent more people from being... being..."

"Being what?" Thomas challenged, coming closer. His proximity brought that familiar scent with it—a mixture of sports deodorant, sweat, and something more unique that was purely Thomas. Simon was overwhelmed with a wave of desire and an involuntary physical reaction he could barely suppress. It felt so good.

"Lost? Like me?"

"You went mad," Simon said, his voice soft with pain. "The hallucinations, the nightmares... they consumed you, Thomas. The doctors couldn't do anything."

Thomas shook his head, now so close that Simon could feel the texture of his sports shirt, the way the synthetic material gleamed in the strange light of the eclipsed sun. "I didn't go mad, Simon. I woke up."

He reached for Simon's hand and gave him a French kiss. Simon could feel the slight chalk traces on Thomas's fingers, remnants of the magnesium powder he sometimes used during his fitness training.

"The dream world doesn't make you weaker," Thomas continued. "It makes you stronger, more complete. You just have to learn to embrace it, instead of fighting it."

Simon could no longer control himself. He pulled Thomas into an embrace, breathed in his scent and buried his face in the hollow of his neck, breathing that intoxicating mixture of scents—sweat, synthetic fabric, that hint of new plastic and glue from his trainers who had always fascinated Simon, but he'd never dared admit.

"I miss you," he whispered, his voice broken. "Every day. Every second."

Thomas's arms closed around him, strong and protective. "I've never really been gone, Simon. The dream world is always closer than you think. Be free with me. Now."

Simon clung desperately, his fingers gripping the smooth, cool material of Thomas's shirt, a sensation that both comforted and aroused him. He wanted to hold on to this moment forever, wanted to lose himself in the warmth and solidity of Thomas's body against his.

"Come with me," Thomas whispered, placing a hand under Simon's chin, forcing him to look up. "Let me show you what you're really trying to destroy."

Simon couldn't refuse, could not refuse Thomas anything. He let himself be led, their hands firmly intertwined, to the edge of the gaping portal in the middle of the lake.

Thomas pulled off his Nike's and socks, placed them carefully on the ground, then stepped barefoot into the water that behaved like a solid surface under his weight. Thomas now wore only gleaming swimming trunks. Simon followed, fascinated

by how vivid all this was. The unforgettable sex in the changing room at the swimming pool flashed by.
"Look," Thomas said, pointing to the depths beneath them. "Look carefully."
And Simon observed. He saw a world that was simultaneously strange and wonderfully familiar. He saw possibilities, infinite patterns of what could be, of what was and what had never been. Not only that, but he saw origin and destination, intertwined in a tapestry of dream substance.
"This is where I am," Thomas said softly. "Not lost, not insane. Just... on the other side."
Simon's heart filled with wild, desperate hope. "Can I come to you? Can I bring you back?"
Thomas's face softened with a melancholic smile.
"There's no 'bringing back', Simon. But there is a union. There is balance. There is a world where dreams and reality meet, strengthen each other."
But as he spoke, something began to change. A shadow appeared in the depths beneath them, growing, stretching like an ink drop in clear water. Thomas's expression changed from warm to concerned.
"We don't have much time," he said urgently. "It's coming."
"What's coming?" Simon asked, feeling the growing fear that stiffened Thomas's body.
"The nightmare you're creating," Thomas replied. "Not the Underworld, Simon. Your fear of the Underworld."
The shadow took shape, a monstrous wolf form of pure darkness with no clear features except a gaping maw and claws reaching upward. Simon pulled at Thomas's hand, trying to draw him away from the creature now rapidly moving towards the surface.
"We have to get out of here!" he cried. "NOW!"
Thomas shook his head, sadness clear in his eyes. "It's too late. We can't run from what you've created yourself, Simon."
The shadow broke through the surface, not with a splash, but with torn reality, as if it were tearing the substance of the dream itself. In a moment of pure horror, Simon saw

it stretch out, its claws closing around Thomas's ankles. "NO!" Simon screamed, desperately gripping Thomas's hands. But the creature's force was irresistible. He felt Thomas's fingers slipping from his, centimetre by centimetre, despite the strength with which he held on.

"Remember me, Simon," Thomas said, still calm despite the monster pulling him down. "This is your nightmare. Not mine."

Their fingers slid past each other, the last touch, and then Thomas was gone, swallowed by the shadow that returned to the depths, leaving nothing but ripples on the mirroring surface of the lake.

Simon fell to his knees, a cry of pure despair tearing from his throat, a sound so raw and anguished that it shocked him awake from his dream.

Simon shot upright in his bed, bathed in sweat, his heart pounding as if it wanted to break out of his chest. He gasped for breath, his tongue dry, his hands trembling. It was still dark in his bedroom, the only light coming from his alarm clock display—03:17.

He fought to get his breathing under control, but images from the dream kept flashing through his head. Thomas's smile. The tangible texture of his sports shirt. The scent of his new trainers. The warmth of his hand. And then that terrible separation, the fingers sliding apart, the monster dragging his beloved to the depths.

Simon became painfully aware of his physical state—despite the horror of the dream's end, his body had betrayed him with an enormous erection for Thomas. He felt grief and arousal simultaneously, and above all, overwhelming confusion.

Was this just a dream? Or was it a message? Was it really Thomas, somehow communicating from the Underworld? Or was it just his guilt and desire playing a cruel game with him?

He threw off the sheets, staring at his erection. Somewhere out there was the young werewolf, Finn De Wulf, who looked so disturbingly like Thomas.

"What are you trying to tell me?" he whispered to the night.

The night, gave no answer, but his right hand, however...

reached for his phone.

HALLO?

Simon peered at his phone in the darkness of his bedroom, the digital clock on his bedside table now showing a cruel number: 3:41. Going back to sleep wouldn't work, and wanking didn't seem like the solution either. His fingers moved over the screen as if they had their will, searching for a number he'd never meant to save, but had kept anyway.

Finn De Wulf.

The image of Thomas, sucked into the darkness by that monster, still haunted him. The dream had been so real, so painfully detailed. He could still smell the synthetic scent of the sports shirt, feel the soft texture of the material against his fingertips. Before he could fully reason his action, he'd already dialled the number.

It rang three times before being answered. "Hello?" Finn's voice was sleepy but alert, like someone used to wake at strange hours.

"Finn? It's Simon."

A brief silence. "Simon? It's... wait, it's nearly four in the morning. Has something happened?"

Simon closed his eyes, suddenly aware of the absurdity of his action. "No. Yes. Sorry, this was a mistake. I'll—"

"Wait," Finn's voice interrupted, now fully awake. "No problem. I was awake anyway." A clear lie, but kindly meant.

"You weren't," Simon said, forming a small smile despite himself.

"Okay, not quite," Finn admitted, and Simon could almost see him smiling on the other end of the line. "But now I am. What's wrong?"
Simon hesitated. How do you explain that you're calling someone because you had a nightmare about your dead ex-boyfriend, who looked terribly like the person you're calling? "I couldn't sleep," he said finally.
"Ah," Finn said, and there was a playful tone in his voice that Simon hadn't expected. "So you thought, let me call that pizza-delivering werewolf I took on a date? A logical choice."
Simon felt caught out, but also strangely relieved by Finn's direct approach. "When you put it like that, it sounds pretty deranged."
"A bit, yeah." Finn's laugh was warm, unexpected. "But hey, we all have those nights."
A comfortable silence fell, a peace Simon hadn't expected, especially given their history.
"I had a dream," Simon finally confessed. "About Thomas."
"It's okay." Finn paused. "Was the dream... very intense?"
Simon sighed, relaxing somewhat against his pillows. "Yes. I saw him again, exactly as he was. His sports clothes, his smile. It was as if he were real. And then..." He swallowed hard. "He was dragged into the darkness by some kind of monster. I couldn't save him. Yet again."
"Sounds pretty traumatic," Finn said. "Is that why you're calling me at this ungodly hour?"
There was warmth in that question, no reproach. Simon found himself smiling. "Partly. And partly because..."
"Because?"
"Because you look like him," Simon confessed. "Not just physically, but... something about your energy. How you move, how you talk. You share the same passion for sport."
"Hmm," Finn groaned softly, and Simon could almost imagine him lying in a comfortable bed and not his own improvised mattress in the boathouse. "Is that why you... you know that night?"
"No!" Simon sat up abruptly. "Or... maybe a bit.

I don't know. Everything's so confusing now."
"I'd say so, yes. And even with identical twins there are character differences, so you don't know me well enough to assume I'm a copy. I'm convinced I'm not. I grew up without a father, on a scholarship."
The silence fell again, but not uncomfortably. Simon listened to Finn's breathing, found a strange comfort in its regularity.
"Tell me about him," Finn said eventually. "About Thomas. How did you meet?"
Simon was surprised by the request, but began talking anyway. "At the university swimming club. I was there for fitness, he was there for competition. He was... radiant. Always full of energy, always laughing."
"Sounds like someone who could make you happy," Finn encouraged.
"Even on my worst days, he could make me laugh." Simon rolled onto his side, the phone clamped between ear and pillow. "We knew it immediately, really. Even at the first training session, there was a connection I'd never felt before. My family had always had candidates of 'good breeding' in mind for me, so it was... complicated."
"I can imagine complicated," Finn said, a bit bitterly. "My coming out on my eighteenth birthday wasn't exactly a celebration."
"Tell me," Simon encouraged, genuinely curious.
Finn told him about that fatal birthday cake, the boys from the football team, the friend who wouldn't acknowledge him once everything became public. Simon listened attentively, struck by the parallels with his experiences.
"But you were brave," Simon said when Finn finished. At least you stood up for it. I hid it, for years."
"Until Thomas came."
"Until Thomas came," Simon confirmed. "He made it worth being brave."
They talked on, minutes turning into half an hour, then an hour. Simon talked about his family, his strict upbringing, the pressure to be perfect. Finn shared stories about his mother,

about the neighbour boy he'd had secret feelings for, about his experience with Mathieu at the gym.

Somewhere halfway through the conversation, Simon realized he felt more comfortable than he had in months. There was something about Finn—a directness, an honesty that cut through the façades Simon had so carefully built. That was at least different from Thomas, who always remained a bit reserved and insecure.

"Do you still have a morning lecture later?" Simon asked, realizing how late it had become.

"Mmm," Finn grumbled, clearly tired but unwilling to hang up. "And then my shift at Lina's shop in the evening."

"Shame. Otherwise, I'd suggest you could come round."

The suggestion hung in the air for a moment, loaded with possibilities.

"Would you want that?" Simon asked, his voice softer now.

"Yes," Finn replied simply. "Despite everything... yes."

Simon's heart skipped a beat. "Even after what I did?"

"Look," Finn said, "I won't deny that what you did was fucked up. But I've experienced enough to know that people are more complex than one moment, one action. You're calling me in the middle of the night because you had a nightmare, not because you have a plan. That says more about who you are than you might realize."

Simon closed his eyes, suddenly overwhelmed by emotion. "Thank you," he whispered.

"No problem. But if you drug me again, I'll fully transform into a wolf and bite your arse off. You've been warned."

Simon laughed, a real, genuine sound he barely recognized himself. "Deal, but my arse might come in handy later."

"Okay. I really have to sleep," Finn said with audible regret in his voice. "Maybe we can..."

Finn stopped abruptly mid-sentence. Simon heard rustling and then a voice—Morpheus, he realized.

"Trouble in paradise?" came the sarcastic voice of the cat on Finn's side. "Romantic telephone interludes with the enemy aren't exactly according to the script, little wolf."

"Go away, Morpheus," Finn hissed softly, his hand over the microphone, but not well enough to muffle the sound.
"Finn?" Simon sat up, suddenly alert. "Everything okay there?"
The silence on the other end of the line was deafening. Then, so soft, Simon almost missed it: "I have to let you go. Sleep well."
"Finn?" Simon called into the phone. "FINN!"
The connection was broken.

PREPARATION

Morning broke with a drizzling rain that made the cobblestones of Bruges' streets glisten in the early light. In the boathouse, Lina, Ingrid, and Morpheus were awake early, partly due to the intimate phone conversation Finn had conducted as if they were in dreamland. Finn avoided every glance in the first few minutes.

"The eclipse begins in about seven hours," Lina said, her fingers dancing over an old map of the Minnewater on which she'd marked strategic positions. "Laurent will start his ritual around 14:30, so the climax coincides with the total eclipse at 14:42."

Morpheus sat at the corner of the table, his amber eyes following Lina's movements. "And meanwhile we have a werewolf making cosy phone calls with the enemy in the middle of the night," he observed, his tail swishing in Finn's direction.

Finn felt a blush rise to his cheeks. "It wasn't how it sounded."

"Oh? So you weren't talking to Simon Laurent at three in the morning, whilst he, may I remind you, possesses an artefact with which he wants to destroy the dream world?" Morpheus tilted his head. "How did it sound then, Romulus?"

"It was..." Finn hesitated, searching for the right words. "Complicated. He had a nightmare about his ex."

Lina looked up from the map, her expression soft but concerned. "Simon is emotionally vulnerable. That

makes him unpredictable, but also... approachable."
"Exactly," Finn nodded. "I think there's a possibility he... might listen."
"Or," Morpheus interjected again, "he's manipulating you again, using your feelings against you, and preparing a new trap. But hey, what do I know? I'm just a cat of nearly five hundred years old who's seen countless human tragedies unfold through exactly this kind of naivety."
"Come on, Morpheus," Ingrid said calmly, her old eyes wiser than her eccentric appearance suggested. "Finn's connection with Simon could be an advantage. If there's even a small chance, Laurent could be convinced..."
"Then we avoid confrontation," Lina finished. She looked at Finn. "Do you think he would listen? Really listen?"
Finn thought about the phone call, about the vulnerability he'd heard in Simon's voice, about the pain of loss they shared. "I think he could listen. If we can show him what Thomas was trying to tell him in his dream."
"That the Underworld isn't his enemy," Lina nodded.
"Strategically speaking," Dreamer said, who had watched silently from his corner until now, "a diplomatic approach gives us more options. But we must be prepared for resistance."
"The Guardians are in position around the Minnewater," Morpheus reported, suddenly more serious. "They report that Laurent's team is installing the final machines. And there's something else... Antoine and an older man in an expensive suit have arrived."
"Victor Laurent," Lina said grimly. "Simon's uncle. The real power behind the Laurent family."
"Which means our time is running out," Finn concluded. He looked outside, where the rain was slowly stopping, and the clouds were opening to let more light through. "We have to go."
Lina nodded and began putting on her purple velvet coat, now decorated with small protective amulets. The silver cacao bean around her neck glowed softly with light, resonating with the golden counterpart Ingrid wore.

"I've made something else for you," Ingrid said, walking to Finn. She produced a leather bracelet decorated with a small wolf symbol. "It's not a cacao bean, but it will help keep your wolf side in balance during the confrontation."

Finn took the bracelet, feeling how the leather was warm, as if it had life. "Thank you."

Morpheus jumped from the table and stretched extensively. "Forgive my earlier sarcasm," he said, which for him passed as an apology. "Although I still think telephone conversations with the enemy at three in the morning are a questionable tactic, I appreciate your attempt at... diplomacy." He looked directly at Finn. "But be careful. The Laurents have learned to manipulate for generations."

"I'll be careful," Finn promised.

They left the boathouse in a sombre mood, the gravity of what was coming weighing on their shoulders. Outside waited two Guardians—Dreamer in his full, majestic form, and a slender, silver fox whose coat seemed to glisten even in the muted morning light.

"Come," Lina said, her voice now filled with determination. "We have a choice to make. A world to save. Perhaps two."

And together they began their journey to the Minnewater, where the future of dreams and reality would be determined within hours.

AWAKENING

Robert Maillard opened his eyes in his hospital room, his consciousness finally returning after days of forced slumber. His gaze was clear, sharper than ever, as if he was looking through more than just physical eyes.

"Devos," he whispered, his voice still hoarse. The duty officer standing by his door jumped up, clearly shocked by the sudden revival.

"Mayor! You're... you're back!"

"How long?" Maillard asked, sitting up in his bed, pulling at the IV tubes in his arm.

"Seven days, Mayor. The doctors said..."

"No time," Maillard interrupted. "It's happening now."

Chief Inspector Devos was brought in within fifteen minutes, his face a mask of professional determination that barely concealed his confusion.

"Mayor, you should rest. The doctors advise—"

"Antoine Leblanc," Maillard interrupted, now sitting fully upright. "I authorize a priority detention warrant."

Devos hesitated. "What charges should we include in the warrant, sir?"

"Attempted murder. Contamination of food supply. Conspiracy." Maillard's eyes had a strange, almost luminous quality. "And if that's not enough, add disruption of interdimensional peace."

"Sir, I must point out that this last charge has no basis in current criminal law or any known jurisprudence," Devos observed carefully.
Maillard grinned, but there was no humour in his expression. "It will be recognized today, Devos. Listen carefully. Leblanc and his accomplices are at the Minnewater. They're trying to do something that could destroy not just this city but both worlds."
"Both...? How would you know that?"
"No time for explanations. Take a unit, go to the Minnewater. Create a perimeter, keep civilians at a distance. There will be... things you can't explain. Accept that. Focus on protecting people."
Devos, who had known Maillard for twenty years, had never seen him like this—the mayor had always been calculating, political, cautious. This man seemed possessed by a clarity that was both frightening and convincing.
"And Leblanc?"
"Arrest him. Antoine Leblanc. He's more dangerous than he appears."
Devos nodded once, sharply. "And Lina Vandevelde?"
A small smile crossed Maillard's face, the first sign of warmth since he'd awakened. "She's trying to save the world, Devos. Give her space to do that."
"Simon Laurent gave me the order earlier because he had a private event planned at the Minnewater."
Twenty minutes later, three police vehicles arrived at the Minnewater, sirens silent but lights flashing. Devos stepped out, his experienced eye taking in the situation—the strange machines set up around the lake, the unnatural darkness of the eclipse, and something he couldn't explain... movements and lights and forms that shouldn't be there.
"Set up a hard perimeter!" he called. "Implement closure protocol, Bravo! No inbound or outbound movement without authorization from the duty officer! Support unit on standby!"
His men moved with swift efficiency, placing barriers, driving tourists and civilians away from what was clearly a danger-

ous situation. "Something amazing is happening right here!" protested an American tourist, camera at the ready. "I believe I saw a wild animal! It was wild, man!"
"Precisely why you must stay at a safe distance, madam," Devos replied curtly in his language. His eyes searched the water surface where activity seemed concentrated—Laurent's machines, and what looked like three figures on the other side of the lake.
"What are your tactical instructions, Inspector?" asked a young officer beside him, visibly out of her comfort zone when confronted with phenomena outside regular training protocol.
Devos thought of Maillard's words. "We maintain public order and safety. Adopt defensive formation and monitor the situation. Subject Vandevelde is declassified as a suspect—all surveillance units informed."
In the distance he saw Antoine Leblanc, confused and frightened. Two officers moved in his direction, handcuffs at the ready.
"Careful," Devos spoke softly, whilst glancing towards the centre of the lake. He'd served Bruges his whole life, thought he knew all the city's secrets. Now he realized some secrets ran deeper than he'd ever suspected.
"What's happening?" the young officer asked.
"Change," Devos replied simply. "Hold the line. Whatever happens, we're here to protect the city."
"Inspector Devos," the officer said, "you need to get back to dispatch. One Kaylee Mendoza is in the interview room with information about the poisoning."
"Right."

ECLIPSE

Bruges awakened in chaos.

Police sirens wailed in the distance whilst the sky above the city slowly darkened—not ordinary cloud cover, but the moon beginning to slide before the sun.

The Minnewater lay before them, a liquid mirror reflecting the first shadows like ink on black velvet. But to Finn's eyes it was more than that—he could now see the undercurrents, the subtle ripples not caused by wind or movement, but by the breath of another world whispering against the thin membrane of reality.

"The Lake of Love," Lina whispered, her voice a muted melody that harmonized perfectly with the soft lapping of water against the old stone shore. "So named by people who saw only the surface, never realizing that what they called 'love' was merely a shadow of the true connection that dwells here."

"What is it really?" Finn asked.

"A tear," Ingrid replied, her old eyes reflecting the profound wisdom of centuries. She held her head high, the golden cacao bean around her neck pulsing stronger than ever. "A tear from the Underworld when it was separated from our reality, a drop of pure emotion that burned a hole through the fabric of dimensions."

The mist creeping over the water was like breathing silk, tangible veils dancing in patterns too complex for the human eye to fully comprehend. Each gust of wind carried whispers, half-thoughts of beings living on the other side.

Finn stared into the depths and saw stars moving that weren't in the sky—points of light living within the water itself, like an inverted universe stretching beneath them instead of above.

"Careful," Lina warned, placing a hand on his arm when he leaned too far over the edge. "The Minnewater hungers for dreams. It will swallow your entire consciousness like a thirsty man downs a glass of water, if you come too close without preparation."

The wind tugged at Lina's purple coat, making the fabric move like the wings of an exotic bird. The silver cacao bean around her neck resonated with the hidden rhythms of the water, pulsing powerfully against her breastbone.

In the distance, along the other shore, they could see Simon's setup—machines and devices in cold geometric formations, an affront to the flowing, organic nature of the Underworld slumbering beneath.

"The eclipse is beginning," Lina whispered, looking at the sky where the moon was now visibly beginning to slide before the sun. It was still subtle—a small bite from the perfect circle of sunlight—but the effects were already noticeable in the quality of light, the temperature of the air, and especially in the thin barrier between worlds.

They moved further around the lake, staying hidden in the shadows of the trees. From their hiding place, they could now see Simon himself, moving between the devices with the authority of a conductor before an orchestra. Beside him stood Antoine and Arianne, plus a handful of men in dark suits with unmistakable weapon bulges under their jackets.

"He's targeted the place where we opened the portal," Lina whispered. "His energy reflectors are positioned to isolate and interfere with that point."

"And now?" Finn asked, feeling a strange chill as the eclipse progressed, now covering about a quarter of the sun.

"Now we take our position," Ingrid replied, producing a small pouch of silver sand. With the skill of someone who had done these hundreds of times, she began drawing a complex figure on the ground—a pattern of concentric circles with Maya symbols between them.

Lina closed her eyes and stretched out her arms, the silver cacao bean now vibrating in an increasingly rapid rhythm.

Around the lake, the Guardians began to gather, almost invisible to normal eyes but perfectly clear to Finn's heightened senses. Dozens of magical beings, each with its own unique form, but all united in one purpose.

"Remember what Kaxil said," Morpheus spoke, suddenly appearing beside Finn in his humanoid shadow form. "The Laurent boy isn't the only player here. There's something else. Something older."

Finn looked sharply at the cat-spirit. "What do you mean?"

Morpheus squinted softly. "There are forces at work that even Laurent doesn't understand. An old enemy I once fought before..."

On Simon's side of the lake, activities became more urgent. It was clear he felt the presence of the Guardians, even if he couldn't see them all. His men moved faster, checking cables and positioning reflectors with growing urgency.

The sun was now almost a third covered, and the effects became noticeable in the physical world. A strange, half-dark quality fell over Bruges, not like ordinary twilight, but something else—a kind of between-light that gave the world a dreamy, surreal quality.

"It's almost time," Lina said. "The eclipse begins at 14:30. That's when Laurent's ritual begins, and when we must intervene."

"How?" Finn asked.

Ingrid stopped her intricate ground drawing and stared directly at him. "You must decide, Finn De Wulf. Before the eclipse reaches its climax at 14:42, you must choose which path you want to follow."

An enormous responsibility fell over him, heavier than any physical burden he'd ever carried. "And if I make the wrong choice?"

"There is no wrong choice," Dreamer spoke, now standing beside him, his coat glowing more than ever. "There are only different paths, different possibilities."
A sudden ripple passed over the water surface of the Minnewater, and then everything stiffened—the air, the water, even sound seemed muffled, like a universe holding its breath.
"He's begun," Lina whispered.

BACK ROOM

The Bieratelier was anything but the sort of establishment where one would expect to find a man like Victor Laurent. Located on two Wijngaardstraat, directly opposite 'Dreams of Lina' (an irony that had briefly curled Victor's thin lips), the small café was notorious for its eccentric decoration—hundreds of colourful bras from tourists hung like strange trophies from the ceiling, whilst the walls were covered with currency from around the world, each note accompanied by a handwritten anecdote.

The place was usually overcrowded, noisy and exuberant, but precisely for that reason, perfect for a meeting that had to go unnoticed. Who would look for a Laurent in such a plebeian environment? It was perfect camouflage—hidden in plain sight.

In the dark back room, officially reserved for "beer tastings" but unofficially available to whoever paid the right price to the proprietress, sat Victor Laurent, his slim, aristocratic figure impeccably dressed in a tailored suit that cost more than the average Bruges resident earned in a month. The boisterous bustle of the café penetrated only mutedly to this small room, which was precisely why Victor had chosen this place—close enough to the action to react quickly, but isolated enough for privacy.

Before him stood a glass of Atelier 6, the artisanal house beer with its characteristic amber colour and subtle vanilla notes.

Beside the glass lay a tablet displaying streamed images from a surveillance camera aimed at the Minnewater, and a small, modified communication device that looked like a luxury walkie-talkie, but with military-grade encryption.
The device crackled. "The setup is complete," came Antoine's voice through the small speaker. "Your nephew hasn't asked me anything suspicious."
"Perfect," Victor replied, his voice low. "He has no idea that his ritual is merely preparation for ours."
"Of course not," Antoine replied. "Simon is too limited in his vision. He wants to seal off the dream world, like generations of Laurents before him. But we..." there was a short silence, followed by a low, amused laugh, "we see the true possibility."
Victor nodded, though Antoine couldn't see him. "Not seal off, not unite, but control. The dream world as an inexhaustible source of power, under our control."
"The equipment is ready," Antoine confirmed via communication. "As soon as Simon's ritual weakens the barrier, we hijack the energy for our purpose."
"And De Wulf?" Victor asked.
A brief silence followed. When Antoine spoke again, his voice had a strange quality that was palpable even through the device's distortion. "His blood is a crucial component, yes. But I've made... additions to your nephew's formula. Ingredients much older than Maya knowledge."
Victor's eyebrows drew together. "You're going outside our agreement, Leblanc."
"Only where necessary for optimal results," Antoine replied smoothly. "The world as we know it is about to change, Mr Laurent. I'm merely ensuring we're on the right side of that change."
From outside came the rumble of thunder, though no rain had been forecast. The eclipse was progressing, and with each disappearing second of sunlight the feeling of tension grew more intense, like electricity building up before an inevitable discharge.

On the tablet, Victor could see Simon moving between his devices, unaware of the betrayal forming around him. Antoine stood at the edge of sight, apparently following Simon's orders, but with a subtle deviation in his movements that didn't escape Victor's trained eye.
"It's time," Victor said, consulting his pocket watch. "Simon will begin now."

"Then so will I," came Antoine's voice, now lower, almost factual, without the previously present subservience? "You might want to consider leaving that room, Mr Laurent. When the barrier breaks... there could be unexpected side effects within a radius of several kilometres."
Victor raised an eyebrow at this sudden concern, but he was no fool. He stood up, emptying his glass of Atelier 6 in one large gulp. "I'll arrive at the lake within ten minutes. Be ready."
"Oh, I certainly am," Antoine replied, before the connection was broken with a finality that made Victor pause momentarily.
With a last glance at the tablet, which now showed Simon in deep concentration as the eclipse progressed, Victor left the back room, his glass the only evidence of his presence.

BUBBLE

On Simon's side of the lake, the jade cacao bean now glowed with unhealthy intensity—a sickly green glow that hurt the eyes. He held the artefact aloft, and a beam of pulsing energy shot out towards the centre of the lake.

"Now!" Lina cried.

Ingrid threw a handful of silver powder into the air, where it hung like a cloud of microscopic stars. Lina raised the silver cacao bean, which now pulsed, harmonizing with Ingrid's golden counterpart.

And around the entire lake, the Guardians moved as one, forming a living chain of magical energy that enclosed the water's perimeter, a counterweight to what Simon was trying to achieve.

The beam from Simon's artefact hit the water in the centre of the lake. It began to boil and swirl, but not naturally—more like a wound in reality itself becoming infected.

"He's using your blood," Lina called over the growing sound of wind and churning water. "He's activating it with the jade key, trying to use the wolf essence to permanently separate the two worlds."

Finn felt it—a strange, sick sensation in his blood, as if something was being drawn from him, used against his will for a purpose opposite to his nature. He groaned, half-sinking to the ground, his head pounding with sudden pain.

"Fight it," Ingrid encouraged, her voice unexpectedly powerful for such a fragile-looking woman. Her palms now glowed with golden light, the energy of the key around her neck flowing through her entire body. "It's your blood, your essence. He can't fully control it without your permission."

Finn gritted his teeth, his vision narrowing to a tunnel. In the centre of the lake, where Simon's energy was focused, a dark vortex began to form—not the golden, vibrant portal from before, but something more corrupt, colder. A hole that didn't lead to the Underworld, but to... nothing. An absolute void that would swallow both worlds and then separate them forever.

"Now, Finn!" Lina called. "What's your choice? I need your power to know which ritual to perform!"

Finn staggered forward, staring across the lake at Simon, whose face, even at this distance, was a mask of intense concentration and triumphant certainty. He thought about what he'd seen in the Underworld—the endless possibilities, the freedom, the connection that could exist between all things if the walls between worlds would fall.

"Union," he said, his voice surer than he felt. "I choose complete union of the worlds. Not Laurent's separation, not the current limited connection, but complete harmony. Let the barriers fall. Let dreams and reality become one."

Lina's face showed a moment of surprise, followed by something that looked suspiciously like relief. "You're certain?"

"Certain enough," Finn replied, now standing upright despite the pain coursing through his body. "I'm tired of half-lives and half-truths."

But before Lina could react, something unexpected happened. The dark vortex in the centre of the lake changed—not responding to their intention, but to another force. The whirlpool became purplish, toxic, and began expanding in an unnatural pattern.

"That's not Simon's work," Morpheus suddenly realized, his head turning sharply towards the other side of the lake. "That's..."

"Antoine," Ingrid finished grimly. "He's hijacked the ritual!"

They looked to the other side, where confusion clearly reigned. Simon conflicted with Antoine, arguing over a control panel, whilst Arianne stood between them, her face a mask of surprise and growing realization.

"We have no time to wait," Lina decided, her voice hardened by determination. "Finn, you must get the jade key. Now!"

Without hesitation, Finn moved into action, but not along the shore—that would take too long. Instead, he jumped straight into the water.

The moment he hit the surface, Finn felt a strange change. The water was no longer entirely liquid, not entirely physical. It felt more like a dense mist that could bear his weight. With growing confidence, he realized he could run across it.

And that's what he did.

Finn ran across the water, his body changing as he moved. Unlike his normal, painful transformations, this was smooth, natural—the barrier between worlds was already so thin that the Underworld's rules were beginning to seep through. His body took on an intermediate form—not fully human, not fully wolf, but a perfect harmony of both.

Across the lake he could see Simon's face change from concentration to shock, to something more complex—anger mixed with an almost painful recognition as he saw Finn coming across the water, half-transformed.

"Stop him!" Antoine screamed at the guards, who now drew weapons—some conventional pistols, others stranger-looking devices clearly designed for magical confrontations.

But the Guardians were faster. They intercepted every man who tried to shoot at Finn. A massive black raven swooped on Arianne, who had drawn a small silver crossbow. With a wild wing beat, it knocked the weapon from her hands.

"Not exactly foolproof, are they?" the raven snapped with a voice suspiciously like Morpheus's, but deeper, older. "Perhaps next time invest in better personnel, Ms Insurance?"

Arianne backed away, her eyes wide with the realization that nothing was, as she'd thought it was. "This... this wasn't the plan," she stammered. "Victor said we'd only seal off the dream world, not... this." She looked at the purple vortex growing ever more corrupt.

Finn was almost at shore when Antoine made a strange movement with his hand. A wave of dark energy shot towards Finn, hit him in midair, and threw him back to the middle of the lake.

"The Wolf goes no further," Antoine grinned, his hand now raised, showing strange, black lines that hadn't been there minutes earlier. "He's mine now."

Simon stared with growing horror at his ally. "Antoine, what have you done? This wasn't the plan!"

"Plans change, mon ami," Antoine replied, his voice deeper, richer, with an accent that was no longer entirely French, but something older. "Seal the dream world? Why destroy what you can control?"

Finn struggled in the middle of the lake, trapped in a field of dark energy that held him like a fly in a web. His transformation accelerated, but not in the harmonious direction from before—there was something peculiar in Antoine's magic that tried to twist his being, distort his essence.

"Lina!" he called in panic.

On the other side of the lake, Lina responded immediately. With a powerful gesture, she threw her hairpin into the air, which transformed into an elegant flying broom. She jumped on it and shot like a comet into the air, circling over the lake towards Finn.

But Antoine was prepared. With a new hand movement, he sent a tidal wave of energy upward, which hit Lina's broom and sent it tumbling.

"Non, non, non," he grinned. "Nothing stands in my way, little witch."

Simon stood frozen, his fingers still clenched around the jade cacao bean that now pulsed erratically, responding to the chaotic energies.

"It's over, Simon," Antoine said, extending his hand. "Give me the key. Your little family crusade was always doomed to fail. You never saw the whole picture."

Simon looked at Finn, trapped in the centre of the lake, at Lina

struggling to regain control of her broom, at the purple vortex growing larger and more threatening.
At that moment, he remembered the dream—Thomas, gripped by darkness, dragged to the depths, and his own powerlessness to save him. Now he saw Finn in the same position, and a tearing pain cut through his chest.
"No," he murmured, his fingers stiffening around the jade cacao bean. "No. Not again."
With a scream of pure, unrestrained emotion—so uncharacteristic for the always controlled Laurent—Simon broke free from his paralysis. He ran to the edge of the water, the jade key high above his head.
"Finn!" he called. "Catch!"
And with all the strength he could muster, he threw the jade cacao bean through the air, over the lake, in the direction of the trapped werewolf.
Antoine roared with fury and gestured wildly. Dark lightning shot from his fingertips, chasing the artefact through the air. But the key, now free from Simon's influence, moved with its intention, dodging the dark magic, spiralling through the air in a trajectory that defied all natural laws.
The artefact reached Finn, who stretched out his hand in a last desperate attempt. His fingers closed around the jade cacao bean just as the moon completely covered the sun, the total eclipse began.
And then everything went white.
An explosion of pure light erupted from the centre of the lake, blinding in its intensity. The dark vortex tore open, but not in the twisting, corrupt manner of Antoine's ritual, and also not in the neat separation of Simon's original plan.
It was an opening, a union, a seamless confluence of two worlds.
From the light appeared Finn, floating above the water, in his hands the jade cacao bean that now pulsed, agreeing with the silver and golden counterparts on shore. His form was transformed—neither human nor wolf, but something new, something complete. His eyes glowed with golden light, his body

surrounded by an aura reminiscent of dew in the morning sun.
"NO!" Antoine screamed, making wild gestures that now seemed to have no effect. "This cannot be! The formula was perfect! The ritual was—"
"Based on a half-understanding of the truth," a new voice interrupted.
From the light behind Finn appeared a figure that no one but Morpheus recognized—Kaxil, the Keeper of Dreams, manifested in the physical world for the first time in centuries. His golden form glowed with inner light.
"Yaluk," Kaxil spoke, looking directly at Antoine. "Or do you now go by the name 'Antoine'? How many masks have you worn through the centuries, old enemy?"
Antoine's—or Yaluk's—face contorted into a mask of fury and hatred. "Not enough to escape you, apparently." His skin began to change, the black lines spreading, growing, his form changing into something barely human anymore.
"But it's too late," he grinned, his voice now lower, more resonant than before. "The gate is open. The union begins. But not as you planned."
With a final, wild laugh, Antoine/Yaluk threw himself backward, into the vortex of light, disappearing into the stream between worlds before anyone could stop him.
Simon stood motionless on the shore, his face a mask of bewilderment. "What... what happened? What did he do?"
Kaxil descended beside Finn, who still floated above the water. "He fled, to depths where even I cannot follow him. Not now, anyway."
"But the ritual..." Lina began, now back on her broom, hovering beside Finn.
"Is complete," Kaxil finished. "The union you sought has begun. The worlds are merging, not chaotically as Yaluk wanted, but harmoniously as the Wolf chose."
"And Antoine?" Finn asked, his voice richer, deeper in this transformed state.
"It never really was Antoine Leblanc," Morpheus replied, now back in his full panther form, larger and more powerful than

they'd ever seen him. "He was Yaluk—an ancient god of chaos and destruction. A being I fought long ago and thought I'd destroyed." There was a strange mixture of guilt and anger in his eyes. "There's an even greater conflict coming."

The eclipse reached its peak—the sun completely hidden behind the moon, only the corona visible as a flaming ring at the edge. The air was filled with a strange, bluish glow, and around the lake things began to change.

Trees that had been ordinary oaks and willows began to glow with subtle light. The water moved with its consciousness, forming shapes and patterns that no wind or tide could explain. And in the air appeared the first signs of what would later be known as 'Dream Veils'—rainbow-coloured bands of light that danced like northern lights, but more complex, more conscious in their movements.

"It's begun," Lina whispered, awe in her voice. "The worlds are uniting."

Arianne Vermeer sank to her knees on the shore, her face marked with shock and remorse. "What have we done?" she stammered. "Victor said we'd only seal off the dream world, that we'd protect humanity from fantasy and madness. But this..."

"This is what was always meant to be," Ingrid said, walking to her and placing a surprisingly kind hand on her shoulder. "It's time you learned which stories are true."

"Where's Victor?" Simon asked suddenly, looking around in growing panic. "He was here at the beginning, but now..."

A quick search confirmed what they already feared—Victor Laurent had vanished in the chaos, probably fled when he saw his plans fail. Or perhaps, more frighteningly, followed to where Antoine/Yaluk had gone.

"That's one problem for later," Morpheus said dryly, his normal mannerisms returning despite his larger, more imposing form. "Let's first face the small fact of THE COMPLETE UNION OF DREAM WORLD AND REALITY, shall we? I suspect this will require some explanation to the mayor."

As if on cue, they heard sirens in the distance—police cars and ambulances approaching, alerted by citizens who had reported the strange phenomena.

Finn slowly descended to the water, the jade cacao bean in his hand, now in rhythmic harmony with the silver around Lina's neck and the golden that Ingrid wore. When his feet touched the surface, the water solidified beneath him, bearing his weight as if this had always been a natural property.

"It's not over," Kaxil warned, his form already beginning to fade, returning to the Underworld that was now increasingly mingled with physical reality. "Yaluk will return, stronger, more dangerous. And you must be ready."

"We'll be ready," Finn promised, his form now slowly returning to his human appearance, though there was something different, more powerful about him than before. "This time, we all fight together."

He looked at Simon, who had hesitantly come to the edge of the water. Their eyes met—wolf and hunter, but now without the enmity from before.

"Together," Simon confirmed softly.

And as the first police cars arrived, Finn, Lina, Ingrid, Simon, and Morpheus closed a circle—a small coalition of the most diverse allies, united to navigate a new chapter in the history of the two worlds. Arianne watched through tears as her nightmare became reality.

The eclipse was ending, the first rays of sunlight breaking along the moon's edge. But Bruges, and the world around it, would never be the same again.

STATEMENT

Bruges Police Station towered as a clinical white and concrete monument at the harbour, its stark lines and glass-and-steel construction a sharp contrast to the mediaeval charm of the rest of the city. Kaylee Mendoza stood before the stern security barrier, a series of detection gates and cameras that separated her from the actual building, nervously turning her iPhone in her hand.

"This is so dystopian," she muttered to herself, her bright pink coat with leopard-print trim absurdly colourful against the sterile grey and white of the surroundings. She took a quick selfie with the building as a backdrop. "Literally, the most unfiltered government aesthetic ever. Not even a single plant to soften the vibe."

A burly male officer at the control desk looked at her with boredom. "May I see your identification?"

Kaylee showed her Brazilian residence permit and was led through a metal detector that protested against her numerous bracelets and the metal details on her designer bag.

"Arms up," ordered an officer with short blonde hair and a facial expression that left no room for discussion. Her voice was sharper than her male colleague's, her posture more forceful. "Bag on the belt. Phone in the tray."

"My phone? No way, I—"
"In. The. Tray." The officer articulated each syllable as if speaking to a disobedient child.
Kaylee rolled her eyes but obeyed, sighing dramatically. She stepped through the gates and was roughly searched by the officer, whose strong hands missed not a centimetre.
"Is this really necessary? I'm just here to file a report," Kaylee protested.
"Standard procedure," the woman replied curtly. "You may proceed."
Kaylee collected her belongings and followed directions to a modern, open reception area. The fluorescent lighting reflected off the concrete walls and cast a pale, unflattering glow on everything and everyone—a fact that made her shudder as she walked to the reception desk.
The young officer behind the desk looked up and attempted a friendly smile, his uniform impeccable, his demeanour less intimidating than the officers at the entrance. He tapped on an ultra-modern keyboard connected to a touchscreen interface.
"Can I help you, miss?" he asked, clearly attempting to appear approachable.
Kaylee straightened her back. She'd practised this speech during the Uber ride here. "I'm here to report an attempted poisoning. Someone tried to make me unalive with drugged chocolate."
The officer finally looked up, his eyebrows drawn together, confused. "To make you... what?"
"Unalive," Kaylee repeated, as if it were the most natural thing in the world. "You know... dead." She whispered the last word dramatically.
"You mean attempted murder?" The officer suddenly seemed much more interested, sitting upright and forgetting his computer.
"Yes!" Kaylee pretended to clap her hands. "That's it. Sorry, on social media we say 'unalive' to bypass algorithms that suppress content with heavy themes. But someone low-key tried to kill me with chocolate. It was so messed up." She opened

her designer bag and produced a small black box, carefully wrapped in at least three layers of plastic film and sealed with duct tape. She placed the object carefully on the counter as if it were an explosive. The officer looked at the officers doing the checks, but they shrugged. Their system had detected no bomb.

"This is the evidence," she declared solemnly. "The rest of the poisoned chocolate. I've triple-wrapped it to prevent contamination. I demand a full forensic investigation. CSI-style."

The officer looked confused at the wrapped package, then back at Kaylee, then slowly pushed a form towards her. "Name?"

"Kaylee Mendoza. With a K and two e's. I'm an influencer. Three hundred thousand followers on Insta, one hundred and fifty thousand on TikTok, you've probably heard of me?" She smiled hopefully.

"Nationality?"

"Brazilian, but I study here in Bruges. Marketing and social media management." She rolled her eyes. "Biggest waste of money ever, honestly. Everything they tell you in the lecture hall is basically outdated before the professor has finished saying it."

The officer noted patiently. "And can you describe exactly what happened, Miss Mendoza?"

Kaylee took a deep breath. "Okay, so. There's this new super fancy chocolate shop that opened on the Market Square—Confiserie du Cygne? A swan as logo? The owner, Antoine, DM'd me that he wanted to hire me for a collab. Very exclusive content, tasting pralines for my followers. Major opportunity, I thought!"

She showed her iPhone with a screenshot of a direct message from an account called @ConfiducygneBruges.

"So I went there, and he gave me this INSANE luxury box of pralines. He said I was the first to taste them, and that they were special. And then I went to the shop of Lina, that other chocolate maker? 'Dreams of Lina', super cute, more old-school vibe."

The officer typed along on the keyboard, but his face now showed clear signs of confusion. "And

where does the poisoning come into this story?"
"I'm getting to that!" Kaylee waved dramatically with her hands. "When I was at Lina's and I tasted that chocolate from Antoine, I felt INSTANTLY weird. Like, hallucinating. I thought there was a talking cat, it was really terrifying. I literally passed out, and when Lina examined me, she said there was something in the chocolate that doesn't belong in chocolate."
"Mrs Vandevelde told you there was poison in the chocolate?"
"No, not rat poison, but drugs? She said it was drugs. She gave me some kind of antidote that made me okay. She said Antoine did it on purpose, that he was trying to poison more people like that."
"So you didn't go to hospital to have your blood tested? You have no medical evidence of poisoning?" The officer seemed irritated.
Kaylee tapped the wrapped package on the counter. "Uh, hello? Direct evidence, right here? I saved the chocolate for forensic investigation. You should be able to get fingerprints from it, poison traces, DNA, everything you do in those crime shows. Where's your forensic team?" She looked around as if expecting a team in white suits any moment.
The officer sighed deeply. "Miss Mendoza, the forensic lab has better things to do than—"
"Better things? Someone's trying to murder people with chocolate, and that's not relevant enough? You know what, I demand my one phone call. I'm going to call a solicitor."
The officer and his colleague exchanged a weary look.
"Miss," Officer Verbruggen said sharply, "firstly, you're not arrested, so there's no 'phone call'. Secondly, we're here in Bruges, not in some American Hollywood film. And thirdly, if you keep insisting on forensically analysing... chocolate," she pointed contemptuously at the package, "without any other evidence of poisoning, then you're wasting police time, which is an offence."
"Excuse me?" Kaylee's eyes widened. "You think I'm making this up? I nearly lost my life for content! I'd never do that... well, not without extensive warnings and disclaimers for my followers."

"Miss Mendoza," Verbruggen said, her voice now dangerously calm, "I think you'd better wait for Inspector Devos. We've had... numerous strange reports in the past few hours, and your story might fit with those."
"Strange reports?" Kaylee looked up from her phone. "Wait, do you mean those super weird lights above the Minnewater? I saw that on my way here! I wanted to stop for content, but my Uber driver said the whole zone was cordoned off by police."
The officer's eyes narrowed. "How do you know about the situation at the Minnewater?"
"Duh, social media?" Kaylee rolled her eyes. "It's literally everywhere. #BrugesMystery trending on X. There are TikTok videos that already have millions of views. People are saying it's UFOs, or a secret government experiment, or—"
"Miss," the officer interrupted, now sitting upright in his chair. "When was your visit to this chocolate maker, Antoine?"
"Three days ago, around half past one? Just before the solar eclipse started."
Officer Verbruggen crossed her arms. "Van Hulle, you've been with the police for less than two years. If you think every stoned student who walks in here deserves special treatment..."
"I. Am. Not. Stoned." Kaylee emphasized each word like her female colleague at reception ordered, her Brazilian temperament beginning to boil. "And you're probably too old to understand it, but I'm a serious content creator with more than three hundred thousand followers."
"Too old?" Officer Verbruggen's eyebrows shot up.
"Yeah, like, no offence, you probably don't even understand how TikTok works." Kaylee smiled sweetly.
Van Hulle suppressed a laugh, earning him a deadly look from his colleague.
"I'm thirty, not dead," Verbruggen snapped. "And I understand perfectly well how—"
"Thirty?" Kaylee's eyes widened in mock disbelief. "That's literally almost double my age. No wonder you don't get why this is such a big deal."
Officer Van Hulle cleared his throat.

"Miss Mendoza, perhaps we could—"
"No, wait," Kaylee interrupted, now amused by Verbruggen's rising irritation. "Let me guess, you're what? Twenty-five? With your 'fellow kids' vibe? Are you still reading the TikTok For Dummies book?"
"I'm twenty-seven," Van Hulle mumbled, clearly uncomforta-ble.
"Wow, you're almost as old as her," Kaylee sighed dramatically.
Officer Verbruggen slammed her flat hand hard on the table. "Enough! Van Hulle, get Devos. Now."
The male officer stood abruptly and disappeared through a glass sliding door, leaving Kaylee alone with the furious Ver-bruggen. She sighed dramatically and returned, apparently unmoved, to her phone, scrolling through her notifications.
"OMG, already more than a thousand reactions to my story," she muttered. "Followers really want to know what's happen-ing at the Minnewater."
As soon as Verbruggen looked away for a moment of an in-coming message on her communication device, Kaylee quick-ly opened the camera app and pointed it at herself, finding the perfect angle despite the terrible lighting.
"Hey besties!" she whispered enthusiastically into the cam-era. "Quick update: I'm literally at the police right now, filing a report about how Antoine almost made me unalive with his toxic chocolate! And plot twist—it might have something to do with those crazy lights above the Minnewater! The police are acting major sus, they're hiding something. And they're treating me like a suspect with this total Karen-energy officer who probably doesn't even know what a filter is. Stay tuned, I'll keep you posted as soon as I know more. Like for part two!"
"What do you think you're doing?" Officer Verbruggen's voice cut through the room.
Kaylee looked up guiltily. "Just... checking my makeup?"
Before Verbruggen could respond, the glass door slid open and Officer Van Hulle returned, accompanied by an older man in a wrinkled suit who looked as if he hadn't slept for days. About twenty minutes passed.

"Miss Mendoza, this is Chief Inspector Devos. He'd like to ask you a few questions," Van Hulle announced, clearly relieved that backup had arrived.
Devos nodded briefly to her. "If you'd follow me to an interview room, please."
"Interview room?" Kaylee's eyes widened. "Am I in trouble? I'm the victim here!"
"This is standard procedure," Devos assured her with a voice that sounded as if he'd repeated this sentence hundreds of times. "We simply need a quieter place to take your statement."
Kaylee hesitated, then shrugged and stood up. "Fine. But I have a sponsored post to do for a vitamin supplement brand in three hours, so let's not make this too long, okay?"
She followed Devos down a corridor to a small room with a table, three chairs, and a mirror on the wall that was so obviously a two-way mirror that Kaylee almost had to laugh. It was exactly like in the police series she binge-watched when she should have been studying.
"Is this an interrogation room?" she asked, her voice rising with excitement as she sat down. "That's so cool! Can I take a photo for my feed?"
"Preferably not," Devos said dryly, sitting opposite her, whilst a younger officer sat beside him with a notepad. "Miss Mendoza, I'd like you to tell me about your interactions with Antoine Leblanc and Simon Laurent."
Kaylee's head shot up from her phone. "Wait, how do you know about Simon? I haven't even mentioned him yet?"
"Please answer the question," Devos pressed, his voice calm but authoritative.
"Okayyy," Kaylee sighed. "Antoine is that new chocolate maker who approached me for a collab. Super fancy French vibe, perfect aesthetic for my feed, you know? He gave me chocolate that almost made me unalive."
"And Simon Laurent?"
Kaylee's cheeks turned light pink. "Simon... I see him sometimes on campus. He's in his final year of law, super hot, that jawline? Ugh." She fanned her hand in front of her face. "An-

yway, I saw him yesterday at Maria's ice cream parlour—with that new pizza delivery guy. They were literally on a date." She frowned at the memory. "Kinda sad, tbh. I've been DMing Simon for months, but he barely responded. And then suddenly there's this random pizza guy..."

Devos leaned forward. "Was this 'pizza guy' Finn De Wulf?"

"Yes! That was his name. Do you know him?"

"Ooh. He's a bad boy, isn't he?" The two officers exchanged a look that Kaylee couldn't interpret.

"Miss Mendoza," Devos began carefully. "We have reason to believe there's a connection between what happened to you and the... incidents at the Minnewater. We need to know if you noticed anything unusual, heard strange conversations, or saw anything at Antoine Leblanc's or with Simon Laurent."

Kaylee thought, her elegant fingers resting on her chin. "Well, when I was at Lina's after I'd eaten that laced chocolate, and I was hallucinating, I saw this black cat that... talked? Like, human words?" She laughed nervously. "But that was obviously the drugs."

Devos's expression didn't change. "And what did this... talking cat say?"

Kaylee stared at him. "Wait, do you believe me? It was a hallucination, obviously."

"I like to let my colleagues have a laugh," Devos said with the voice of an undertaker.

"Uhm, okay? He said something about the chocolate that Antoine had drugged it. And that a whole city full of people would be drugged as part of a plan?" She shook her head. "But it was just a trippy hallucination. Cats don't talk."

"Of course not," Devos agreed, but his tone suggested otherwise. "And before you came to the police, did you speak to anyone else about this incident?"

"I posted stories," Kaylee said, as if it were the most obvious thing in the world. "But I didn't mention Antoine's name because I don't want a defamation lawsuit. I only tagged him as 'that fancy new chocolate maker' and warned my followers to stay away for now."

"May I see those posts?" Devos asked. Kaylee gave him her phone, unlocked on her Instagram profile. Devos and the younger officer viewed the series of short videos in which Kaylee dramatically described her experience, including the near "unalive" incident and her warnings about the chocolate maker.

"How many people have seen this?" Devos asked, returning her phone.

"Hmm, about eight thousand nine hundred views so far? It's becoming one of my most viewed stories ever. The algorithm loves drama."

Devos now also rubbed his chin. "Miss Mendoza, we'd like to keep you here whilst we investigate this case further."

"Wait, what?" Kaylee's eyes widened. "Am I arrested? Do I need a solicitor? Is this because I'm brown? Because I'm Brazilian?"

"You're not arrested," Devos assured her hastily. "We want to protect you, in case Antoine Leblanc finds out you've filed a report. And we may have more questions as our investigation progresses."

"So I can't leave? That really sounds like an arrest," Kaylee protested. "And what happened at the Minnewater? Does it have something to do with Antoine's drugged chocolate? Is it some kind of mass poisoning? Is that why you want to cover this up? Because there'd be a panic?"

Devos sighed deeply. "Miss Mendoza, I assure you that—"

He was interrupted by a powerful vibration. Kaylee's phone, still in her hand, vibrated so violently it seemed like it wanted to jump from her palm.

"What the hell?" Kaylee stared at the device. "It's never done anything like—"

The screen lit up with an intense, blue light, much brighter than normally should be possible for a phone screen. All three stared at the device, bewildered.

Suddenly, a message appeared, but not in the normal way. The text seemed to float above the screen, like a hologram:

> "THE WORLDS UNITE. THE DREAM VEIL HAS FALLEN. THE CHOICE IS MADE."

"What. The. Actual. HELL?!" Kaylee almost dropped her phone. "Is this a hack? Is this some sick joke?"
Devos stood abruptly. "Stay here," he commanded, and hurried from the room, the younger officer on his heels.
Kaylee stared at her phone, which had now returned to normal, as if nothing had happened. With trembling fingers, she opened her camera app again.
"Guys," she whispered, her voice now really trembling. "Something INSANE is happening. My phone just went completely berserk with a creepy message about 'worlds uniting'? The police have run away like scared little bitches. I think this has to do with those weird lights at the Minnewater—"
The door flew open and Devos came back in, now accompanied by three other officers.
"Miss Mendoza," he said curtly. "I must ask you to stop livestreaming. This is a matter of national security."
Kaylee's mouth fell open. "National security? Seriously? Why? Have aliens made contact? Is this a government cover-up?"
"Give me the phone," one of the new officers commanded, extending his hand.
"What? No way!" Kaylee pressed her iPhone against her chest. "This is my livelihood! You can't just—"
"We can, and we will," the officer said. "Either you give us your phone voluntarily, or we confiscate it as evidence."
"Evidence? Of what?" Kaylee jumped up, her Brazilian temperament now fully unleashed. "I'm the victim here! Someone tried to poison me, and now you're trying to silence me?"
She stepped backwards, still protecting her phone. "I know my rights! I want a solicitor! Now!"
"Miss—" Kaylee Mendoza's live feed was going mental.
"And not just any solicitor," Kaylee added, getting a sudden idea. "I want Simon Laurent."
The room fell dead silent.
"What did you say?" Devos asked slowly.
"Simon Laurent," Kaylee repeated, her chin up in defiance. "He's almost graduated in law, and he's the best in his year. If you're not going to explain what's go-

ing on, then I want him here to defend my rights." The officers exchanged uncomfortable looks, whilst the camera was black, but the audio was still streaming. Hundreds of messages were coming in.
"Miss Mendoza," Devos said finally. "I'm afraid Mr Laurent is currently... unavailable."
"What do you mean?" Kaylee demanded. "Is he also arrested? Is he here? Is he part of this whole mess? Was Simon dodgy with Antoine? OO MM GEEEE was that why he was at the Minnewater?"
Devos seemed to struggle with how much to say. "We currently cannot—"

He was interrupted again, but this time by a loud cracking that echoed through the entire building, followed by what sounded like a gigantic gust of wind. The lights flickered, went out, and then came back on—but in a strange, bluish tint that bathed the room in a dreamy light.
"What was that?" the younger officer whispered.
Kaylee looked at the window of the interview room that looked out onto a small courtyard. What she saw made her breath stop.
"O. My. God." She pointed speechlessly. The daylight disappeared. Outside the window floated what looked like a small, gleaming being, no bigger than a hummingbird, but clearly intelligent. It had a form reminiscent of a miniature human made of pure light, with wings that beat in a rhythm that reminded Kaylee of a heartbeat. It looked curiously inside, head tilted like an interested child.
"Is that a... fairy?" Kaylee stammered, laughing at herself. "Am I still hallucinating?"
Devos walked slowly to the window, his face a mask of disbelief and... recognition?
"The worlds have united," he mumbled.
"What does that mean?" Kaylee asked, but her question was overshadowed by a new series of sounds—sirens, voices shouting over each other, and what sounded like collective exclama-

tions of amazement and shock from outside the police station.
"We have to go," Devos decided, turning to the other officers. "Set up a perimeter around the centre. No journalists within five hundred metres of the Minnewater. Contact the mayor and tell him it's happened, exactly as he predicted."
"What's happened?" Kaylee pressed, now completely confused. "Someone has to tell me what's going on!"
Devos looked at her, as if suddenly remembering she was there. "Miss Mendoza, you stay here until we have the situation under control."
"But—"
"This isn't a request." His voice was finally sharp. "One of my officers will stay with you. This is bigger than your social media presence. Oh my god!"
With those words, he left the room, most of the other officers following, except one young officer who remained uncomfortably by the door.
Kaylee sank back into her chair, speechless for the first time. She looked at the small light being outside the window, which now seemed to be drawing figures in the air with its fingers, leaving light trails that slowly faded.
"This is real, isn't it?" she asked softly to the remaining officer. "I'm not hallucinating?
The officer shook her head and tried to compose herself. "It's quite real. We're getting reports of... beings, lights, and other phenomena from across the city."
"But what does it mean? What did Devos mean by 'the worlds have united'?"
The officer shrugged, clearly as lost as Kaylee. "I only know what I've heard from other officers. Something about a confrontation at the Minnewater, between Laurent, Vandevelde and others. Something about a choice that was made. And that... nothing will ever be the same."
Kaylee turned her gaze back outside. The small light being had been joined by two others, and together they now danced in complex patterns, like some kind of communication or celebration.

With a determination, she rarely showed in serious situations, Kaylee raised her phone, the camera aimed at the dancing light beings.
"Sorry, Inspector," she whispered. "But the world needs to see this."
Her feed went viral and was picked up by all television stations as amateur footage from influencer Kaylee Mendoza.
Two hours later, the interview room had been transformed into a sort of impromptu command centre. A large plasma TV had been brought in and now showed news footage of what was being described worldwide as "the Great Union". Kaylee's follower count had quadrupled in the last two hours. Kaylee had been joined by two officers: young Van Hulle, who nervously fiddled with his tie, and a new officer—a sharply dressed woman in her late twenties who had introduced herself as Maes.

Digital maps of Bruges were projected on an interactive screen on the wall, with red markings indicating the areas where the "phenomena" were strongest. The Minnewater stood at the centre, surrounded by concentric circles of decreasing intensity.
"This is literally insane," Kaylee said, staring at the television, where a shocked newsreader showed footage of floating light beings above Amsterdam's canals. "Is this everywhere?"
"No, it started in Bruges," Officer Maes explained, her voice professional but less aggressive than Verbruggen's. "The epicentre was the Minnewater. But it's spreading, like... well, like ripples in a pond."
"And it was caused by a 'choice'? Made by whom?"
Van Hulle and Maes exchanged a look.
"Devos talks about a Wolf, a Witch, and a Hunter," Maes replied carefully.
"I thought at first they were code names," Van Hulle added, clearly trying to sound approachable. "But after what we've seen today... I don't know anymore."
"You're really such a millennial," Kaylee said, shaking her head at Van Hulle. "That awkward older energy try-

ing to fit in like you understand my generation. Probably had a MySpace page as a teenager, right? And now a TikTok account where you film yourself making dad jokes."

Van Hulle's face turned red. "I'm just trying to—"

"And you," Kaylee turned to Officer Maes, "let me guess, you're one of those elder millennials who thinks she's still relevant because she knows what an Instagram filter is?"

Officer Maes's neutral expression tightened. "Miss Mendoza, I suggest you focus on the situation instead of age differences. We're in the middle of an unprecedented crisis here."

"Oh please," Kaylee snorted. "If anyone here is taking the situation seriously, it's me. On my socials, I've informed more people about what's happening than your entire police force. My update video already has 3 million views."

Kaylee's phone vibrated again, this time normally. She looked at the screen and her eyes widened.

"My video has 4 million views," she whispered in disbelief. "My hashtag #GreatMerging is trending worldwide."

Before Devos could return to confiscate her phone, Kaylee had already uploaded the dancing light beings with a simple caption: "This is real. No filter. No edit. #GreatMerging #BrugesMysteriousLights"

"You shouldn't have posted," Ceulemans said, but without real conviction. "Devos will be furious."

"People have the right to know," Kaylee replied, and for the first time that day she sounded completely serious. "If the world is changing, we can't hide that."

The door swung open and Devos entered, accompanied by none other than Mayor Maillard himself, who looked remarkably well for someone who according to rumours had been in a coma for weeks.

"Miss Mendoza," Maillard greeted her with a formal nod. "I understand you're the one who first raised the alarm about Antoine Leblanc's... activities."

"Uh, yes?" Kaylee stood up, suddenly nervous in the presence of such an important person. "He gave me drugged chocolate. Hallucinations and stuff."

"Indeed," Maillard nodded. "And thereby you played, without knowing it, a crucial role in the events that led to what is now known as the Great Union."
"Wait, what?" Kaylee's mouth fell open. "I literally just ate some chocolate and then filed a report when I almost went unalive."
"Unalive?" Maillard looked confused.
"She means die," Devos translated.
"Ah," Maillard nodded, before returning his attention to Kaylee. "Through your allergic reaction to Antoine's special ingredients and your quick response, Lina Vandevelde was able to develop an antidote. And through your social media posts, others were warned, which undermined Antoine's plan to cause mass hysteria."
"O-okay?" Kaylee looked confused. "So... am I a hero or something?"
"In a sense," Maillard smiled. "And that's why we're here. Although Chief Inspector Devos's actions in detaining you were justified given the circumstances, you're naturally free to go. But we'd appreciate it if you'd be present at a... briefing, let's call it that, about the new reality we now find ourselves in."
"New reality? Do you mean those weird light things?" Kaylee pointed to the window, where now a whole swarm of the small beings danced.
"That, and much more," Maillard nodded. "We're about to hold a press conference, and your social media reach could be... useful in spreading the right information."
Kaylee's eyes lit up. "Wait, you want me to officially cover this for my followers?"
"With certain guidelines, yes," Maillard confirmed. "In exchange, you'll get exclusive access to information and... demonstrations that no one else will have."
"OMG!" Kaylee almost jumped up and down. "That would be INSANE for my metrics! I'd be the first with exclusive content about this whole..." Kaylee's words changed into a hysterical squeal and hopping little steps that any teenage girl would be proud of.
Devos and Maillard exchanged a look somewhere between

amused and desperate.
"Indeed," Maillard said dryly. "So, are you interested?"
"Yes Queen!" Kaylee grabbed her phone. "When do we start? What's the vibe we're going for? Serious news? Educational? Mysterious?"
"Regarding the tone," Maillard began carefully, "We'd appreciate it if you'd emphasize calm and wonder, rather than fear or panic. This is an... evolution for our world, not an apocalypse."
"An evolution," Kaylee repeated, already forming ideas. "Got it. Avatar vibes, but real life."
"And regarding your question about Simon Laurent," Devos added. "He is indeed involved, but not as a suspect. In fact, you'll meet him during the briefing, along with Finn De Wulf and Lina Vandevelde."
Kaylee's cheeks went from light pink to red. She turned abruptly to Officer Maes, who was observing her hysterical outburst.
"What?" Kaylee asked defensively.
"Nothing," Maes replied with a faint smile. "It's just... interesting how your expression changes at the name Laurent."
"That's totally not true," Kaylee protested, her blush deepening. "And even if it were, that's not your business, boomer."
"I'm twenty-seven," Maes said dryly.
"Exactly my point," Kaylee shot back. "Practically prehistoric in influencer years."
Van Hulle suppressed a laugh, earning him a deadly look from his colleague.
Kaylee turned back to Maillard. "So I'm meeting Simon? Is he also... involved in this whole supernatural stuff?"
Maillard nodded. "More than you can imagine, Miss Mendoza."

WORLD NEWS

"...and we now switch live to Katrien Verhaegen at Bruges town hall."
The image changed to a young reporter looking directly into the camera, her microphone firmly gripped, whilst behind her a crowd of journalists clustered together.
"Thank you, Johan. I'm standing here in front of the town hall, where an emergency meeting is taking place about what are cautiously described as 'unusual phenomena' that have occurred in and around Bruges since the eclipse. According to eyewitnesses, the phenomena began exactly after the eclipse." She consulted her notepad. "Local authorities, in cooperation with scientists from Ghent University, have issued a statement speaking of 'atmospheric anomalies' and 'mass suggestion'. The mayor, Robert Maillard, is meanwhile awake and informed, according to the city spokesperson."
The image switched to amateur videos of the rainbow-coloured patterns above the city, children pointing at small luminous beings above the Minnewater, and an oak in Astrid Park whose leaves subtly glow in the dark.
"Religious leaders speak of a miracle, sceptics of mass hysteria, and social media is full of theories from alien intervention to secret government experiments. Whatever the explanation may be, the phenomena seem to be spreading, with first reports from Ghent and Antwerp

of similar light patterns and unexplained phenomena." The reporter looked aside briefly, listening to her earpiece. "We just heard that the mayor has postponed his press conference. According to a spokesperson, federal authorities have requested coordination for a joint response to what is now called a 'supra-local phenomenon'."

She turned back to the camera, her face professional but with barely concealed excitement. "The situation remains highly uncertain, but one thing is clear: the events that began during the solar eclipse in Bruges have changed the world as we know it. Back to the studio, Johan."

"Thank you, Katrien..."

The television was turned off.

Antoine Leblanc—or the being that had worn that identity—stood before a mirror. The black lines under his skin were now prominent, a network of dark veins with lives of its own.

"They think they've won," he whispered to his reflection. "They think the union is as they wanted."

His laugh was cold, hollow. "But they don't understand what they've released. What crawls through the cracks? What I will become."

From the shadows behind him stepped Victor Laurent, his face ashen with exhaustion and fear. "You deceived me," he said, his voice barely audible. "This wasn't our plan."

"Plans change," Antoine/Yaluk replied, his eyes now completely black. "Evolution is necessary, Victor. I evolve. The world evolves. The question is: do you evolve with it?"

Victor stared at him, the full implications of his alliance with this being finally dawning on him. "What are you?" he whispered.

Antoine's smile grew wider, unnatural. "I am the end. And the beginning."

FOUR DAYS LATER

The Church of Our Lady stood majestically in the afternoon light, her centuries-old spire now decorated with subtle, rainbow-coloured light patterns that no one had created, but which had appeared on the third day after what some now called "The Union".

In front of the church, a crowd had gathered—a group of about twenty people, dressed in black, organized in a circle around a small, hovering light orb that flickered anxiously in their midst. They sang religious hymns, holding up crucifixes and other symbols.

"Devils from hell!" their new leader shouted, a man with a fanatical gleam in his eyes. "Back to where you came from!"

The small light spirit flickered weaker in what was clearly fear. Around the circle a growing group of onlookers had gathered, some filming with their phones, others shouting at the black-clad group to leave the being alone.

"They're not devils, you idiot!" a young woman with purple hair called out. "They're beings from the Underworld! Read the news!"

"The Underworld IS hell!" the leader bit back. "This is God's punishment for our sins! These demons must be cast out!"

The tension rose visibly. Police had arrived but kept their distance, clearly uncertain how to respond to this unprecedented situation.

At that moment, Finn, Lina, Simon, and Ingrid arrived at the church, following Morpheus in his cat form.
"They've had it trapped in a circle of holy salt since this morning," Lina said, pointing to the small, anxiously flickering light spirit in the centre of the exorcism attempt. "An old method, but surprisingly effective against beings of pure energy."
"We're four days after the eclipse, we must intervene before this xenophobia escalates," Finn decided, moving forward.
The tension was almost tangible, an electric charge in the air. The black-clad group increased the volume of their singing, whilst the protest from the onlookers grew louder. The trapped light spirit flickered in obvious pain.
"Stop!" Finn called, his voice deeper, more confident than before, his being-side showing through. "This being means no harm!"
The leader of the group turned around. "Who are you to interfere with God's work? These demons must be driven back to hell where they came from!"
"It's not a demon," Lina said, stepping beside Finn. "It's a light spirit, a natural being from the Underworld. It's as frightened as you would be if you were suddenly thrown into a strange world."
"Lies from the sorceress," the man hissed. "We know who you are, Vandevelde. Your family has practised devilish arts for generations. This is your work!"
The tension rose. In the crowd, voices began to get louder, pushing and pulling visible on the flanks.
Suddenly, Simon stepped forward, his face calm but determined. "I am Simon Laurent," he announced, his voice carrying over the square. "My family has studied the evil you fear for generations. And I can assure you—this is not evil. This is a new chapter in our history."
A whisper went through the crowd at the name Laurent—even here, his family name carried weight.
"Let us free this being," Simon continued, stepping closer to the circle. "Let us show that humanity is worthy to be part of this new, greater world."

The leader of the exorcists hesitated, confused by this unexpected intervention. At that moment of indecision, Finn stepped quickly forward, his hand extending over the salt circle. The small light spirit reacted, flashing with renewed energy.

"Break the circle," Finn said, acting on instinct. "A simple interruption is enough."

Simon bent down, swept a small opening in the salt line. Immediately the light spirit leaped upward, free from its prison, spinning in a grateful spiral around Finn and Simon before rising higher.

The crowd reacted with mixed emotions—some cheered, others stepped back in fear, and the exorcists looked on with anger and confusion.

Before the leader could make a new accusation, a huge black panther with amber eyes appeared from nowhere. It growled low, menacingly, its shadow form growing to almost double size.

The group of exorcists screamed in panic and fled, shouting about "the devil himself" having appeared. Within seconds, the square was largely empty, only the bravest remaining at a safe distance.

Morpheus, satisfied with his intimidation, shrank back to his normal cat size and began ostentatiously washing himself. "A kitty miss," he chuckled, clearly enjoying the chaos he'd caused. "Or perhaps just right on target?"

"You enjoy this far too much," Lina scolded him, but there was a smile in her voice.

"Someone has to bring some cheerfulness to this apocalypse," Morpheus replied. "And since I'm the only one with a healthy sense of humour..."

Finn looked at the sky, where the freed light spirit now danced with others of its kind, free and safe, at least for now. "This was just the beginning," he said softly. "These confrontations will keep coming, whilst people struggle to understand."

"Then we'll have to be present at every confrontation," Simon replied. "Until understanding grows, until fear diminishes."

Lina nodded, her face serious but hopeful. "There will be costs, Finn. Not everyone will survive or accept this union. Some will fight to the bitter end."

"And some will flourish like never before," Ingrid added, pointing to a young woman at the edge of the square whose hands subtly glowed with a soft light, her face a mask of wondering joy at this discovery.

"We're only a few," Simon observed, looking around at their small group. "And the challenges are immense."

"But we're not alone," Finn replied, pointing to the Guardians who, invisible to most people, gathered on the rooftops around the square. "And more importantly—we have each other."

He looked at Simon, an unspoken question in his eyes.

Simon hesitated, then extended a hand to Finn, a simple gesture that formed a bridge over generations of enmity between their kinds. "Together," he confirmed softly.

And as they walked back through the streets of a Bruges that would never be the same again, the Wolf, the Hunter, the Witch, the Gossip and the Shadow Cat sealed an alliance that would protect not only their city, but the entire newly united world they had created.

SIX MONTHS LATER

Summer had returned to Bruges, but it was a summer unlike any the old city had ever known. The trees in Minnewater Park glowed at night with a soft, pink light. The swans on the canals were sometimes accompanied by water spirits with translucent, undulating forms. And above the city, always, danced the subtle, rainbow-coloured light patterns now known as the "Dream Veils".

In 'Dreams of Lina' it was busier than ever. The once small chocolate shop had expanded to the adjacent building, the walls decorated with informative displays about the connection between chocolate and the Underworld. A small light spirit—the same one they had freed from the exorcists—had found a permanent home in a specially designed lantern beside the counter.

Finn stood behind that counter, elegantly dressed in the new, violet-blue uniform of the shop. His movements were smooth, confident—the last six months had brought about a transformation in him that went beyond just the physical. He had found his place, not only as an assistant in the shop, but as a bridge between worlds.

The door swung open, the bell ringing with a melody that subtly changed depending on who entered. This time it was a lullaby in minor—Simon's signature.

"Busy today?" Simon asked, his eyes warmer, his demeanour

more relaxed than they had ever been during those first, tense encounters.

"Tourists," Finn beamed. "They come from all over the world to see 'the epicentre of the Great Union'." He playfully rolled his eyes at the dramatic term the media had coined.

"Well, this tourist has news," Simon said, leaning closer over the counter. "The international regulatory commission has finally reached agreement on Beings classification. All beings with consciousness, whether they come from our world or the Underworld, have equal rights in the European Union as of today."

Finn's face lit up. "That's fantastic! Where's Dreamer? He should hear this."

"He already knows," Simon replied with a small smile. "He was at the signing in Brussels. Apparently gigantic, talking white wolves make an impression on EU commissioners. Who'd have thought?"

They laughed together, an easy familiarity between them that had grown from the shared experiences of recent months. What had begun as manipulation and mistrust had slowly evolved into respect, then friendship, and then... something more?

Lina emerged from the back room, carrying a tray of fresh pralines. "Simon! Just in time for the new batch. Maya Twilight Blend, with a hint of star bark."

"Star bark?" Simon raised a critical eyebrow. "Is that what I think it is?"

"Bark from the star trees in the deep Underworld," Lina nodded. "The first officially imported ingredient under the new trade treaties. Completely legal, sustainably harvested, and..." she offered him a praline, "absolutely divine."

"Are these trees then ecologically processed?" Simon asked half-mockingly.

"These trees have an inexhaustible source of life energy," Lina laughed, her voice melodious and lyrical like a poem, "they're not processed, what you take away grows back immediately, like stars that never fade, like dreams that always return." She winked.

Simon took a cautious bite, his eyes closing at the taste sensation. "Incredible," he said under his breath. "It tastes like... chamomile tea and something I can't even describe."
"Exactly the intention," Lina laughed. "Now that the worlds are united, entirely new culinary horizons are opening up."
A small group of students entered, hesitating at the door. Finn beckoned them in kindly.
"First time in 'Dreams of Lina'?" he asked with a friendly smile. "Come in, we don't bite." He paused, his eyes briefly gleaming with that golden light. "Well, not unless you dream of it." He exchanged a look with Simon.
Whilst Finn guided the students, Simon led Lina to a quiet corner of the shop.
"There's something else," he said, his voice softer, more serious. "My contacts at Interpol have noticed a pattern. Disappearances of individuals with... specific characteristics."
"What kind of characteristics?" Lina asked, her attention immediately sharpened.
"People with natural connections to the Underworld. Dreamers with extraordinary clarity. And..." he hesitated, "werewolves."
Lina's eyes narrowed. "Antoine."
Simon nodded. "And presumably my uncle Victor. They vanished without trace after that day at the Minnewater, but there are indications they're operating from Switzerland."
"They don't give up," Lina said softly. "The union wasn't what Antoine wanted. He wanted control, not harmony."
"Exactly," Simon confirmed. "And what he couldn't achieve by sealing off the dream world, he might now be trying to achieve via another route."
Lina mused, looking through the window where the Minnewater was visible, gleaming in the spring sun, the crystal membrane now a permanent but almost invisible presence in the centre. "We must warn Finn. And Ingrid."
"I've already informed Ingrid," Simon said. "She's busy strengthening the security measures. But Finn..."
Their gazes went to where the young werewolf was enthusiastically explaining to a group of students how special

pralines were made for beings with non-human physiology. "He's worked so hard to help build this new world," Lina said softly. "To help people and beings live together. I hate to remind him of the dark side of what we've done."
"But we must," Simon replied. "He's still a target. Perhaps now more than ever."
At that moment, Finn cast a glance at them, as if he'd picked up their conversation with super hearing. His wolf senses were sharper than ever, now that he no longer had to suppress them. His eyes met those of Lina and Simon, a questioning gesture in his eyebrows.
"Tonight," Lina decided. "We'll tell him tonight, after closing time. And then we make new plans."
Simon nodded, his face serious but determined. "The struggle for balance between worlds isn't over yet, but at least..." he stared at Finn, a warmth in his eyes that would have been unthinkable six months ago, "we're fighting together now."
Lina smiled, a small but genuine expression of hope. "Together," she confirmed. "And this time we're prepared."
Outside, above the old rooftops of Bruges, the Dream Veils formed a complex, spiralling pattern—a natural phenomenon according to some scientists, a manifestation of cosmic consciousness according to others. For ordinary citizens it was simply a reminder of how the world had changed, a daily encouragement that reality was bigger, more complex, and more wonderful than they had ever thought.

Deep in Switzerland, in an underground laboratory far removed from curious eyes, Antoine Leblanc—or what had once been Antoine—stood before a large, crystal container filled with a dark liquid. The lines under his skin were now a network of dark veins that crawled over his entire body. His eyes, once brown, now had a strange, purple glow.
"Six months," he whispered to the liquid in the container. "Six months since Bruges. But soon..." A smile spread across his face, an expression that had nothing human left in it. "Soon the real transformation will begin."

The form in the container moved, as if in response to his words. A hand pressed against the glass, fingers spreading in a gesture reminiscent of a reach for freedom, or perhaps for dominion.

Behind Antoine stood Victor Laurent, aged and greyed in these six months, his face marked with lines of exhaustion and something that looked suspiciously like fear.

"Are we certain we can control this?" he asked, his voice barely more than a whisper.

Antoine turned around, his purple eyes glowing in the half-darkness of the laboratory. "Control?" he repeated, as if tasting a new, strange concept. "No, old friend. We don't control it."

His smile widened, revealing teeth that were now sharper than humanly possible.

"We become it."

And in the container the liquid grew darker, the vague form within growing, expanding, waiting for the moment it would be released into a world that, despite all its recent wonders, wasn't yet ready for what Antoine Leblanc had truly become.

In Bruges, unaware of the growing darkness, Finn, Lina, Simon, Ingrid, Morpheus, and their allies lived in the dream of a united world, not yet realizing that dreams, even united with reality, could still turn into nightmares.